STACY KESTWICK

Edited by Kay Springsteen
Cover design by Hang Le
Formatting by Pink Ink Designs

wet

Prologue

Holding my breath, I eased open the lid of the small velvet box, barely able to contain my excitement. The afternoon sunlight streaming through the windows of our downtown Nashville loft hit the diamond ring, speckling the walls with tiny prisms.

Damn.

The air left my lungs in a surprised whoosh. That was some rock. I plucked the ring with the larger-than-expected center stone from its blue cushioned bed, pinching it between my thumb and forefinger, and examined it the way one would inspect a dropped contact lens. The cushion-cut center diamond had to be at least two carats. And the side stones, another carat easily. "Wow," I whispered, fighting the huge smile overtaking my face. I thought about slipping the ring on, wanting to see how it would nestle between my fingers, but I held back. I would only have that first moment once, and it should be after I said *yes*.

Returning the ring to the box, I replaced it exactly the way I'd found it, tucked under a stack of trouser socks in my boyfriend's top dresser drawer, next to a tangle of power cords and chargers for his various pieces of tech. A laptop, iPod, GoPro camera, and two different sized tablets littered the top of his dresser.

I knew it. Asher *was* planning to propose. I squealed and jumped up and down like a little girl. When I'd gotten home early today—my scheduled afternoon photo shoot had to be canceled after a morning thunderstorm soaked the outdoor venue—I couldn't resist taking advantage of the empty apartment to do a little snooping. Asher had been acting funny the last few weeks, fiddling with his computer and that top drawer, stopping whatever he was doing when I walked in the bedroom. I had been suspicious at first, but, really, this was *Asher.*

Predictable was Asher's middle name.

He'd graduated summa cum laude two years ago from the University of Tennessee, his parents' alma mater, and returned home to Nashville as expected to join his father's prestigious accounting firm. He got his hair cut at the same place he had since he was seven. Ate the same turkey-and-cheddar sandwich for lunch every day. Had the same best friend since middle school. He was solid and steadfast, and I loved that about him.

Asher took the trash out. Opened my car door. Let me pick the radio station. Always paid the check. He was the epitome of what mothers hoped their daughters found in a man. Security, sweetness, and respect wrapped up in a lightly muscled, perfectly combed package. And predictable didn't mean boring. We heated up the bedroom twice a week, occasionally spicing it up with lingerie or strawberries and cream, on Tuesday and Friday. Sometimes Saturday too, if it was football season and the University of Tennessee won their game.

On those nights, Asher would yell, "Touchdown!" as he came inside of me. It was cute.

He was cute.

We were cute.

We were that couple. Best friends in high school who turned into more at college. The one that never argued and had already picked out the names of our future children—first a boy with his daddy's charm named Michael, then a sweet apple-cheeked girl named Molly. Even our siblings got along. His older brother and mine had been college roommates at Vanderbilt.

I was the more rebellious one. Secretly getting a tattoo at seventeen. Earning a management degree at Vandy, like my brother Simon, but starting up a photography business upon graduation instead of joining my parents and brother in the music business like everyone assumed I would. Asher had been supportive, urging me to move in with him so he could help me out financially while I got my company off the ground. Never complaining about my crazy hours. Helping lug all my equipment around to shoots until I made enough money to hire my own assistant. Tolerant of my frequent visits to the South Carolina coast to visit Rue—my college roommate and best friend—for long weekends of girl time.

Beaming at the realization that I would most likely be engaged to the perfect guy in the next three weeks, I floated around the loft, daydreaming, touching the few hodgepodge holiday decorations we had scattered around. I bet he'd tuck it in my stocking, I mused, as I unpacked the new 800-thread-count sheets I'd bought us after lunch, an early Christmas present to ourselves. I planned to put them on the bed and don a red bra-and-panty set to be the bow on top of his surprise gift—it was Tuesday, one of our usual frisky days. The new satiny soft sheets had felt sensual when I picked them out, a nice little change from the standard cotton percale we had now.

As I fluffed the last pillow, I heard the apartment door opening. Confused, I glanced at the clock. The red numbers glowed 2:15, and Asher didn't normally get home until 5:30. Asher's voice echoed through the loft, and I started to answer when I realized he wasn't talking to me.

"Dude, that last video was smokin'! When's the next one?" I recognized the voice of Jameson, Asher's best friend. I bet Asher would ask him to be his best man. And then Jameson would walk Rue down the aisle. They'd look cute together. Maybe raspberry and black for wedding colors. What kind of flowers were raspberry? Not daisies. Lilies? Roses, maybe?

I tuned out the sound of Jameson and Asher talking, lost in my wedding fantasy, until one of them saying my name snagged my attention. " . . . Sadie still has no idea?" Jameson talking again. How cute, they didn't think I knew about the ring. I rolled my eyes. Guys were so dumb. Like I hadn't figured out that was coming.

Asher had been extra sweet and affectionate lately, and the sex had been steamier than usual. Plus, we'd been together, officially, for three years now. Time to start thinking about settling down.

Asher scoffed. "Hell, no. And after I propose, can you imagine the footage from that night?"

"Think you'll be able to get her to do some new positions?"

"I think she'll do anything I ask her to after I put that giant rock on her finger." The smugness in Asher's voice had a vulgar, calculated tone I wasn't used to.

Positions?

Footage?

Crinkling my brow, I crept closer to the bedroom door. Jameson's slightly nasal reply—why had I not noticed how grating his voice was before?—mixed with the dust motes floating in the air.

"What about Rebecca? When's the next one with her?"

Rebecca?

My head snapped back. Rebecca was my photography assistant, a cute junior from the local community college I'd hired a year ago when she'd needed a job to help with tuition.

One of them snorted. "You know as soon as I make her my fiancée, she'll be dying to take a trip down to Reynold's Island to show off the ring to Rue. I'll set it up for then. Probably before New Year's if I'm lucky."

"You're a fucking bastard, Ash." Jameson made it sound like a compliment. "You plan on keeping it up after you're engaged?"

"Why wouldn't I?"

"I dunno. Don't you think it's a little different if you do it after you pop the question?"

That was Asher's drawn-out sigh. I recognized it.

"I've thought about that. Maybe stopping the stuff with Becca on the side. But, seriously, the sex is so fucking hot. And Becca lets me do stuff that Sadie won't."

"Like what?"

"Like maybe I don't share everything I film with you guys."

They laughed long and hard. I wrapped my arms around my middle, my breathing shallower, my legs feeling weak.

"Want a beer, man? Dad's out of the office the rest of the day, let's call it quits early and play Madden at your place." There were some thuds, then two loud pops followed by slow hisses. Beer cans. I slid bonelessly to the floor by the window, picturing Jameson's identical loft down the hall.

"For real, though. Sadie doesn't suspect? How do you manage to get away with it?"

"I'm sweet. Considerate. Loving. The perfect boyfriend. Seriously, Jameson, if you tried it sometime, you'd probably get some action of your own instead of having to jack off to mine. Sadie eats that shit up. With Becca, though, it's different. More raw, more intense, more—" Grunts and slapping sounds echoed off the high ceiling. A lone tear hesitated at the corner of my eye, waiting for permission to trail down my cheek.

"Yeah, Becca's tits are pretty epic. And her legs—"

Asher interrupted. "And her ass and her mouth and her tongue. Yeah, dude, I know *exactly* what I'm doing with her."

"Shit, man." Awe radiated from Jameson. "You've, like, studied this or something?"

Asher laughed. "Yeah, dude, I totally studied fucking in college. And, trust me, I got an A."

A phone rang. Not Asher's ringtone. Numbly, I heard Jameson answer and, a few minutes later, the door slammed in the front of the loft. The guys leaving.

I was frozen on the floor, that stubborn tear still clinging to the hope that this was all a nightmare, and it didn't really need to fall. I drew in a shaky breath, suspended in disbelief.

This wasn't happening. This wasn't Asher. This wasn't the guy who rubbed my feet after a long day and packed me snacks to take to work. The guy who told me I was hot no matter what I was wearing. The guy that whispered in my ear at night that I was his other half and made sure I always had extra batteries and memory cards before a big shoot.

Shit. Footage. Hadn't Jameson said something about footage?

My attention shifted to the laptop, and I moved across the room, grabbing the sleek computer and settling on the new sheets that I no longer planned on christening tonight.

Opening the screen, I hesitated at the password screen. What would he use?

My fingers pecked out the letters, and I hit enter. The home page appeared. *Touchdown,* I thought.

I ignored the software icons and looked at the file folders in a row across the bottom of his screen. The first four yielded nothing, but the one labeled *Work Proposals* had two subfolders labeled 1001 and 1002. After clicking on the first one, thumbnails of video files lined the screen, each meticulously labeled with dates. Opening the most recent, I saw an ass—*my* bare ass—walk across the screen. The camera was aimed at the bottom two-thirds of our bed. The bed I was sitting on.

In shock, I slid to the floor, away from what was playing on the screen. It was earlier in the summer. I could tell by my tan lines. I watched, stunned, as I crawled across the bed, over Asher's naked body. You couldn't see our faces. My hair was in a messy ponytail, and Asher kept his face turned toward the windows, away from the camera. I squinted at the screen. I had noticed that vague change in his behavior. How he often faced that way during sex in recent months.

Fucking bastard. And I did not mean that as a compliment. As my onscreen self lowered onto Asher's erection, I closed the video.

I clicked on the other folder, the one labeled 1002. Again, video thumbnails neatly organized by date popped up in a box. Picking one at random, I double-clicked.

My bedroom, same view as before. Only, that wasn't me bobbing between Asher's spread legs. That big-breasted, pale skinned girl was my assistant, Rebecca, who I had considered a little sister.

I exited the video immediately, bile rising in my throat. The bottom of the file folder cheerfully informed me the folder contained forty-one items, dating back just over five months, to July fourth.

I gagged, dropped the computer, and rushed to the bathroom.

When I emerged thirty minutes later, throat raw from acid and tears burning my eyes, I walked back to the laptop and cradled it carefully in my arms, the metal still warm, before returning to the bathroom. Taking a deep breath, I tossed the computer in the bathtub. My steps never faltering, I retrieved all the tech gear I could find of Asher's, filling the tub with shades of silver, gray, chrome, and black. Walking down the hall to the closet that held our washer and dryer, I snatched a bottle of detergent and a jug of bleach and returned to our bathroom. I drizzled the electronics with both liquids until the bottles were empty and then turned the shower on high, leaving the curtain wide open.

Packing my stuff haphazardly into whatever luggage and duffle bags I could find, I made four trips to my red Wrangler before I just couldn't stand to be in that loft we'd shared any longer. Making one last trip to our bedroom, I dug out that shiny piece of coal from under Asshole's trouser socks and tossed it on the middle of the bed.

Just so he would know I knew exactly what I was walking away from.

As I peeled off down the road, heading south toward the Carolina coast, I had one last fleeting thought.

There was nothing left in that loft I would miss.

Except those sheets. Bastard owed me a set of sheets.

chapter one

I'M DONE BEING A *vegetarian.* As I eased into my morning run with little enthusiasm for the three miles left to go, I concentrated on putting one foot in front of the other while avoiding the washed-up jellyfish that dotted the mostly empty beach. *So done.*

I needed to get laid. And soon. If I was starting to compare my currently meatless love life to a diet, I was in trouble.

My feet pounded over the wet sand, and I tried to focus on the sunrise coming up over the Atlantic instead of my appetite, but this morning, even the sun was pissing me off. It was colder than I had anticipated, the sun's rays weren't doing jack to warm me up, and the damn angle of the light reflecting off the water was partially blinding me. My sunglasses were sitting in the cup holder of my Jeep, forgotten as usual.

Tipping my water bottle, I took a swig, wishing it were hot coffee instead. I sighed and pushed my pace faster, skipping the slow jog I usually started with in favor of flat-out running, wanting my goose bumps to go away. I should have added a light jacket to my flimsy tank and shorts combo.

Popping my ear buds in, I looked down at my phone and debated which playlist to pick. They were loosely organized by letter instead of genre. I was thinking maybe M this morning. John Mayer, Maroon 5, Matt Nathanson, Jason Mraz, and Mat Kearney. My M playlist was one of my favorites. Maybe it would cheer me up. I selected it then tapped the random button.

"The Cave" by Mumford and Sons started, and I couldn't help but roll my eyes. Even my music was talking about being a meat eater. It was a sign. Time to move on.

I hadn't had sex in five months. Five long, hard months. Damn it! My starved libido latched onto those adjectives with greedy fingers—long, hard, *fuck*. The motion of my thighs rubbing together as I ran made me crave a different kind of friction altogether.

I mean, I had been taking care of things myself, but I hadn't had an actual sweating, panting, thrusting guy in that length of time. Shit, there I went again. *Length*. My vagina was lonely.

And horny.

This dry spell wasn't my fault. After all that shit had gone down with Asshole, I hadn't even wanted to look at another guy for months. I shuddered at the memory and pushed him from my mind. He didn't deserve anything from me anymore. Not even a single disgusted thought.

I sidestepped to miss a glob of jellyfish, almost rolling my ankle, and the sound of a mournful bay from up ahead caught my attention. Squinting, I could see a huge black and tan dog running up and down the waterline, a piece of driftwood in his mouth. Out in the ocean, a handful of guys were surfing the early morning waves. The glare from the sun made it hard to get a good look at any of them, but I could see bare chests and muscles, and my pulse kicked up a notch. *My missing food group.*

They must've been locals.

Reynolds Island wasn't very big. It was one of South Carolina's barrier islands, mixed in with Fripp, Kiawah, and Edisto, cuddled between Beaufort and Charleston. It was prime real estate, though. Property values were ridiculous, especially oceanfront. Unless you had bought the property over thirty years ago, odds were, you were doing pretty well for yourself.

The beach here on the south side of the island was where the locals and the wealthy summer transients stayed. It was easy to tell which houses belonged to which group. The transients had huge oceanfront mansions. Show-off houses. Farthest south, toward the jetty, were the more reasonably priced houses the local working class occupied. To the north were the rental properties and the Water's Edge resort. I lived with Rue midway down the island, in one of the rental properties, even though Rue was considered a local since she'd moved here permanently after she finished her MBA last year. I was a local now too since moving in with her five months ago, in the wake of that mess with Asshole.

The baying dog—some kind of hound—ran alongside me for a distance as I passed the surfers. Slobber flew from his jowls, and his long droopy ears flapped like wings. As big as he was, I think he was still a puppy. His paws were huge for his size, and his skin hung on his frame. A surfer called out eventually, and the dog turned back.

I didn't bother to really study the guys, after my initial ogling. One thing Rue had drilled into me, was that locals weren't for flings. That's what tourists were for. Hot guys delivered weekly, ready for a hook up, and already prescheduled to leave, erasing the chance of awkward future run-ins.

A fling was exactly what I needed. While I didn't distrust men now as a whole, the thought of starting up another relationship just seemed like too much damn work. I wanted something easy. Disposable. If a relationship was equivalent to a five-star restaurant, then I was searching for the nearest drive-thru.

Rue had an almost foolproof system in place. There were three bars on the island—two frequented by tourists, and one by locals. She stuck almost exclusively to the tourist bars, picked out her flavor of the night, then went back to his place. *Always* to his place. It was that simple.

And it worked. Rue went through men like Halloween candy, unable to pick a favorite and in a hurry to try them all. And they all seemed just as eager to sample her, no strings attached. She had been begging me to go out with her, and I was finally ready to cave. It was time to see if I remembered how to flirt, in any case. *Appetizers,* my dirty mind chimed in.

Zoned back out to my music, I reached the jetty at the end of the beach, where the sand disappeared into coastal scrub. I hadn't meant to run this far, which meant I had even longer to go to get back. *Great.* Taking a break, I bent over at the waist and tried to catch my breath. I downed a third of my water bottle and looked out over the Intracoastal Waterway, my chest heaving from exertion.

The sun was higher now, so I was no longer half-blind from the reflection off the water. And I had warmed up, sweat darkening the part of my sports bra under my breasts. I eyed the waves, knowing the cool water would feel refreshing, but stayed where I was, safely on shore. I was afraid of the ocean in a vague, but very real sense. Who knew what kinds of dangerous things lurked under that murky surface, just out of sight?

Taking one last deep breath, I turned back the way I had come, following my footprints still visible in the sand. It was official. Starting tonight, I would be following a new Atkin's based diet. Meat friendly.

I grinned. Rue would be thrilled. We'd hit the bars, and after a good one-night stand or two, I should be feeling as good as new. Surely orgasms were the equivalent of nature's vitamins? All those endorphins?

Partway back, with my calves aching, the craving for Krispy Kreme hit hard. Since I had run at least a mile more than I'd planned, splurging on a hot glazed breakfast seemed like a fabulous idea. Krispy Kreme doughnuts might be the only thing I craved as much as sex. I picked up my pace.

Macklemore played in my ears, and I smiled and matched my stride to the beat, covering ground quickly. A nervous crab guarded his hole but darted away when I got too near. Silly crustacean, I was just as scared of him as he was of me.

The spot where the surfers had been was just up ahead, and I saw the giant puppy still playing on the beach. He spotted me and started loping my way, his tongue lolling to the side. I glanced out at the waves rolling in, but I didn't see the surfers anymore. The dog reached me and jumped up, his sandy paws knocking my water bottle out of my hand and bringing me to a stop, his tail wagging furiously.

I knelt down, rubbing his huge ears, murmuring to him. "Hi there, big boy. Who do you belong to? Did they forget you out here?"

The hound rolled to his back, begging for a belly rub. I played with him for a few moments, looking around for the guys from earlier. Surely the dog belonged to one of them.

Finally, I spotted a lone surfer floating out just past the breakers. Cupping my hands around my mouth, I hollered at him. A light morning breeze was blowing inland, so I wasn't sure he could hear me over the waves. The dog zipped up and down the waterline, baying with delight. It sounded more like the noise a seal made than a bark.

The guy was floating on his back. I waved my arms at him and yelled again. Still nothing.

I turned back to the dog, who was crouched beside me with his head down and his hindquarters up in the air, and wrestled with him for the piece of driftwood in his mouth. He surrendered it without much of a fight. I threw it as far as I could, and he raced for it, bringing it back and dropping it at my feet. He knew how this game worked. I threw the stick a couple more times, laughing at the dog's antics.

I was about to start running again when I turned back to the surfer. Still floating. The wind whipped strands of my ponytail in my face, and I batted them away. In fact, he hadn't moved at all. I frowned, putting my hands on my hips, and walked to the foamy edge where the waves rushed the shoreline. What the hell was he doing out there?

When a wave cresting early crashed over him and he still didn't react, my lifeguarding instincts kicked in.

"Shit," I muttered, toeing off my running shoes and tossing them toward higher ground, along with my phone and ear buds. Gasping at the coldness, I waded out into the surf until I was submerged waist deep, then dove into the waves. After I passed the breakers, I swam toward him with practiced strokes, angling a little to account for the current trying to pull me farther away. A surfboard was floating a few feet from the guy. Behind me, the dog howled.

The surfer's feet were just in front of me, bobbing with the swells, and I went to swim around him to approach him from behind, but my arm brushed along his calf. Flinching, he folded in on himself, jackknifing in the water. His foot slammed into my gut, right in my solar plexus, and the air whooshed out of my lungs.

"What the fuck?" The surfer jerked upright.

Coughing and sputtering, I treaded water and tried to inhale, not getting any air. I wheezed, spitting salty water back into the ocean.

Managing to look both irritated and concerned, the surfer grabbed me around the waist, lifting me a little higher out of the water. I glared at him as I hacked my lungs up, realizing he could more or less stand by hopping along the bottom as the waves sucked at us. Shoving his arms away, I tried to copy him, but my head went under when I put my toes on the sand, and I swallowed a mouthful of water.

The guy yanked me back up, anchoring me against his side this time, his arm across my ass, fingers tight on my hip. His other hand brushed at the hair plastered to my face. Turning away from him, I continued coughing, my lungs burning. I tried to inhale through my nose. My eyes watered, and my mouth hung open like a fish, but all I could do was focus on trying to breathe. In. Out.

"You okay?" His hand moved to grip my ribs, holding me against him, keeping my head out of the water. I nodded, closing my eyes as my lungs remembered how to work. My hands clutched his broad shoulder.

Getting some much needed oxygen, my focus narrowed to the solid slab of his muscles pressed against my stomach. I was straddling his side, my pelvis snugged up to his hip and my legs tangled around his. It was closer than I'd been to a guy in months. Unexpected desire flared where my sex rubbed his skin, my shorts the thinnest of barriers. The waves jostled us, teasing me with the friction.

Peeking from under my lashes, I watched him shove the surfboard, and it caught a wave, riding to the shore. His biceps flexed under my fingers, the muscle hardening. That small motion snapped me back to reality. Humping a possible drowning victim wasn't appropriate, no matter how good he felt between my legs.

Taking another tentative breath, I pushed against his shoulder, trying to create some space between us.

"Don't think so," his deep voice rumbled in my ear. Rearranging me, he cradled me in his arms like a child and started moving toward the beach.

Wait, what the hell is he doing? Stiffening, I struggled to free myself.

Drops of water fell from his hair and the tip of his nose, splashing down on my face, making me blink. The sun was behind him, blocking his facial features. His arms tightened around me.

"Let go of me!" I sputtered and squirmed within his grasp.

"Nope. You have trouble breathing and keeping your head above the water at the same time. I'm scared to see you try to walk." He chuckled.

I glowered up at him. "You kicked me."

"After you attacked *me* out of the blue. It was an accident."

"Attacked you? I was saving you!" I smacked his shoulder. He didn't even flinch.

"From what? Floating?"

"You were just lying there—not moving, not responding. I called out to you, and you didn't answer. I thought you were hurt!"

He moved through the water, holding me easily against his chest. I tried not to notice how warm his skin felt under my fingers, but I shivered, hunching closer. Now that I could breathe again, the chill from the ocean became obvious.

Like my hard nipples under my sports tank.

I glanced up at him, but still couldn't see his eyes because of the damn sun again. His mouth had quirked up on one side though, and he was looking down at me.

"So you thought you would rescue me?" he asked.

"Something like that," I muttered, realizing how ridiculous that must seem to him, considering he was the one carrying me out of the water. "I can walk, you know."

He made a noncommittal noise in his throat. Pressed this close to him, one arm wrapped around his shoulders, the other resting on his chest, embarrassment warred with awareness of how very caveman his actions were. A small part of me couldn't help but feel an answering thrill.

We reached the shore, and the dog bounded over, my shoe in his mouth. The guy frowned. "Yours?"

Huh? I tore my eyes away from the cords of his neck and glanced at the furry behemoth again. "He's not yours?"

"Not the dog. The shoe."

"Oh. Yes," I said dumbly.

"General Beauregard! Drop it," he ordered. The dog whined but obeyed, dropping the shoe and watching us with sad, droopy eyes. "Good dog." His voice warmed several degrees and filled with affection as he praised the animal.

I raised an eyebrow. "General Beauregard? Really?"

"What's wrong with that? It's a good, strong Southern name," he countered, his own accent sounding only slightly Southern, more like it was acquired, not born and bred into him.

We stared at each other. I could finally see his eyes. They were beautiful—a clear blue with chips of gray mixed in, his thick eyelashes spiky from the ocean. I lifted myself higher, trying to get a closer view. He tilted his head, and his gaze drifted down my face, stopping on my mouth. My tongue responded, slipping out to lick my salty bottom lip.

"You know," he said, "There are easier ways to get my attention."

It took a second for me to realize his implication. I narrowed my eyes. "Excuse me?" The tone of my voice should have been a warning to him, but he didn't seem to catch it. I might have been horny, but I wasn't desperate.

He shrugged. With torturing slowness, my body slid along his as he set me on my feet. I shivered from the loss of his warmth and crossed my arms over my chest, trying to hide my nipples. Standing on solid ground, his height became more obvious. My head came up to his chin, making me eye level with his throat. I shook my head at him and turned to look at the dog instead. "Egotistical ass," I said under my breath, annoyed.

"You seriously thought I was drowning? In chest-deep water?"

"You seriously thought I was so overcome by lust, I attacked you in the ocean?" I mimicked his tone.

"It's happened."

I stared at him before rolling my eyes. Plopping down on

the beach, I grabbed my wet shoes and with shaky hands tried to brush some of the sand from them. I was freezing.

He dropped to his haunches beside me, picking up my right foot. Long gentle fingers brushed the sand off my foot, taking a second to trace my tattoo. I had a paper airplane with a dotted line trailing it that made it look like it had flown in a loop. His finger followed the path of the plane, and I felt another shiver that had nothing to do with the temperature. He looked up at me as he worked my foot back into my shoe and tied the laces for me—double knots. "What's it mean?"

"Escape," I answered after a beat. It wasn't the truth, but it's what I wanted to do at the moment. I gazed at his shirtless body, my eyes drinking in his lean, ropy muscles and his sun-darkened skin. His torso was sculpted without being bulky, and a half-sleeve of Japanese style waves cascaded down his left arm, tattooed in black and gray. I couldn't decide if my attraction to his body or my irritation with his ego bothered me more.

Scowling, I picked up my other shoe before he could help me with it too. I shoved my foot into it, not bothering to untie the laces in the first place. Scooping up my phone and ear buds, I stood and turned to leave. "You're welcome, by the way," I tossed over my shoulder.

He caught my elbow, stopping me. "For what?"

I spun back, yanking my arm free, annoyance winning out. "For trying to rescue you! Clearly, no one else was around to care if something happened to your sorry ass. I dragged myself out into the water, and I never go into the water, and you think it's some dumb ploy—"

"Why don't you go into the water?" he interrupted, head cocked to the side.

"I—I just don't," I stammered, flustered that he'd caught that.

"Scared?"

I glared back at him, refusing to answer.

"Really? Why?" He seemed amused.

"It's not the water I'm scared of. It's what I can't see in the water that bothers me. Jellyfish, sharks, stingrays—who knows what else is in there just waiting to get you."

He laughed. "Yeah, you'll have to get over that."

"Whatever. It's not your problem." I shrugged. Before he could say anything else to me, I popped my ear buds back in and started running. Not running away, I told myself. Just running to warm back up and get to Krispy Kreme faster.

My stomach growled on cue. I was starving. As I snuck a quick look back and saw him still watching me, I tried to convince myself doughnuts were the only thing I was craving.

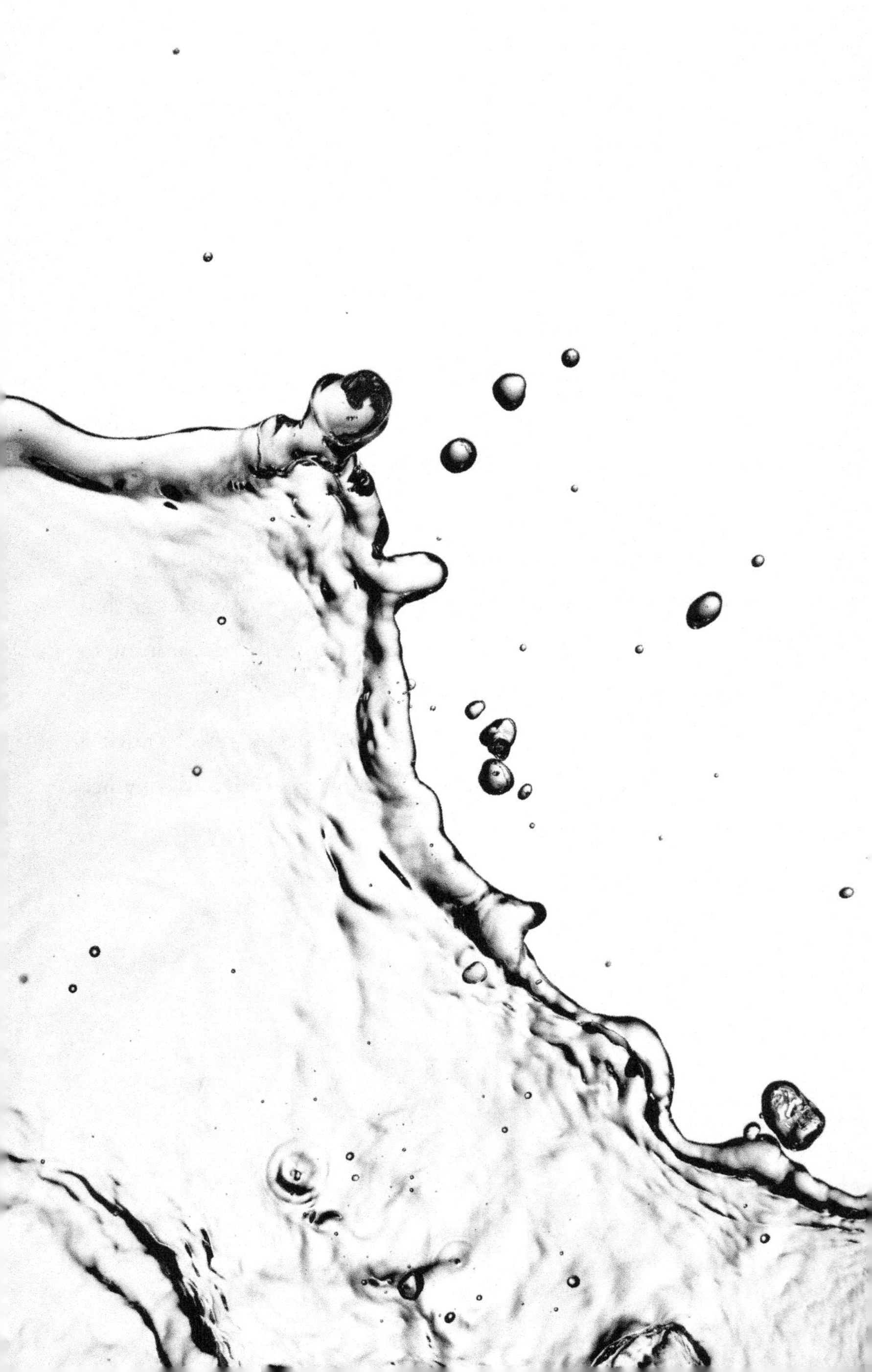

chapter two

LATER THAT NIGHT I stood in my room, fidgeting in front of the mirror and waiting for Rue to deliver her verdict. The blue halter gave me decent cleavage while leaving my upper back bare, and the white skirt was flirty but short. My makeup was smokier than normal, and I'd taken the time to straighten my hair and treat it with an anti-frizz serum that was probably not strong enough to withstand the evening humidity, but, really, that was asking for a miracle.

I adjusted my push-up bra. And, seriously, this bra was a push-up champion. Like, it wasn't doing any on-the-knees girlie push-up. Oh, no, this bra was a one armed, feet spread—*hoorah!*—kind of push-up bra. My girls were looking as good as unsurgically possible. I was fervently hoping they would help compensate for my rusty flirting skills.

Rue inspected me, hand on her hip. She was stunning, of course. She had on a purple jersey dress that softly hugged her curves and made her waist seem tiny. To clarify, Rue always looked curvy and tiny-waisted. She was letting her twins go free tonight and easily had me beat by a good cup size. Still, she was rocking that dress something fierce. Her dark brown hair was hanging in big loose curls, and earlier in the week she had dyed the ends hot pink. It should have looked ridiculous, but on her, it was both girly and edgy. The pink ends brushed the tops of her breasts and drew attention there. The guys were going to be lining up for her tonight. And I hoped that whichever hottie picked her had a cute wingman who needed a little company too.

"I think the problem is the shoes," she decided. She went over to my closet and rummaged around until she found a pair with taller heels. "Here, try these with it."

I traded shoes and did a slow spin for her. She nodded, satisfied. "You'll get laid. Probably someone more preppy than bad boy, though. You still look too wholesome."

"I know. I can't pull off the whole sex kitten vibe like you can," I grumbled.

It was an old joke between us. But there was no real animosity. I tamed her down somewhat, and she pushed me out of my comfort zone. She got us into trouble and, well, yeah, she *always* got us into trouble, and I was there following right behind her. Full disclosure, she was the one to get us out of the trouble too. Proof? I'd been pulled over for speeding seven times since starting college. I'd been ticketed three times—the times I'd been in the car solo. When Rue was with me, she batted those pretty brown eyes of hers or turned on the waterworks, and once, the cop had apologized to us.

Rue had been pulled over six times and had yet to get a single fine.

She was the master. I was a terrible student.

"It's a gift." She shrugged, nonplussed.

I checked my purse one more time, making sure the condoms were tucked inside, along with my phone. I didn't bother to put away the two discarded outfits Rue had vetoed earlier. The rule was no flings at the cottage. Hook ups were conducted strictly at the hotel or rental house of the guy. It made both clean up and exit strategy that much simpler.

We were going to Anchor, one of the two tourist bars on the island. Rue preferred it over the other place, Porthole, because the drinks were better, less watered down and higher quality alcohol. We'd waited until nine to start getting ready to make sure we'd have plenty of options by the time we got there.

Anchor was the island spot to see and be seen. It had a long curved bar, concert style lighting, and a large, two-level dance floor in the back. A live deejay played there most nights during the summer and on the weekends the rest of the year. As we walked in, one of the bartenders nodded at Rue, pointed at her hair, and gave her a thumbs-up. Rue smiled at him and motioned to me. "That's Jason. If anyone gives you trouble, let him know, and he'll take care of it for you." The bartender had a shaved head and stubble, a look that worked for him, and I repeated his name to myself. He lifted his chin in acknowledgement and turned back to the girls almost falling over the bar trying to get his attention.

We snagged a table close to the dance floor so we could check out the scenery. The place wasn't at capacity, since it was still late spring and tourist season was just starting, but there were over a hundred people out there. Rue was murmuring to me about a pair of guys wearing Clemson shirts over near the deejay booth when shots materialized in front of us. Rue turned to look at the two guys bearing gifts and lifted an eyebrow.

"You looked thirsty, and we thought we'd take care of that for you," the one in the blue polo said, eyeing Rue like she was his last meal. "I'm Eric, and this is my cousin Jared. Your hair caught my eye. You seem spicy, and I love playing with fire. Dance with me?"

Rue glanced at me and winked. She downed her shot, grabbed Eric's hand, and headed for the dance floor. I glanced at the guy who must be Jared. He grinned at me, his gaze lingering on my legs. At least he appreciated my best feature. "Wanna dance?"

Jared was tall and lanky with buzzed hair and a button down shirt rolled up his forearms. His nose appeared to have been broken before, and his smile was crooked but sweet. He was adorable. And really, I wasn't feeling picky.

"I'm Sadie," I told him, as we drank our shots and then followed after Rue and Eric.

Jared took my hand and led me to the middle of the dance floor. Pulling my hips close to him, he faced me and began to move to the music. He danced well for such a tall guy, not awkward at all. That boded well for later, I mused.

"Do you live here or are you visiting?" He leaned close to my ear to speak, his breath warming my neck.

"Visiting." I lied without an ounce of guilt.

He nodded and then seemed content to drop the conversation. His hands slid around to the small of my back and dipped low, sitting right above my butt. My hands ran up his arms to his neck, and my hips swayed with the beat of the techno club music. His hair was surprisingly soft considering its short length, and he smelled good, like expensive cologne. I sighed and shifted a little closer, so our hips were almost touching. I'd forgotten how fun this part of being single was.

Rue walked past with Eric, and she flashed me a thumbs-up sign. I grinned at her and then turned back to Jared. We danced for over an hour, watching each other through half-closed eyes. Thank God he wasn't one of those guys who made weird faces while he danced or checked out other women the whole time. He focused on me.

The song changed, and he spun me around, pulling my butt flush to his hips and grinding with me. His erection grew and pressed into me through his pants. I smiled to myself and rubbed against him, dipping low and slowly shimmying back up. A deep groan vibrated through his chest against my back. His fingers tightened on my hips, and he leaned down and brushed his lips over the shell of my ear. I shivered and melted back against him.

When the song faded, we headed to the bar, threading our way through the crowd. Jared caught the bartender's attention, and the man brought us bottles of Yeungling. Jared hadn't even checked with me first. I tried not to be irked and reminded myself it wasn't his manners I was interested in. Priorities. He smelled good, wasn't sweating like a pig even after all that dancing—another good indicator for later—and he was buying. So far, so good.

The pair of barstools we roosted on next to each other sat close enough my leg was pressed against his. His hand on my lower back was warm and rubbed lazy circles while we exchanged basic info. He was a grad student taking a vacation before starting a research project this summer at Clemson, only here for two more days. Perfect.

He stared at my mouth as I tipped my bottle up and swallowed the last of my beer, following the line of my exposed skin down my neck to the valley of my cleavage. I lowered the bottle, drawing out the motion. He made a noise in his throat, and his arm tightened around my back. Leaning over, he pressed his lips to the sensitive skin just below my ear. My eyes drifted closed. God, it felt good to be touched again.

"You want to come back to my place for awhile? My room has a great view of the ocean." His voice was huskier than before.

I nodded as I slipped off the stool, not even caring that his line was lame. We both knew what was going to happen. Jason the bartender caught my eye as I headed out the door, sending a text to Rue as I walked. I dipped my head to let him know I was okay, and he winked back in acknowledgement.

Jared was staying at the resort, and the ride to the hotel was relatively short. He put his hand on my leg as he drove us back and with one finger traced a meandering path up and down my thigh, flirting with the hem of my skirt.

When we got to the elevator, we stood in the back and kissed softly, experimentally, behind an elderly couple who were oblivious to our actions. His hand cupped the back of my head and tangled in my hair. I wrapped my arms around his waist and leaned into him, his lips moving over mine, tasting me with the slow slide of his tongue. We didn't even pause when the couple got off two floors below our stop.

After fumbling with the key card in the slot, Jared pulled me inside and pressed me to the back of the door, not going any farther into the room. He shoved both hands into my hair, tilted my head to the side and started to devour my mouth, his tongue probing everywhere at once. The urgency caught me off guard, and I dropped my purse at my feet, but I tried to go with it, running my hands down his chest and slipping them under his shirt to grab his sides.

"Oh, Christ, you're so hot," he murmured, licking down my neck while his busy hands reached for the hem of my shirt and yanked it over my head. Apparently, we were in a hurry. His hands rushed up to capture my breasts, squeezing them together and pushing the tops up. He nuzzled into them, placing sloppy kisses as he went. It was like he was trying to touch every part he exposed. Neck, check. Cleavage, check. Pulling the lacy cups down, he sucked a nipple into his mouth, while pinching the other one to the point of pain. I winced and removed his hand, which he seemed to take as a sign, because that hand dropped to my thigh, before sliding back up to my panties. His fingers rubbed the lace he found there, his middle finger pressing into my folds. Okay, that felt good. Now we were getting somewhere.

I tipped my head back, pushing my chest farther into his face, and moved my hips in a slow circle. He pulled at my nipples with his lips, sucking them into hard points. With his other hand, he kneaded my ass. I tugged at his shirt, and he broke away from me long enough to rip it over his head and throw it into the dark room behind us.

Wrapping my arms around his chest, I scraped my nails down his back, and he shuddered against me. His insistent tongue pushed back into my mouth, stroking mine. When he pulled back a little, I fought the urge to wipe the extra moisture from my face. He reached into his back pocket and pulled out a condom. Holding it between his teeth, he dropped his pants and boxers in one quick movement. I couldn't get a good look at him before he pressed his hardness up against my panties and ground against me. My skirt was still around my waist.

After sheathing himself, he pulled my underwear to one side and bluntly pressed at my entrance. I guess foreplay was over. I was only kind of wet, and he grunted as he tried to work himself inside me, while I bit my lip at the uncomfortable pinching sensation. It had been awhile for me, but he didn't feel very big, and he pushed himself in without too much difficulty.

Burying his face in my neck, he grabbed my hips and rocked into me, pushing me harder into the door. After a half a dozen thrusts, he stiffened, jerking inside of me.

What the fuck? Already?

Sighing with satisfaction, he kissed my shoulder and leaned against me, pinning me with his weight. His chest rose and fell against mine as he took slow deep breaths. After pressing his lips to my neck one last time, he slipped out of me and took a step back.

"Sadie, Christ, that was great. Thanks." His hand reached out to cup my cheek, his thumb stroking me. "I'm gonna jump in the shower real quick. You good?"

Was I good? Um, no, dickwad, I was not good.

"Yeah, I'm good," I lied, fixing my underwear and smoothing my skirt back down. "I think I'm just gonna go."

He tipped his head and drew his eyebrows together. "You sure? We could go for round two in a little bit."

"I, uh, have an early morning. Spa appointment." I reached down for my shirt, and pulled it back over my head. I just needed to get out of there.

Details. Details were important. Rue had tried to teach me, but again, I failed to learn the lesson. Lame line, uncreative in the bedroom. Fumbling the room key, lack of finesse. Not making sure I finished, total douche.

He nodded his understanding and leaned down to kiss me. I turned at the last second, and he got the corner of my mouth. We hadn't even made it past the damn doorway. Hadn't even taken my clothes off. What. The. Hell.

Grabbing my purse from where it had landed by my feet, I mumbled something as I opened the door and fled, my face burning with annoyance and frustration. I stalked back to the elevator, which was mercifully already on my floor, and leaned against the stainless steel interior, feeling its coolness seep into my back and upper arms, raising goose bumps on my heated skin. I ground my teeth together as I waited impatiently for the elevator to lower.

Three floors down, the car stopped, and a man stepped on. Glancing up at him, I froze.

It was the surfer from earlier today.

I wanted to laugh, only it wasn't funny. He looked wonderfully disheveled. His hair was mussed, his lips swollen and red, his shirt not quite straight. Dipping his head, he zipped up his jeans, the movement unhurried, then ran a hand through his messy brown hair. My cheeks flamed. It was obvious what he was coming from.

He glanced over at me, and recognition lit his face. One side of his mouth lifted in greeting as his eyes raked over me. "I take it your evening went as well as mine?"

"Best sex ever. You?" I smiled at him sweetly and said the words slowly, as if I was savoring them.

"It was better the first time." He shrugged. "And you're lying."

I narrowed my eyes at him. "Am not."

"Then why are you already sneaking out and not spooning?"

I opened my mouth and then closed it. I didn't really have a good answer to that. And truth be told, I loved to spoon.

He nudged my shoulder. "Don't worry. You'll have better luck next time."

I snorted. Oh God, I snorted. What was wrong with me?

And why was the elevator moving so damn slow? An eternity later, the elevator dinged, the door slid open, and I stepped out with as much dignity as I could muster, moving across the tiled lobby as fast as I could on my spiky heels. I called back over my shoulder to him, "Have a good night."

"I already did. Twice. But thanks." His answer floated to me as I walked away.

I scowled as I exited the resort and headed for the sidewalk that would take me back toward my cottage. Home was closer than my car, so I turned that way. I could get my car in the morning.

Two blocks from the hotel, a vehicle slowed down as it passed me. Alarm bells went off in my head as it rolled to a stop and parked just ahead of me, but on the opposite side of the street. I watched it nervously and came to a standstill, gripping my purse. It was late, and I was alone. The street lights kept it from being dark, and Reynolds Island was pretty safe, but my heart rate still picked up.

The truck door opened, and it was him again. Seriously? Three times in one day? He jogged over and stopped next to me.

He smelled like sex and sweat. I was still horny and pissed off from earlier, and his obvious satisfaction needled. "Now what?" I demanded.

"Look, it's late, and my grandma would kill me if I just ignored you and let you walk home at night by yourself. Can I give you a ride?"

My mind flashed to an image of him on top of me, braced on his elbows, pumping into me with abandon, his hard flesh bared to my eyes. I bit my lip, my gaze falling to the front of his jeans. What was I thinking? I had just been naked—well, partially naked—with another man.

He cleared his throat and smirked. "That wasn't what I was implying, but I can offer you that as well, if you'd like."

I shook my head, embarrassed to be caught staring, and answered coolly. "Sloppy seconds isn't really my style. And we don't know each other. I don't even know your name."

"West Montgomery, at your service." He grinned and formally offered his hand.

I shook his hand, feeling a spark straight down to my toes. *God, I'd like to have him at my service.* "Sadie Mullins," I responded, the manners ingrained in me .

"Well, Sadie Mullins, if you're done picturing me naked, we can go. Your place or mine, either works for me."

I rolled my eyes at his audacity. I mean, yeah, I had been, but he couldn't know that for sure. "Are you always this cocky?"

"Only around beautiful women who stare at my package. Or touch it. Or suck—"

"Okay, okay, I get the point."

"Not yet, you don't. But maybe one day. If you're nice to me."

I stared at him for a beat, crossing my arms in front of me. "Does all this bullshit actually work for you?"

"Usually."

"It won't work on me."

"It will. Eventually. I tend to grow on a person." He wiggled his eyebrows at me.

"Are you capable of driving me home without molesting me?"

"Me? You're the one with the history of launching yourself at me. You've already mentally screwed me too, I can tell. You have the look."

"The look?"

He leaned closer and whispered in my ear. "I have this effect on women. Not my fault." He tucked a strand of hair behind my ear, letting his fingers drift down my neck as he straightened up.

"Maybe I'm immune to your charm."

Taking my hand and pulling me toward his truck, he looked at me, his eyes burning into mine. "We'll see."

We reached the side of his truck, a surprisingly beat up old Ford pickup. After climbing into the seat, I turned to shut the door only to find him leaning into the cab across me, buckling my seat belt. He patted my thigh. "Safety first."

"What happened to keeping your hands to yourself?" I shot back.

"You know you liked it." He grinned as he closed my door and jogged around to the driver side. "But to apologize, I'll let you pick the radio station."

He cranked the truck, and I leaned over to change the dial, adjusting it to my favorite local rock station. I glanced up to see if it was okay with him and caught him sneaking a peek down my shirt. "Hey!" I smacked his arm.

"Now who can't keep their hands to themselves?"

Ignoring his comment, I told him which street and cottage number to head to, eight blocks over, knowing he would think

I was just a tourist by its location. He nodded. "One of the Hawthorne's houses, huh? You have good taste. Of course, since you're into me, we already knew that."

I sighed. "You're impossible."

"Would you prefer it if I were a possibility?"

Maybe. I didn't answer, and we spent the rest of the ride in silence, me staring out the passenger window and him sending me questioning glances. I could feel the weight of them, but I stubbornly refused to turn and acknowledge him. When he pulled up outside my cottage, I started to reach for the door handle, but he grabbed my arm and stopped me.

"Wait." He jumped out and ran around the truck again, opening my door for me. He just stood there and studied me, as if I were a puzzle he wanted to figure out. "You okay? The guy you were seeing earlier, he didn't hurt you, did he?"

"No. He didn't hurt me. I promise," I assured him, when he continued to look at me with concern. *He also didn't get me off, and now I'm still horny, and you're standing here next to me looking completely edible but completely off limits.* I sighed and moved around him, heading up the steps to the front door. All the houses were built on stilts to keep the living premises higher above the water line. At the door, I paused and turned back. He was still standing by the truck, watching me, a look on his face I couldn't decipher. "Thanks for the ride. That was sweet of you."

He grunted. "Trust me, Sadie, I'm not sweet." He climbed back into his truck and roared off down the street, the darkness taking him away from me.

I moved through the cottage, getting ready for bed on autopilot. Shoes kicked to the corner, clothes tossed over a chair, makeup removed. Sleep eluded me, and I lay in bed for a long time, tossing and turning. Unable to get the image of West out of my head when I closed my eyes. I pictured my hands running through his close-cropped brown hair, staring into his blue-gray eyes, his mouth descending to mine. I imagined the play of his muscles as he moved over me, settling between my thighs, his fingers tracing a path down my body to my core, wet and waiting for him. I fantasized about what happened next.

Groaning with frustration, I squeezed my eyes shut, banishing him from my mind. I knew what I needed before I would be able to sleep. Grabbing my phone, I queued up my S playlist. Ed Sheeran, Sia, Seal, Shaggy, Sean Paul. Then I lay back on my pillows and my hand drifted down under my panties. Sometimes, when you wanted something done right, you just had to do it yourself.

chapter three

I SIGNALED TO KENDRA, the other lifeguard at the Water's Edge resort, that I was taking my ten-minute break and headed over to the tiki-hut poolside bar to grab a bottle of water. It was early yet on Wednesday morning, and only a handful of kids splashed about in the pool with their mothers hovering mere inches away, so Kendra and I were feeling pretty redundant. "Take twenty," she called out, sounding bored.

I plopped down on a barstool, and Theo handed me a sweaty bottle. "Slow morning, huh?" he commiserated.

I had met Theo when I started earlier in the week, and we'd hit it off right away. Theo was adorable, with his big puppy dog eyes and a curly mop of black hair that desperately needed a trim. We'd bonded during break time, making fun of the girls who spent all week doing nothing but laying by the pool getting a tan, rotisserie chicken style, hoping to catch the eye of the cute guys wandering around, but too lazy to actually get up and flirt.

I nodded my agreement and sipped from the cold bottle, looking down the path to the beach. Not much going on down there either. Most of the younger crowd was either still asleep or hung over from the night before. Only the families with small children and the retirees were out this early.

Theo leaned his elbows on the bar. "Up to anything exciting this week?"

I wiped my mouth with the back of my hand. "Not really. I still don't know many people around here other than Rue, and she travels for work a lot." Rue helped companies manage their online presence, mostly through social media, but she sometimes helped design websites too. This week, she was in Chicago, consulting with a new gourmet popcorn company.

Really, it was sad. I'd been here for five-and-a-half months and barely knew anybody. Of course, I had spent the winter wallowing in self pity and doughnuts, until my dwindling savings account forced me to reevaluate my hermit-like tendencies and seek actual employment. True, I had been a wedding photographer in Nashville, but capturing a bunch of lovesick fools promising each other forever wasn't real high on my to do list these days, and it took awhile to build up a client base with photography. With my lifeguarding background, and Rue's connections to the manager at the Edge, she'd managed to hook me up with a job. It was enough to keep me busy and put some money back in my pocket while I figured out my next move.

"Want to hit the gym with me tomorrow morning?" Theo offered. "I had a client cancel his training session, so I have an opening. No charge, and it'll get you out of the house for awhile."

"You're a trainer?" I was surprised. Theo's logoed t-shirt was snug enough on his frame for me to recognize he worked out, but I didn't realize he took it so seriously.

He looked wounded. "Yes. Is that so hard to believe?"

"No. Well, maybe." I squinted at him. "You're just so nice."

"You can be nice and still get good results. But I can do mean too, if that's how you like it." He wiggled his eyebrows at me.

"What time?" I asked, giggling at his face.

"Seven."

"Seven?"

"I'll even take you to breakfast afterwards, my treat."

"Can we get Krispy Kreme?" I brightened.

He looked confused, like the two couldn't possibly go together. "Doughnuts? After a workout?"

"What's the point of burning all those calories if you can't indulge a little?"

"We'll get doughnuts if you don't wimp out during the session," he countered.

"Deal."

THE NEXT MORNING, I dressed carefully for my workout. Compression leggings to show off my legs, a new shockingly bright pink sports tank, and my hair pulled back in a perky ponytail. You could always count on cute guys being at the gym, Theo included. It wouldn't hurt to look my best. I even swiped on some waterproof mascara before walking out the door.

Theo was on the treadmill when I walked in, and he raised his eyebrows as he looked me up and down. "You here to look pretty or break a sweat?"

"Can't I do both?"

"We'll see, I guess," he said. He looked like he was regretting the invite, but I could hang with the best of them. He'd figure that out soon enough.

He stepped off the treadmill and used the bottom of his damp top to wipe the sweat off his brow. I got a quick peek at his abs. Better than I expected. He dropped his shirt and caught me looking, grinning at me.

After filling up my water bottle at the water fountain and grabbing a towel, I was ready. We started with a one mile jog on the treadmill to warm up, and then he had me do a series of twisting lunges using the Bosu ball. Moving on to upper body, I swung a small kettle ball until my arms felt like jelly. I kept trying to glance around at the other guys in the free weight area, but Theo kept us on the mats in front of the mirrors on the other side of the gym. We'd run through several of the leg machines, and I suffered through squats holding a barbell on quads that were ready to collapse. I turned toward the mirror again, trying to check out the guy using the captain's chair.

Theo snapped his fingers in my face, jerking my attention

back to him. "Sadie! What is going on with you? Yes, you look hot. Yes, the other guys are looking at your butt as you squat. Happy, now?"

I flushed and stared straight ahead while I finished out my set, focusing on my form while he watched me. We switched to crunches on the decline bench until my abs screamed for surrender. Finally, he took mercy on me, and I sat on the mats, stretching out my legs and moaning.

We didn't talk much until we were settled at a table at Krispy Kreme, with hot coffees in hand and a small box of warm, freshly made doughnuts between us. Theo tilted back in his chair, studying me. "So," he said. "What was all that about at the gym?"

I looked at him, puzzled. "What are you talking about?"

He shot me a pointed look. "You were acting like you've never seen a guy flex before. You were practically drooling at one point."

Okay, I thought I had been a little more subtle than that. "It wasn't that bad," I protested.

His lips quirked. "If you say so."

I studied the steam rising from my latte and chewed my lip, and Theo folded his arms across his chest, waiting me out. "I'm just not doing well in the guy department," I admitted.

He let the legs of his chair drop back down and chuckled. "I find it hard to believe you're having trouble attracting a guy."

I picked up a doughnut and nibbled, the glaze melting against my tongue. *Heaven.* Stalling, I watched Theo devour a doughnut in three bites, trying to decide if I wanted to discuss the details of my stagnant love life.

"Oh God!" he groaned in ecstasy, his mouth full. "These are amazing." He grabbed another one and inhaled it while I tried not to laugh. He took a swallow of coffee, picked up a third doughnut and dipped his chin down. "You know you want to tell me. You're a girl. You're dying to talk about it."

I made a face at him. "Fine. But if I tell you, you can't make fun of me."

"Promise." He put one hand over his heart and held up the other like a Boy Scout.

I sighed and gave him the condensed version of what happened with Asshole and my strike-out with Jared. "And then, to top it off, as I was doing the walk of shame, I ran into this guy West again, who clearly had a better night than me and—"

"Wait. West?" Theo interrupted me, raising his eyebrows. "West Montgomery? Are you the girl who attacked him on the beach?"

I felt my cheeks warm. "I did not attack him," I said through gritted teeth. "I was trying to save him. And how do you know about that?"

"I was surfing with him earlier that morning. When he came in to grab breakfast, he was talking shit about some girl launching herself at him in the water, and that he had to drag her back out. Said it was a shame he didn't get a chance to do mouth-to-mouth."

I didn't think it was possible to turn any redder. "Right," I mumbled, trying not to picture West's lips fused to mine, sharing the same breath. "So, anyway, my luck with guys has turned to crap. I think something's wrong with me."

Theo shook his head. "There's something wrong with everyone. You're fine."

"Oh, yeah? What's wrong with you?"

His eyes turned sad, and he didn't answer right away, fiddling with his doughnut. "I let the right girl get away," he said, almost sounding embarrassed. "I was too chickenshit to make a move, and by the time I was ready to, she was already with somebody else. I missed my shot."

My heart broke for him. He looked like a kicked puppy. I reached over and squeezed his hand. "Her loss, Theo."

"Yeah. Sure." He laughed without humor.

We were both quiet for a few minutes, engrossed in our own thoughts. "Well, aren't we just pathetic?" I mused, just to break the heavy silence.

Theo narrowed his eyes and set his jaw and let my sentence hang for a moment. "No, we aren't. There's nothing wrong with either of us."

"Except the lack of romance, you mean?" I arched an eyebrow.

"Maybe that's fixable. I mean, we're both available, we've already seen each other half-naked at the gym—"

I made a strangled sound in my throat. Where was he going with this?

"Let me take you out this weekend," he said, catching me off guard.

I looked at him, flustered. I hadn't really gotten that vibe from him, like he was interested in me that way. He couldn't quite meet my eyes and the tips of his ears were red. "Look," he started.

"Maybe I'm not who you pictured yourself with, but I like you. I feel comfortable with you. Maybe it'll turn into something, and maybe it won't, but either way we'll have a good time. We can catch a movie then grab some ice cream on the boardwalk. It'll be fun. Whaddaya say?"

He looked at me hopefully, and I found myself grinning back at him. "Sure." Why not? What did I have to lose? And it's not like I had anything better to do.

"Saturday at seven?"

"Sounds good. I'll text you my address."

"It's a date!" He winked at me then shoved the rest of the doughnut in his mouth, licking his fingers. Such a guy.

After playing phone tag all week, Rue answered my call Thursday night. She'd left early the morning after we went to Anchor for her trip, so we hadn't had a chance to debrief yet. I rehashed my previous weekend with her. She about died laughing when I recounted my run-ins with West. "West is such a player," she said, when she caught her breath. "I don't think I've ever known him to have a girlfriend. Although he is gorgeous, I'll give you that."

"Tell me about it," I said.

Rue had spent her summers at Reynolds Island growing up, so I wasn't surprised she knew who West was. She recounted a few rumors she'd heard about girls doing stupid stuff to get his attention. He sounded like an arrogant horn dog with attention span issues. Figured. The hot ones always were.

"So, any other prospects out there? I take it Jared is gone."

"Yes, thank God. What about Eric?"

"Eh, nothing to talk about there. He had hairy toes. It was weird." Rue found something wrong with every guy, whether it was a date or a hook up. She was searching for the perfect man and refused to stop until she found him.

I paused. "Why were you looking at his toes that closely? You know what, never mind, don't tell me."

"You going out this weekend? Or do you want to have a girl's night when I get back?"

"Actually, I have a date Saturday," I announced.

"Oooohhh, with who?" she squealed with delight.

"Theo, from work. Do you know him?"

"Yes! Aw, he's a sweetie! I wouldn't have picked him for your type, but he's a step up from Asshole." My ex was never mentioned by name anymore. He didn't deserve such kindness.

"Sweet isn't my type?" I was a little offended.

"No. You like to argue too much."

"I do not!"

"See what I mean?" she pointed out.

I huffed. "We'll see."

"Just remember," she warned, "He's a local. No hook ups. Dating for real, yes, casual sex, no."

I rolled my eyes, even though she couldn't see it. "Yes, Mother."

She giggled. "I'll see you Sunday then. Have fun!"

ON SATURDAY NIGHT, the doorbell rang promptly at seven. *Two points for him,* I thought, as I moved across the living room to the front door. I loved our house. It was a quaint little three bedroom place with an open floor plan, so the kitchen, living room, and dining room were one big space, with driftwood gray walls and nautical blue and white furnishings. We had a screened sun porch off the back of the kitchen and a big hammock tied between two live oaks dripping with Spanish moss in our small yard. Since the whole cottage was on stilts, we just parked under the house.

I'd slipped on my favorite green sundress and wedges for the date, leaving my hair to fall in its natural partly curly, partly wavy riot around my shoulders. My make up was subdued, just mascara and lip gloss. Checking my reflection in the entryway mirror one last time, I smoothed the front of my dress, took a deep breath, and opened the door.

Theo was leaning against one of the porch columns while he waited. He straightened when he saw me and came forward, giving me a hug, and my nerves vanished. This was just Theo. "You look really nice," he said, grinning at me, one of his dark curls falling over his eye. He pushed it back, a movement I could tell was habit for him.

"You're looking pretty good yourself," I returned, smiling. He was wearing the standard island guy uniform—a polo, plaid cargo shorts, and leather flip flops. I locked the front door, and we were ready to go. Theo held my hand as we walked down the steps and opened my car door for me, waiting until I slid inside before closing it behind me. A perfect gentleman.

At the theater, we picked a comedy with Jason Segel, and he held hands with me during the movie too, lacing our fingers together. The connection felt warm and easy, but that was it. My palms didn't sweat, and my heart didn't race. I tried not to let that bother me, tried not to remember the tingle I'd felt when my skin had connected with West's out in the water. I definitely didn't relive, in slow motion, that endless slide down his body when he'd set me back down on the shoreline, the way he'd kept his hands on me a beat too long after I was steady. It never even crossed my mind.

After the movie let out, we meandered along the boardwalk that the north half of the island was known for. "So, Sadie, has lifeguarding always been your dream job?" he teased me, as we interrupted a group of seagulls picking at spilled popcorn, their loud caws berating us.

"Of course!" I said with fake enthusiasm. "And haven't you always wanted to be a bartender at a frozen daiquiri bar?"

"What higher calling is there?" he agreed, before turning more serious. "No, really, what do you want to do here?" He seemed genuinely interested in my answer.

"Photography," I said, a hint of wistfulness creeping into my voice. "It's what I was doing back in Nashville. Wedding photography, mostly. But ever since that mess with Asshole, I've wanted to change my focus. Portraits maybe, or more commercial stuff."

"Have you talked to Grady about maybe doing some work around the resort?" Grady was our manager and Rue's friend who'd gotten me the job.

"No. I barely know the guy, and I already owe him for the lifeguarding job. I didn't want to push my luck by asking for any other favors."

"Nah, Grady's cool. Actually, he was surfing with us that morning you met West too."

I groaned. "Great."

"Well, he doesn't know it was you," Theo assured me.

"Hopefully, we can keep it that way."

"I'll talk to him for you. I bet he can come up with something."

"Theo, you don't have to do that!" I protested.

"No biggie. Just leave it to me."

I stopped walking and wrapped my arms around him, giving him a big hug. Maybe there were still some good guys left in the world. "Thank you," I whispered, giving him a quick peck on the cheek.

Whistles and catcalls interrupted our embrace and had me pulling back in embarrassment. A group of guys were strolling up the boardwalk toward us. "Benedict!" one of them called out.

Theo grinned as the group approached. "Guys. What are y'all up to tonight?" Theo did one of those complicated guy handshakes, ending with a back slap, with a guy who had a blond faux hawk and pierced lip.

"Heading to the Wreck to hang out, shoot some pool," the same guy said. "Who's the chick?"

Theo's arm snaked around my waist, pulling me to his side. "Trevor, this is Sadie. Sadie, these are the guys. Trevor, Dylan, Wyatt, and you've already met his brother, West." Theo pointed to each in turn, but my attention was snagged when he said the last name.

West. My eyes locked on his. He was wearing a baseball hat pulled low over his eyes, and it made him seem softer, less potent somehow. His jawline was scruffy, like he hadn't shaved in a day or two, and I couldn't help but wonder how it would feel against my face. He stared at me, his expression a mix of confusion and surprise, and then his eyes dropped to my hip, where Theo's hand rested. The muscle in his jaw clenched, his hands curling into loose fists at his side.

Wyatt whistled and gave Theo a high five. "Good job, man." Wyatt looked like a more boyish version of West, but with longer, darker hair instead of West's close-cropped style.

The other guys greeted me, but I didn't really hear them. "Sadie," West acknowledged with a dip of his chin, my name rumbling over his lips. It felt like a caress, like he had reached out and stroked me. I smiled back, the tip of my tongue sneaking out to wet my dry lips, and he seemed riveted by the small action. His eyes darkened, and then he swallowed and looked away.

"We're headed to get some ice cream," Theo said. "You guys want to join us?"

West glanced back at me, down to the hand on my hip, then back up. "No," he said, sounding almost bored. "Besides, Grady's meeting us soon. We'll catch you later, Benedict." He started to walk away, not waiting for the other guys. My face burned, and I felt guilty, like I had done something wrong, which was ridiculous, of course. I refused to turn and watch him leave, even though I swear my body could tell the difference as he moved farther away, my awareness of him lessening.

The others trailed after West, and Theo and I started walking again, his arm falling back to his side. "Benedict?" I questioned.

"My last name. I played pee-wee football with most of those guys. Well, not West and Grady, because they were older, but we went by our last names there. It kind of stuck for me."

I hummed an acknowledgement, then returned to our previous conversation, refusing to let myself think about West. "So, Theo, if bartending isn't the goal, what are you working toward?"

He shrugged. "I'm still trying to figure that out. I couldn't afford college like those guys, so I've just been working and saving. I want to be my own boss someday, not have to answer to anyone but myself."

I nodded. I could understand that. It was part of the appeal of photography. Setting your own schedule, working as hard as you wanted, knowing your success or failure depended only on you. I could definitely relate.

We walked farther, laughing at each other's stupid jokes. We bought waffle cones and stood licking the melting gelato, watching the sunset over the water turn the sky a delicious shade of coral. I wished I had my camera. I snapped a quick photo with my phone, but it wasn't the same.

Back at my house, we climbed the steps to my front door when my stomach twisted with anxiety. Would he try to kiss me? I wasn't sure how I felt about that. We stopped on the porch, and I dug my key out of my purse, letting it dangle from my hand. "Theo, I had a great time tonight," I said.

He smiled and stepped a little closer, taking each of my hands in his. "Me too." Staring into my eyes, he took a deep breath, letting it out slowly. "Okay, moment of truth."

He leaned in and pressed his lips against me, moving them gently over mine. It was nice, but there was no spark. *Bummer.* We broke apart and stood there facing each other, holding hands, foreheads touching.

Theo whispered, "Wow. That really didn't do anything for me. How 'bout you?"

I laughed in relief that we were on the same page. "You do have nice lips," I offered as a consolation.

"And you have a nice ass, so why can't this just work? Hold on a sec."

He grabbed my butt and pulled our pelvises together and ground against me for a moment. I looked at him in confusion. He sighed and shook his head. "Nope. I mean, don't get me wrong, you're hot, and I'd lay you in a heartbeat if I didn't have to see you at work and—"

I cut him off. "Friends?"

Theo nodded. "Definitely. See you at the gym Monday morning?"

I smiled at him and squeezed his hand. "I'll buy the doughnuts this time."

He groaned. "No more doughnuts. I'll take you to this little café I know. They have good omelets."

"But I like doughnuts."

"How 'bout this? I train you for free four times a week, and you buy breakfast. We'll eat healthy three days a week and splurge for doughnuts on Wednesdays."

I narrowed my eyes. "We'll only train three times a week, and we'll get doughnuts on Mondays and Wednesdays."

Theo sighed then nodded in defeat.

"Ahhh." I grinned. "A man after my own heart. We are going to get along just fine, Benedict."

chapter four

I blew my whistle at the rowdy preteen boys running around the pool having a water gun fight. "Walk! No running!" I hollered for the nineteenth time in the last hour. Their moms were either absent or oblivious after too many of Theo's daiquiris, I wasn't sure which. It'd been a Friday from hell. Fridays always sucked during the summer because all the weekenders were just arriving, and the kids were extra rambunctious from being cooped up in the car.

Around eleven, two guys thought it would be funny to pick me up and pretend to throw me in the pool, which had resulted in Theo vaulting over the bar and coming to my rescue, much to the delight of the teenage girls. And since lunch, this creepy older man had been pretending to read a book while ogling the same three teenage girls who had swooned over Theo, as they lounged on their chaises wearing only the skimpiest of bikinis. The man even offered to rub more sunscreen on them. Twice. Luckily, they were smart enough to decline, and the second time he offered, one complained to her mom, who reported him to management. Now, the creepy old guy had wandered down the beach path, probably searching for some other prepubescent body to fantasize over. Gross. Kendra was a saint and had spent the last twenty minutes patiently explaining to a woman that the pool used a salt system, and her baby would be perfectly safe from carcinogenic toxins if she got wet.

I eyed the tiki-hut wistfully, pulling my hat off long enough to swipe at the sweat beading on my forehead. A daiquiri sounded pretty good right about now.

Theo waved to catch my attention and pointed to his phone. I walked over to my beach bag for my cell and saw a text from him.

Theo: A bunch of us are going to the Wreck tonight. Wanna come?

Me: What's the Wreck?

Theo: You haven't been to the Wreck yet? It's Wyatt's bar. The ultimate hang spot. Super casual.

Me: Can I bring Rue?

Theo: A bar can never have too many hot girls.

Me: Pervert.

Theo: Just sayin.'

Me: We'll meet you there. I'm sure Rue knows where it is. What time?

Theo: I'll be there around 8, but whenever.

I tapped out a quick message to Rue, knowing her phone was

always within reach.

> **Me: Want to go to the Wreck tonight?**
> **Rue: I haven't been there in ages. Sounds fun! What time?**
> **Me: Theo said 8?**
> **Rue: Ok. See you at home later!**

This day might be redeemable, after all. Friends, alcohol, and more alcohol. Just a few more hours. Closing my eyes, I searched for a moment of Zen. I concentrated, breaking down the moment. The feel of the sun heating my skin competing with the cool breeze ruffling my ponytail. The smell of sunscreen, salt, and pheromones. The crash of the distant waves, barely audible over the ear-splitting screech only very small children are capable of making. A loud splash and the feel of water cascading over my ankles ruined the rest of my illusion. Rolling my shoulders, I opened my eyes to my headache-inducing reality.

With her hands fisted on her hips, Kendra was glaring at the boys making machine gun noises who had just made a pair of toddler princesses cry, so I tucked my phone away and slipped into the role of bad cop. I confiscated all the water guns, ignoring their protests. "I'll take these, thank you. Next one who runs, gets it!" I threatened in a cheerful voice, keeping the biggest one in my hand. The kids looked pissed and went off to whine to their parents. Tough. The posted rules said no water guns. That meant—surprise—no water guns.

Six o'clock finally rolled around, and Kendra and I hung the *Swim At Your Own Risk* sign on the lifeguard stand and clocked out. As we walked to the employee lot, I mentioned the get together at the Wreck later, and she perked up. "The Wreck? The guys there are always a blast! I'll see you there later." She waved as she headed off to her champagne-colored Camry.

When I got home, Rue was already there, her hair wrapped in a towel from the shower. She was moving between the master bedroom that she occupied and the third bedroom, which basically functioned as our overflow closet. Her bedroom was on the other side of the cottage from my room and the spare bedroom, which shared a bathroom. It was a good thing we didn't have a lot of visitors, since my bathroom was the only other one in the house except for Rue's private one in the master suite. I kept it super clean; everything was tucked into the drawers below the sink. I didn't like the idea of my toothbrush and other toiletries being exposed to everyone's grimy hands.

She had three hangers of clothes in each hand and was looking at them, frowning at the colorful array of shiny, glittery, and sequined dresses. It looked like Nordstrom's had puked an after-five rainbow in her bedroom.

"Those look pretty dressy. I thought Theo said the Wreck was laid back," I said, wrinkling my nose at her choices.

"It is." She pouted. "That's the problem. I can never figure out how to get that casual look. I like dressing up. It's not my fault I have good taste."

I walked by her into the third bedroom and grabbed a pair of snake print shorts and tossed them to her, causing her to drop the hangers she was holding. "Find a black top and some shoes, and be done with it. Quit over thinking." She looked at the shorts and twisted her lips in indecision before walking over to the rack of tops that were hers, organized first by color, then by sleeve length, then by fabric. She left the other clothes lying on the floor in the hall. I picked them up for her and draped them over the futon by the window. I never put them away correctly, and it made her crazy. "Whatever. Figure it out," I said. "I'm hopping in the shower."

I washed my hair and took the time to use an exfoliating body scrub to really get all the layers of sunscreen off my skin. It smelled like watermelon. So did my shampoo. It was knockoff store brand stuff, but whatever. It worked. My legs still felt pretty smooth from this morning, so I didn't bother to shave again. It was only two weeks into May, but I already had a nice tan going. I smiled at my reflection as I wrapped my hair in a towel like Rue and padded to my room, letting the steam escape into the hall.

Rue plopped onto my bed, wearing the snake print shorts and a black lace strapless bra, her dark brown and pink hair now dry and hanging straight and glossy down her back. I eyed her dubiously. "I doubt it's *that* casual, Rue."

"Shut up." She made a face and threw a lobster-embroidered pillow at me. My room was decorated with a nautical feel, like most of the cottage. A pale blue quilt covered my bed, punched up with brightly colored throw pillows, and a battered sea chest acted as a bench at the foot. The headboard was made of iron and painted white like the wicker dresser and nightstand, and a pair of weathered aqua oars crisscrossed over the bed. The bottom half of the walls were covered by white bead board, but the top half were painted a deep navy. Burlap curtains filtered the light coming in through the windows. The room looked like it belonged in an issue of Coastal Living magazine. I loved it.

I slipped on a pair of cutoffs that hugged my butt like a second skin and threw on a white skinny tank and a sheer pink top over it. "There, was that so hard?" I asked her. She made a face at me and left the room again to finish getting dressed. Bending over at the waist, I unwrapped my towel and rubbed some of the water out of my wet hair. I scrunched some fancy brand name sea spray product I'd found on clearance into it and went back to the bathroom to at least partially blow dry it.

I was finishing with my makeup when Rue appeared again, fully dressed and carrying two glasses of her famous rum-spiked basil lemonade. A slouchy black top and black espadrilles tied around her ankles completed her outfit. She looked stunning, as always. Rue was delicate and petite with pale skin and miles of curves, and nothing ever looked bad on her. I'd hate her if she wasn't my best friend. We sat on the couch and sipped our drinks, pre-gaming.

"So why haven't we been to the Wreck yet?" I asked, crunching an ice cube.

"The ratio is off. It's more like two-thirds locals, one-third transients. The other two bars are the opposite. Plus, I like to dress up, and you don't really dress up to go to the Wreck."

"Do you even own a pair of cutoffs?" I asked, amused.

She scrunched up her nose as she thought about it. "Yeah, I think. They're designer, though."

"Of course," I mocked.

"Oh, shush. I like nice things. There's nothing wrong with that."

I took a long drink and didn't answer her. There really wasn't anything wrong with it, and she could afford it all without even blinking. Plus, I was often the recipient of her generosity and had access to her legendary shoe collection, so who was I to talk? We finished our drinks while she bounced some ideas off me for the popcorn company. It was kind of hard to make popcorn sound exciting, though, so I wasn't much help.

I let Rue pick out a pair of braided leather sandals for me to wear, since she wrinkled her nose at the old rubber flip flops I had planned on wearing, and then we left. Rue had the top down on her Mercedes convertible, the weather was perfect, plus I had no idea where we were going, so she drove. I used the hair tie I always had around my wrist to tie my hair back until we got there, so it wouldn't morph into a giant rat's nest. Rue's hair still looked perfect, of course. As I finger combed my own slightly damp strands, I convinced myself I was rocking the sexy, tousled look. It could be true.

As we got out of the car, I saw the Wreck for the first time. Rue had mentioned it'd originally been called The Shipwreck, but the Ship portion of the sign had fallen off and was leaning against the building. The clapboard wooden structure looked like it had seen better days, and the metal roof was rusted in spots. Cars filled the parking lot, though, and loud music was drifting out the open door.

When we got inside, I could see why Theo described the place as laid back. The tables were simple wooden picnic tables, and the scarred plank floor was littered with peanut shells. Red Coleman coolers full of unshelled peanuts sat on a bench next to plastic kids' sand pails and shovels for customers to help themselves. The walls were made from reclaimed boards of different colors and sizes, but it was hard to tell from all the graffiti. Scribbles covered the walls and tables in a colorful tangle.

I spotted Theo across the room watching a game of pool and waved. He laughed and shook his head at one of the guys from the boardwalk the other day—Dylan, maybe?—and then headed toward us.

"You made it," he said, giving me a hug and a quick kiss on the cheek.

Rue and Theo greeted each other and caught up on the local gossip while I finished looking around. The bar was off to the side, and bits of paper fluttered above it. In the back there were a handful of pool tables, as well as an old foosball table and a new-looking air hockey game. A dance floor was to our left, and through a pair of open doors a deck overlooked the marsh behind it, lit by strings of light. This was more my kind of place than Anchor. It felt comfortable. Easy.

I leaned into Rue, bumping her hip. "I'm going to the bar. You want a shot or a mojito?" I knew I wanted a margarita.

Theo shook his head at us. "You have to try the grog."

Rue half-groaned, half-laughed. "I'd forgotten about that. He's right. We have to get the grog."

I furrowed my brow. "Okaaay. I'll go get us some . . . grog."

Theo squeezed my side. "Just tell them you want a pitcher and to put it on Grady's tab. He's buying tonight."

I felt Rue stiffen next to me. "Grady's here?" She whipped her head around, looking for him, and ran her fingers through her hair. It was what she did when she was nervous.

"Yeah. Tonight's all on him. Drinks here first, then we're all headed back over to his place later for an after party. You remember how to get there, right, Rue?"

"Yeah," she clipped out. "I remember."

I gave her a quizzical look. I'd have to remember to ask her about Grady later. She was acting weird.

Theo pointed out which table he'd claimed, and I headed to the bar. As I got closer, I realized the fluttery paper things hanging above the bar were actually dollar bills thumbtacked to the beams above it. Dollar bills with graffiti. I was still trying to figure out what the writing on the bills was when I reached the bar, my head twisted up and to the side to stare at one dollar in particular. Block letters spelled out, *Are you a lieutenant? Because you just made my private stand at attention.* What? The one next to it asked in bold Sharpie, *Do you work at Subway? Because you just gave me a footlong.*

"They're pick-up lines."

I jerked my head down at the sound of the deep voice. It almost looked like the voice belonged to West. Good Lord, was I so sexually deprived that now I was conjuring him up as the bartender? I blinked. It was him. "What?" I asked, smoothing a wisp of hair from my face.

"The dollar bills. They're pick-up lines. If a line works for a guy, he pins it up. Sort of as a favor to his fellow man."

"Are any of your lines up there?" I asked without thinking, glancing up again like I'd be able to spot one.

He spread his arms wide, gripping the edge of the bar from the service side, and grinned, his eyes crinkling in the corners. He had several braided rope bracelets on his right wrist. They looked worn, the colors more muted than vibrant, like he never took them off. "Nope. Want to know why not?" His shoulders stretched the material of his t-shirt, and my eye was drawn upward to his tattoo peeking below the sleeve.

"Why not?" I parroted, distracted.

He crooked his finger at me and bent down like he was going to tell me a secret. I leaned over the bar halfway to meet him. Cupping his hand around my ear, his fingers brushed my hair, and he whispered, "I don't need a line."

Amused, I drew back and quirked an eyebrow, ignoring the way my scalp tingled where his fingers had just been. I made a big show of studying him, my eyes lingering on his chest and shoulders. "Because you're just that good, right?"

"Maybe. I mean, you followed me here, didn't you?"

"Sorry to disappoint you, but I followed *Theo* here. Guess you'll have to settle for second place." He scowled. His obvious jealousy made me feel desirable, powerful. I couldn't help wanting to needle him further. "There is something I need from you, though." I licked my lips, leaning forward again. I made my voice low, sultry. "Something only you can give me." His smile grew beneath half-closed eyes, and he crossed his arms over his chest, his biceps flexing. "I need a pitcher of grog. And put it on Grady's tab," I finished, keeping my tone even.

His smile faltered for a moment before the arrogant smirk slipped back in place. Turning his back to me without a word, he began scooping fruit from a cooler. I couldn't help my eyes from tracing the line from his broad shoulders, down his tapering back, and over the curve of his ass. He was a prime example of what a man should look like, and he knew it too, damn him. The play of his muscles as he added ice and topped it with something red from the bar gun made me bite my lip with appreciation and yearn to reach out for him and stroke the length of his spine to see how he would react to my touch. He finished and turned back, breaking me out of my daze, and presented me with a full plastic pitcher of what looked like Kool-Aid with fruit salad floating in it.

I wrinkled my nose. "What is it?"

"Punch with Everclear-soaked fruit."

My eyebrows rose.

"Be careful. It packs more of a wallop than you'd expect."

"I'm sure I'll be fine, but thanks anyway."

I grabbed the pitcher and wove through the full bar to the table Theo had pointed out, being careful not to spill any of the bright red drink on myself. When I got back to the table, Kendra had arrived too, looking adorable in an ikat sundress.

Theo took the pitcher from me and poured us all drinks into the red plastic cups that were stacked on the tables. Rue took a big swallow and headed out to the deck, muttering something about needing some air. Minutes later, Kendra spotted a friend across the room and went off to say hi, promising to come back in a bit. Feeling abandoned, Theo and I stood shoulder-to-shoulder, and he filled me in on the local gossip, pointing out who was together, who hated who, and who to avoid at all costs.

"What about him?" I pointed at a guy with buzzed hair who was staring at Rue intently as he nursed a longneck beer.

Theo shot me a confused look. "That's Grady. You haven't met him yet?"

I lifted a shoulder. "Not officially, no. Rue got me the job, and I did the rest through the HR girl."

"Ah. I'll introduce you later."

"That'd be good, since I did charge my drink to his tab."

We people-watched for awhile, and I tried to pick out a girl for Theo to hit on, but everyone I picked he found something wrong with. He was like the male version of Rue. One girl laughed like a hyena, he said, a pretty redhead had ignored him in high school because he wasn't cool enough, and the last one I motioned to before I gave up apparently had dog breath.

"Fine," I huffed. "What about for me? Whose attention should I try to catch?"

"For short term or long term?"

"Short."

Theo nodded toward the foosball table. "Boone, the blond standing over there. He always manages to stay friends with his flings, so he must be doing something right."

I checked Boone out. He had a lanky frame, great looking lips, and messy hair that looked like it was styled by running his hands through it once or twice before giving up. Not a bad choice, not a bad choice at all. Theo nudged my side with his elbow. "He'll be at Grady's later too." I nodded, but couldn't help myself from looking over at West. He was flirting with a brunette whose boobs were barely contained by her top. Such a typical guy. A little flash of flesh, and they were goners. I tried to ignore the stab of disappointment that he was so susceptible.

Theo laughed. "C'mon." He flung an arm around my shoulder and directed me toward the nearest pool table. "We're up next."

We watched Trevor and Dylan finish up their game. Trevor sank the eight ball, and Dylan claimed Trevor cheated the whole time. "Fuck that, dude, I won. Next round's on you," Trevor told him as they handed off their cue sticks and headed to the bar for shots, with Dylan continuing to give him shit as they walked away.

I knew the rules of pool, but I sucked. Theo took it easy on me and tried to give me pointers, but I was pretty much a lost cause. If I couldn't find an easy ball to pocket, I tried to knock Theo's balls out of position. Then I resorted to flat out trying to mess him up, bumping into his hip and knocking my cue against his as he positioned his shot. He joined in the corruption, tipping my elbow at the last second and bending close to blow in my ear. We were being goofy, and I was on my second cup of grog and feeling a little warm.

I tripped over my own feet and fell against the pool table, giggling when my elbow sent two balls rolling down the felt.

Hearing Theo's hoot of laughter behind me, I twisted and looked over my shoulder, and my eyes drifted past him to the bar again. This time, West was filling a glass with draft and looking in my direction. Was he checking out my ass as I bent over the pool table? His heated gaze traveled down my legs, then back up. I suppressed the urge to give a little wiggle. His eyes trapped mine, and I couldn't look away. The crowd around us faded until all I could see was him.

A primal awareness of him settled deep within me and unfurled, sending tendrils of heat to lick at my core. His eyes darkened, turning more gray than blue, as if he knew what he was doing to me. Suddenly, he jerked his hand and mouthed a curse, looking down to see the beer overflowing and breaking the spell between us.

I pushed myself upright and tried to slow my pulse. Theo was talking behind me, and I forced myself to concentrate on his words. "Sadie, meet Boone. Boone, this is Sadie. She lifeguards over at the Edge with me."

"Nice," Boone drew out the word, making it seem twice as long. He raised his eyes from my rear to my eyes, making me wonder what exactly he was referring to. "You gonna be at Grady's later?"

"Yeah." His obvious interest flooded my cheeks with heat.

"Awesome." He rubbed his hand over the back of his neck and looked around, as if trying to think of a way to prolong the conversation. "Wanna play foosball? I've got the table next."

I wrinkled my nose and tilted my head side to side. "I'm more of an air hockey kind of girl."

"I can work with that. I can definitely work with that." He nodded. "I'll be back for you in a few minutes." He headed toward the air hockey table to make the arrangements.

Theo held up his first, and I bumped it. "Aw, yeah!" he whooped, proud of his wingman skills. I rolled my eyes at him and tried to stifle my mouth from kicking up at the corner. It probably wasn't a good idea to encourage him.

Boone came back for me shortly after, and we decided on best two out of three. Theo came with me to cheer me on, and though I lost the first round pretty spectacularly, I squeaked out a narrow victory in game two. Kendra wandered back over for moral support when she saw what was happening. We were tied in game three and kept trading points back and forth, neither of us getting a lead on the other. Boone and I were flirting and talking shit to each other, Theo was making fun of me, and I could hardly stop laughing. We were posturing like it was life or death who won, and a small crowd had gathered around to watch. Wyatt moved in next to Boone and was trying to coach him, pointing out my weak spots. "The edges, man. She's not guarding the edges."

"Try me," I shot back, bending at the knees and shifting my weight back and forth.

I was having a really great time for the first time in months, a perma-smile splitting my cheeks. It was the first night since the whole debacle with Asshole that I had felt like my old carefree self again. I looked around the table for Rue, wanting to share the moment with her, but I didn't see her.

Boone took advantage of my distraction, and the puck slipped past me, putting him one up on me. Game point. I concentrated, and we went back and forth, the puck sliding furiously between us, ricocheting off the walls. Theo, Kendra, and Wyatt were egging us on. I'd almost scored twice, and I was flushed with excitement.

"You got this, Mullins!" Theo hollered from the corner.

Not to be outdone, Kendra chimed in. "Better watch my girl, Boone. She's got skills."

My mallet slipped a little in my hand, and I lost the rhythm. I tried to regain control, but I was off, chasing after the puck instead of connecting with it. A second later, I heard the hollow *thunk* as the puck slid into my goal. A shout went up on Boone's side of the table, and a couple of the guys raised their arms in the air victoriously and chest bumped, spilling some beer on the floor. No one seemed to care. Boone worked his way around to my side and wrapped his arm around my shoulders, giving me a side hug. "You almost had me. A little more practice, and you might come out on top next time."

"You just got lucky."

"Not yet, but the night's still young," he grinned, pressing a kiss to the side of my head. I punched his arm, and he released me good-naturedly, saying he'd see me later at Grady's, a hot promise in his eyes.

I pulled away from the crowd, still smiling, and passed the bar, moving toward the double doors to the deck so I could find Rue. Normally, she was the life of the party, laughing and joking alongside everyone else. It wasn't like her to be so reclusive. I finally found her curled up on a bench in the corner of the deck, staring out over the marsh at a pelican perched on an abandoned dock piling. I sat down next to her, looking from her to the bird and back again. "He doesn't seem like much of a conversationalist," I pointed out.

She turned to me, her lips twisted and her eyes cloudy. She shook her head and focused on me.

"Hey," I said softly, "Something wrong? We don't have to go to Grady's. We can just go home."

"No! I'm fine. I'm fine," she repeated with more force.

I raised my eyebrows. "You trying to convince me or yourself?"

She looked back at the bird and set her chin. "Maybe both. You ready to go? I saw Grady leave with Marissa awhile ago."

"Who's Marissa?"

Rue shrugged. "His flavor of the week, I guess. I don't really know her. He stopped me to say hi and introduced us. She looks like an anime pixie, all big eyes and big boobs, with a tiny little body."

I tried to contain my smile. "Jealous?"

Rue whipped her head back around to me. "Of her? *Hell,* no! Why would I be jealous? She's just some chick passing through. No one will even remember her next week." She waved her hand dismissively.

I sat there in silence, watching her with a mixture of concern and curiosity. Something about Grady seemed to get to Rue. And I'd never seen a guy get to Rue before. She had her jaw clenched and was avoiding eye contact. "Okay. I guess I'll see you inside in a few minutes then."

I was passing by the bar again to tell Theo we were heading out, when a hand grabbed my elbow. Turning, I found West looking down at me, brow furrowed. "Yes?" I asked.

He crossed his arms over his chest. "You headed to Grady's with everyone?"

"I'd planned on it. Although, I still haven't actually met the guy."

"Grady's a good guy. Just . . ." He paused. "Just be careful there. Sometimes his parties get a little wild."

I lifted the corner of my mouth, offering him a faint smile. "I'm a big girl. I can take care of myself."

He looked at me, his gaze dragging over my face and dropping down to my legs. "Then why do I have to keep rescuing you?"

Raising my eyebrows, I looked at him in disbelief. He lifted his in return, challenging me. Nodding, I licked my lips. "Tell you what, West. If I need rescuing later, you'll be the first one I call." I patted his arm and started to move past him.

"Is that your not-so-subtle way of asking for my number?"

I paused, straightened my shoulders, then continued on without looking back.

His deep laughter followed me, taunting me.

chapter five

When we got to Grady's, Rue left me with Theo and disappeared to the makeshift bar set up in the kitchen. I started to go after her, but Theo caught my arm and steered me in the other direction. "C'mon," he urged. "I'll introduce you to Grady."

I tried not to gawk as he led me through the foyer and into the living room. Grady lived in a show-off house. An *impressive* show-off house. As we entered the main living space, I couldn't help but look up. The ceiling had to be at least three stories high in this room. It was ridiculous. Huge windows showcased the Intracoastal Waterway, where a few boats still zipped around. Sunrises and sunsets would look amazing from here.

This house was more Rue's lifestyle than mine. Her parents' house was a lot like this—echoing rooms, custom drapes, polished floors, clutter-free, dust-free, personality-free. The Hawthorne's rental properties had more character and charm than their actual house, thank God. My upbringing was decidedly more middle class. My parents were sound engineers in Nashville and made a decent living. They didn't work with the big names on a regular basis, but they'd worked with some of them when they were just starting out. My brother was part of the family business, too. I'd broken the Mullins music legacy, and I think they were all disappointed, but not mad per se.

I'd been raised to be independent, since my parents' work hours were so varied, and they weren't entirely surprised I wanted to strike out on my own. Home for me had been an average-sized ranch in a sidewalk neighborhood, where each lot had a matching oak tree in the front yard, the mailboxes were all painted the same shade of off-white, and *custom* was something you did to your truck, not your house.

Theo stopped moving, and I walked right into him, letting out a grunt and snapping my head down. We were standing in front of the guy with the buzz cut from the bar, and perched on sky high heels behind him was a girl who really did resemble an anime pixie. Her short black hair was so glossy it was almost reflective, and her boobs looked like they had special antigravity properties. I tried not to stare and instead focused on Grady.

Well, *shit*. No wonder Rue acted weird around him. The man was gorgeous. And his eyes, my God. He had the prettiest eyes I'd ever seen on a man, with lashes long enough to make any woman jealous and a clear green gaze that seemed to burn through you.

He was mesmerizing. Even just wearing a button-down shirt with the top buttons undone and the sleeves rolled up, he oozed raw masculinity. He was probably deadly in a suit.

"Theo, my man, you finally hooked one?" he teased, holding out a hand to me. "I'm Grady Tomlin. And you're the Sadie he's been telling me about?"

I flushed, not sure what Theo had told him. Surely he hadn't mentioned the incident with West in the ocean? "Nice to meet you," I said, taking his hand. He had a firm grip and looked me right in the eye. I got the feeling he was a man who was always in control.

"Theo tells me you're quite the photographer and that we might be able to utilize your skills at the Edge. I'd love to set up a time to talk to you about it next week. I'd say let's talk now, but I'd rather not mix business and pleasure, and tonight is definitely not about work." He winked, and it was charming, not creepy.

"Of course. Whenever it's convenient for you. Just let me know." I withdrew my hand. Damn, the man was smooth. I was going to have to corner Rue later. "You have a stunning home."

He shrugged. "It's nice. I bought it for the view mostly. Wait 'til we're outside later. Then you'll understand." He tugged on the pixie, and she moved forward. "This is Marissa. Marissa, you've met Theo, and I'm sure we'll be seeing more of Sadie this summer. You're staying with Rue now, correct?"

Marissa smiled at me, all perfect gleaming teeth and big lips. I nodded at him, distracted, and smiled back at Marissa. I wondered if she could talk or if she was just for show.

Grady started to move away, dragging Marissa with him. "If you'll excuse us, we're going to get a drink and then head out to the dock. You guys should join us out there soon. It's a beautiful night."

I watched him go. He had a magnetic quality that made it hard to look away. Theo squinted at me out of one eye and then groaned. "Oh, no! Not you too! Please tell me you're not going to turn into a weird girly little puddle every time he comes near. And he wonders why we don't like to invite him to go places with us."

I shook my head to clear it. "I'm good. I'm good. I just wasn't expecting all that. He should come with a warning or something."

"We need more alcohol. Let's find Rue," Theo said, grumbling.

Suddenly, the full impact of Grady's words registered. I squealed and latched onto Theo's arm. "He wants to talk to me about my photography! That would be amazing!"

Theo just smiled and shook his head. "That's what friends are for, doofus."

Trailing behind Grady into the kitchen, we found Rue flirting outrageously with a Latin-looking guy, giggling and rubbing his arm. "Sadie!" she yelped. "Come meet Hendrix."

I said hi, and Hendrix took my hand, raising it to his lips for a kiss before turning back to Rue and wrapping his arm around her shoulders, dragging her to his side.

Rue giggled again and melted against him while Theo and I stood there in awkward silence and fixed ourselves a drink. Hendrix had pulled Rue against him and was whispering in her ear. She put a hand against his chest, her eyes closed and biting her lip, and nodded to whatever it was he was suggesting.

I squinted at Theo, silently begging him to save us. I did not want to stand here and watch this. Theo tipped his head toward the deck, and I turned, letting him lead the way. We leaned against the steel cables encircling the deck and looked out at the night sky. Now I saw what Grady meant. The view was breathtaking. The stars covered the sky like sprinkles on a cupcake, and below us the waves crashed into the seawall, the sound a soothing soundtrack to the evening. A small pathway to the left led to a dock that stretched out over the water, ending with a tin roof canopy. A few tiki torches lined the path and the end of the dock, and to the right, a bonfire was burning, circled by stone benches where a few couples were snuggled up roasting marshmallows.

An ear-splitting shriek from behind me jolted me upright, and I turned in the direction of the sound. Rue approached, pulling Hendrix out onto the deck with us. "I know!" she cried. "Let's go play dirty truth or dare on the dock. Like old times." She started dragging Hendrix down the steps and turned to pin me and Theo with a wide-eyed look. "You two better be getting your asses down there."

Theo gave a helpless shrug, and we fell in line behind her. She collected people as she went, herding Grady, Marissa, Boone, Wyatt, Trevor, Dylan, and a small group of girls I didn't recognize along the path. We ended up sitting in a loose circle on the dock, and Wyatt and Trevor set down a couple of bottles of liquor in the center. I was sandwiched between Boone and Theo, my knees pressed against theirs. A salty breeze blowing inland whipped my hair in every direction, so I tipped my head back and gathered it into my signature messy bun with the royal blue hair tie from my wrist. When I sat back up, I saw West had slipped into the circle and was sitting directly across from me.

My heart thudded an extra beat, its steady rhythm faltering.

Where had he come from? *Not* that I had been looking for him earlier.

West looked like he'd taken the time to go home for a quick shower. His hair was damp around the edges, and he was wearing an old faded concert t-shirt that was snug around his shoulders. His shirt looked soft, and I had the urge to run my hand over his chest just to feel the contradiction of worn cotton over solid muscle. He caught my eye and flashed a grin. I quickly looked away, flustered to be caught staring. His ego did not need encouragement.

"All right!" Rue clapped her hands and commanded everyone's attention. "For those of you who haven't played dirty truth or dare with us before, here are the rules. One person asks the group a question. If you refuse to answer it, you get to pick your dare. You take a shot, lose a piece of clothing, or kiss somebody. The person who asked the question gets to decide which piece of clothing you lose or who you kiss, if you pick that dare. And most importantly, you cannot, under any circumstances, pick the same dare twice in a row. Although . . ." She paused to look around the circle and let out a drunken giggle. "I'm not sure kissing someone from this group counts as a hardship." She leaned against Hendrix. "Questions will move around the circle to the right." She pointed left but didn't seem to notice the contradiction. "You don't have to answer your own question. Who wants to start?"

One of the girls I didn't recognize piped up. "I will!" She tossed her ponytail over her shoulder and blinked at us from under thick bangs. "Um, have you slept with anyone sitting here?"

Surprisingly, everyone before me answered yes. When my turn came and I said a quiet no, every male head turned in my direction. It was like they could smell the fresh meat. *This is how a mouse must feel, when the cat is half interested in the chase and half with the meal at the end.* To my relief, Hendrix and one other girl answered no as well.

Even though, looking around the circle, I wouldn't mind being hunted by one of these guys, I had a sinking feeling this game might not end well for me.

The other girl who said no was up next. She looked up in the air, as if inspiration would fall down from the stars and land in her open mouth. "So, like, everyone has tattoos these days. So, like, tell us what one of your tattoos means."

Grady had a memorial tattoo for his mom. Marissa had a heart on the inside of her wrist because she "just loved love." Rue caught my eye from across the circle and rolled her eyes at that. Hendrix had a four-leaf clover for luck. Theo didn't have any tattoos, so he ended up losing his shirt. I showed my paper airplane tattoo and mumbled something about a love for travel—another lie. I didn't talk about the real meaning behind it, ever. It wasn't my secret to share.

Rue smirked at me. She turned her back and showed the top

of a peacock feather that curved along her back. "It reminds me that beauty is only skin deep, and that, sometimes, the prettiest things aren't what they seem," she said, with a bite in her voice.

Grady jerked his head around to her and stared, but she refused to meet his gaze. Instead, she wrapped one of her arms around Hendrix's bicep and laid her head on his shoulder. The girl with the ponytail was also tattoo-less and had to give up her shirt, much to the enjoyment of the guys.

More questions followed. When did you lose your virginity? Theo refused to answer and dropped a quick peck on my lips. How old was the oldest person you've slept with? Grady and West shared a look, and both opted for a shot. Weird. Have you ever really been in love? I wasn't sure how to classify Asshole anymore, so I took a shot. So did most of the guys, although Grady and West ended up shirtless since they'd taken shots last time. Rue skipped answering too, pounding a shot of Patron and wiping her mouth with the back of her hand.

When I refused to answer Boone's question about how many people I'd slept with, I chose to lose a piece of clothing. Boone looked me over slowly. He was already down to his boxers. I assumed I'd lose my shirt first, which didn't really bother me, but Boone surprised me. "Take off the tank," he said, leaning close to me. I swallowed and managed to wiggle out of it while keeping on my sheer pink top. My black bra was clearly visible underneath. I'd thought I'd stay covered a little better since I had worn double layers, and I crossed my arms. I couldn't help but glance at Boone next to me, whose gaze was glued to my chest. Peeking down at myself, I realized my position pushed my girls up more than hid them, so I dropped my arms and hunched my shoulders some. Good Lord. Without waiting for the next round, I downed another shot.

I wasn't exactly a prude. A bra wasn't that different from a swimsuit top, and I regularly pranced around in a bikini, albeit a family-friendly one, at work. But this atmosphere felt different. The flickering light. The hormones saturating the salt air. It was intimate somehow. And I'd only ever been intimate with Asshole before. While that night with Jared technically counted, it hadn't felt intimate. We'd been detached, rushed, and impersonal—like I had hoped. Well, okay, I had hoped for decent sex, but the mood had been what I had been looking for. Not this shadowy sharing of secrets and skin and lips.

Maybe I was just getting drunk. I always overthought things when I was drunk.

I hadn't even heard the following question, but suddenly Marissa was telling Boone he had to kiss me. Twisting toward me, he wrapped his big hand around the back of my neck and tilted my face up to his. He clearly was going for more than the quick peck I'd shared with Theo. I sucked in a breath. Lowering his head to me, he grazed his lips over mine, which gave me time to learn the shape of his mouth. My hands grabbed his shoulders for support as we leaned into each other. Boone took it as encouragement because he wrapped his other arm around my back and pulled our chests in tight before slipping his tongue in my mouth. He tasted like tequila. Engrossed in the kiss, the damp slide of our lips, and the pressure of his fingers on my skin, I barely heard the catcalls from behind us, and I was slow to pull back. Boone had a shit-eating grin on his face as the other guys whooped at him. I stared at the bottles of booze in the center of the circle in a daze, surprised I had lost myself in the kiss so thoroughly.

How much had I had to drink again?

The weight of a pair of eyes bored into me, and I peered across the circle at West from under my lashes. His jaw was tight, and he was glaring at me. Raising my head, I glared back. What was his problem, anyway? It was just a damn game.

When the girl with the ponytail chose a dare, she leaned over to Trevor, and whispered in his ear. Rolling his eyes, Trevor laughed. "Whatever. You can kiss West." Hopping up, she skipped over to him in just her underwear and kneeled down. Shooting me one last angry look, West grabbed her in his arms, tipped her back, and shoved his tongue down her throat, kissing her deeply. I watched in stupefaction as her arms clutched at his back and she moaned.

It was just a game. Just a fucking game.

West's hand stole up from her hip to cover her breast. I felt my stomach churn and forced myself to look away. It's just the alcohol, I told myself. But even so, I chugged another shot, anything to distract me from the blatant display. Unable to help myself, I stole another glance toward West and found that Ponytail had just plopped herself down in his lap. His hand was covering most of her naked thigh.

My stomach felt queasy. I wasn't sure if it was from the show

West was putting on or an overabundance of alcohol, but either way, I'd had enough. I got to my feet and slipped quietly down the dock, trying to find my way back to solid ground. When I put one hand out to steady myself, I noticed there were rope lights tucked under the dock railings, lighting the way. I focused on staying between the lines and not looking back. Anger rose inside me, hot and painful, and I stumbled on a loose board.

"I'm fine," I bit out, trying to convince myself. The warm sea air pulled at loose strands of my hair and blew them around my face. I swatted at them and tripped again. God, I was so drunk I couldn't walk straight and was talking to myself. Fucking classy.

When I finally made it to the end of the dock, I veered right, farther from the house and into the welcoming darkness. I made my way to the seawall and bent over it, emptying my churning stomach into the crashing swells below.

I looked down into the pulsing water, watching the patterns the torch light reflections made. It was almost hypnotic, the way it twisted and rippled over the waves. Mesmerizing. Seductive, even. Begging me to come play. But I knew better. Knew not to accept the invitation and get in over my head, where I couldn't see the bottom, couldn't predict what was coming next. That's when you got hurt. From now on, I was playing it safe.

I wiped my mouth with the back of my hand and tucked chunks of hair behind my ears. My feet felt a little steadier as I retraced my steps. It was time to find Rue and go home.

People were making their way down the dock as I reached it. While this wasn't the kind of game ended by crowning a winner, I still felt like I had lost—I just wasn't sure what.

Boone spotted me first and came over. "Hey, I think this is yours," he said, handing me my tank. I hadn't even realized I'd forgotten it.

Embarrassed, I nodded my thanks and ducked behind the trunk of a nearby palmetto tree to fix my clothes. As I came back around, West went by with Ponytail clinging to him like a barnacle. His hands were holding her ass, her legs were wrapped around his waist, and it looked like she had watched one too many vampire movies, the way she was attacking his neck. I stood frozen, unable to tear my eyes away.

Boone moved to my side and slipped an arm around my waist. "Want to check out the bonfire?" he whispered, his lips brushing my ear. I looked up at him, with his shaggy hair tangling in the breeze, and his lanky skateboarder's body. I shivered and let him pull me closer.

"Absolutely."

Two hours and four rum drinks later, I'd lost Boone. We'd been sharing a blanket and snuggling by the fire, giggling at each other and getting more drunk. He'd gone to get us refills, but then he never came back. I wrapped the blanket around myself and staggered up the steps to the porch. Boone was sprawled out on a chaise.

Annoyed, I walked over to him and nudged him with my knee. He didn't stir. I furrowed my brow and nudged him again, harder this time. A loud snore rose from him, and he flopped his arm across his face.

Really? Frowning, I put my hands on my hips and looked around. Grady was studying Boone too. "I think he's out for the count," he said with an apologetic shrug. I stared at Grady, trying through my alcohol-induced haze to figure out what to do now. I eyed the rum on the counter next to him and moved toward it, but Grady grabbed my wrist with gentle fingers before I could snatch the bottle. "I think you might want to hold off on that."

I glared at him. He might be right, but who did he think he was? My boss?

My sluggish brain processed the horrific truth of that thought. I was wasted, beyond wasted, in front of my boss. What was wrong with me? I needed to go home. Now.

I peered around the room, squinting into the bright light of the house. "Where's Theo?"

"Theo?" Grady asked. "He had to leave about an hour ago. Family emergency. Something about his dad."

Damn. I twisted my face in confusion, trying to think.

"It's okay," Grady said, "You can stay here. I have some extra guest rooms."

"Um . . . thanks, no, that's okay. I really just want to go home." I concentrated on not slurring my words.

Wyatt turned around. I hadn't even realized he was there. "I can take you home. I'm DD tonight. You ready?"

Wyatt was my new hero.

"Sure, I just gotta grab Rue." I swiveled my head in both directions but didn't see her right away.

"Oh shit, I forgot about her. I've only got room for one more in my car. Hold on. West! *West!*" Wyatt hollered across the room, and I wanted the floor to open up and swallow me. "You got room for Sadie and Rue in your truck? Or just one and I can take the other?"

West walked over to stand next to us. Ponytail was nowhere to be seen. "I can take 'em both. You might have to help me load Rue though."

My eyes shot to his and tried to focus. "What do you mean help load her?"

West sighed and waved his fingers for me to follow him into the living room. Rue was comatose on the couch, a dribble of drool on her cheek. Grady had followed us too and shook her shoulder gently. She didn't react. Grady and West looked at each other and had some kind of weird unspoken conversation.

Grady glared at West. "Fine, but you owe me." Grady turned to me. "Look, Sadie, she's already passed out here on the couch. I'll get her a blanket and just let her sleep it off here. I can give her a ride home in the morning."

I protested, knowing that Rue would be furious if I left her here. I wasn't sure what was going on with her and Grady, but I didn't think having her wake up to breakfast with him and Marissa was a good idea. I tried to grab her arms and drag her to a sitting position, but couldn't manage it on my own. Giving in, I pulled out my phone and sent an apologetic text to Rue, knowing she'd find it in the morning.

When I looked back at West, I realized we'd be alone in his truck. Or maybe not. Maybe Ponytail was going back to his place with him. God, just the thought of riding with them while they molested each other made my stomach turn. "Where's Wyatt?" I asked him, looking past him to the kitchen where Wyatt had been last. "I can just ride with him then. He said he had room for one."

West shook his head. "He's going the other direction first to take Dylan and Trevor home. It makes more sense for me to just drop you off real quick on the way back to my place."

I stuck my tongue in my cheek and tipped my head to the side, trying to stall. "What about Ponytail? Won't that cramp your plans?"

"Ponytail?" He looked confused. "Oh, Bethany? Nah, she took off with Alexis a few minutes ago."

"So it's just you and me then?"

His eyelids dropped to half-mast, and one side of his mouth curved up. "Just you and me," he confirmed, drawing out the words. "Guess I'm rescuing you again, after all."

chapter six

I WOKE UP TO THE sound of panting. Hot, damp air was puffing against my face. When something wet poked my cheek a few seconds later, I jerked away. Confused, I cracked my eyes open, and staring back at me were the saddest, droopiest brown eyes I had ever seen.

What the hell?

I smothered a scream and struggled to sit up in bed. Blinking against the sledgehammer banging in my skull, I fell back to my elbow and realized two things at once. One—I knew those eyes. General Beauregard was looking back at me, opening his mouth in a huge yawn, drool stretching between his jowls. Two—I was most definitely *not* in my own bed.

Looking down to see a tattooed arm draped over my hips, I was slower to realize the most important fact. I wasn't alone either. The arm moved into a stretch, and the man next to me yawned too.

West.

My elbow fell out from under me, and I laid on my back staring at the ceiling, trying to force my sluggish brain to work. What the fuck happened when I left Grady's?

West leaned over me to rub General Beauregard's ears. "Morning, boy. You ready to go out?" West's voice was a raspy rumble that resonated through me. His bare chest pressed against my left side, and if I lifted myself up the smallest fraction, I'd be able to lick his shoulder. I closed my eyes against the temptation and took a deep breath. I smelled soap, salt, and citrus. I smelled West. I swallowed back a moan.

General Beauregard let out a soft whine of pure bliss and laid his head against me. When I turned to glance at him, his tongue swiped my cheek, and his tail thumped against the floor. West laughed and gave the dog one last pat. "I know, buddy. She does look good first thing in the morning."

My cheeks warmed. And other parts of me did too.

His arm brushed against my breasts as he pulled it back, and my nipples budded in response. He flipped back the covers on his side and padded across the room to a set of sliding glass doors, opening one enough so that the hound slipped out. The sunrise peeked over the ocean through the glass, but it barely registered before my eyes returned to West.

He stood looking out the door in just a pair of boxer briefs. He was all golden skin and lean muscle, with a tight ass hugged by some thin black fabric. I was jealous of that fabric. As he turned back to face me, the grooved definition of his abs was on display, his torso narrowing to a tempting V before disappearing. My eyes dropped lower, taking in the prominent bulge in his shorts. Maybe I was still dreaming. That would explain everything but the jackhammer in my skull. The light dimmed as he drew the curtains and shut out the light.

Slipping back into bed and covering his lower body, he turned on his side and faced me, one arm tunneling under the pillow beneath his head, the other resting between us. I kept my eyes on his fingers and tried to focus. I did a quick inventory of my body. My head was pounding, but the darkened room helped. My stomach was clenching, but I blamed that more on the view than the hangover. I tensed my legs experimentally. My thighs felt . . . fine. Not sore at all. What did that mean? Had the sex been bad? Or maybe he had been like Jared, and the act had been over so fast that my muscles never even got a workout.

"Coffee," I croaked, turning away from him. I couldn't be expected to think clearly without coffee. I sat up on the side of the bed and swayed for a moment. Jesus Christ, my head. Looking down, I saw I was only wearing one of the logoed bar shirts from the Wreck and my underwear. My cutoffs were on the floor near the end of the bed, and I slid them on, grateful for the oversized length of the shirt.

Without looking back, I left the room, figuring the kitchen couldn't be that hard to find. Sure enough, it was just down the hall and to the right. I pushed my wild hair out of my face and squinted around the too-bright room. Morning light filtered through curtainless windows and glinted off the oversized stainless steel fridge. I reached for the hair tie on my wrist, but it had disappeared along with the rest of my clothes.

Coffee. I smelled it. I had to be close. Turning around farther, I spotted it. Just past the retro enamel toaster, a glass pot sat beneath the small coffee maker, filled halfway with steaming brown liquid gold. I plucked a cup out of the sink, not caring if it was clean or dirty, and filled it to the brim. Leaning back against the counter, I inhaled deeply, trying to expel the smell of West from my mind.

As I took my first tentative sip, Wyatt walked into the room, wearing only board shorts. I swallowed the wrong way, coughing and sputtering before setting the cup down behind me, my lungs burning. What was it about these guys that messed with my basic ability to breathe properly? And what the fuck was Wyatt doing here?

Wyatt reached around me to pour himself a cup. "Mornin,'" he said, smiling at me with a knowing expression as his eyes ran down the length of my body.

I looked at him in dawning horror.

Oh. My. *God.*

Did I have a threesome last night?

Wyatt took another swallow and sauntered down the hall toward West's room. He paused at West's open door. "Surfin' in twenty minutes, bro. You coming?"

I felt my face flame at his word choice. Had he already come this morning?

I couldn't hear the rest of their conversation, only their sporadic laughter. *Oh, dear sweet Jesus, don't let them be laughing at me,* I begged. I stared into my coffee cup like it held all the answers and then drank the hot liquid as fast as I could without scalding myself.

Ten minutes later, as I finished my second cup, West came down the hall, dressed in board shorts too. Only board shorts. Were they allergic to shirts? Was I wearing his last clean one or something?

He went to pour himself a cup of coffee and only the dregs were left. My fault. As he refilled the machine, he glanced at me warily. "How're you feeling this morning? Can I give you a ride home?"

A ride. My mind flashed back to his bedroom and his nearly naked body in the bed next to mine. I could almost picture myself under him, his narrow hips flexing between my legs. I peered out the window over the sink instead of meeting his eyes. That's right. I knew where I was. I was only a few blocks from home.

"I'm good," I said. "I can just walk."

West leaned his hip against the counter and faced me. "You sure? It's not a problem. I know—"

"It's fine," I cut him off, lifting my cup for one last swallow. My head was tolerable now.

He studied me for a long minute. "Okay. Let me just grab your clothes." He disappeared around the corner and came back with a knotted, plastic Bi-Lo grocery bag. "I tried to rinse them out for you. I thought about washing them, but that pink shirt felt all delicate and crap, and I didn't want to mess it up."

I took the bag, not understanding what he was trying to explain, but eager to make a fast getaway. "Okay."

He led the way through a cozy but masculine living room to the front door and followed me out onto the porch. Facing him nervously, I wet my lips. "Did we—me and you—or me and you and him—did we . . ." I trailed off, unable to finish my question. When he didn't answer right away, I peeked up at him.

He looked at me with a steady gaze. "Does it feel like me and you, or me and you and him, did anything?" His voice was even, giving nothing away.

I narrowed my eyes at him and straightened my back. Using my sweetest voice, I hypothesized, "Maybe it just wasn't that memorable."

He glared at me. Leaning forward, he grabbed my upper arms, not hard, but enough to keep me in place. He dipped his head close to mine, his lips almost brushing my ear, and in a rough whisper said, "First of all, I don't share with anybody, not even my brother. And, Sadie, trust me, when we sleep together, you'll know it." I pulled back, confused now. He must have seen it, because he crossed his arms over his chest and regarded me with exasperation. "Do you remember anything from last night?"

I looked away from him. "I remember you were going to give me a ride home."

"Right. And then when we got to your house, you puked all over the bushes before you could even get up the stairs. It was such a turn on." He curled his lip in annoyance. "I couldn't leave you alone like that. My grandma would've skinned me alive if she found out I'd left you like that to fend for yourself. I figured I'd bring you back here to sleep it off. You messed your shirt all up, so I put you in one of mine. Like I said, I tried to clean it for you the best I could. I was worried you might get sick again, and I wanted to be close by, so I just put you in bed with me."

I raised my eyebrow at him. "Convenient." My tone was accusing.

He lifted one shoulder in a shrug. "I thought so. Did you know you snore?"

"I do not!"

He smirked but didn't say anything.

I glowered at him a moment longer before my manners grudgingly kicked in. "So, I guess I should say thanks for taking care of me. You didn't have to do that. Most guys wouldn't have."

"I'm not most guys. But you're right, damsels in distress aren't normally my thing. You just seem to need more help than most."

I straightened my backbone. "Excuse me?"

The expression on his face was pure disbelief. "The ocean, the hotel, last night. You should come with a warning label or something. 'Needs saving from herself.'" He chuckled.

"I am perfectly capable of taking care of myself," I sputtered, offended. Who the hell had designated him my white knight in board shorts anyway?

He grinned at me, and I knew he was enjoying this. "If you say so."

I gritted my teeth. "Like I said, I *should* say thanks."

"But you won't," he finished.

I smiled at him, or at least I tried to. It felt more like maybe I bared my teeth before I turned and stomped down the steps to the street, refusing to look back even though I felt his eyes on me until I turned the corner.

THREE DAYS LATER, I skipped down the path to the beach, exuberant. It was Tuesday, my day off this week, and I had spent the whole morning hanging out at the resort and taking pictures. When I'd met with Grady after lunch, I'd had plenty of photos to show him. He'd been receptive and even downloaded two dozen shots off my memory card to show his boss the following week. Rue had helped me come up with some ways to tie in the photography to the Edge's Facebook page, and Grady looked especially intrigued when I pitched that idea. He said he'd be in touch, but that he was pretty sure we'd be able to come up with something that let me get behind the camera lens more. The meeting had gone so much better than I'd hoped.

I headed down to the beach to see what else I could capture for my portfolio before the crowds left. I knew there was a sandcastle contest for the kids finishing up, and I wanted to get some shots of it.

Jackpot. I strolled around the beachfront, squatting low and coercing the kids to pose next to their creations. Their excited faces shining from behind the wet sand mountains were endearing. The innocent glee of the moment came across well in the pictures. I zoomed in on a fiddler crab caught in the moat of one child's abandoned fortress. Snapping a handful of quick shots, I panned up with the camera still held up to my eye.

West's face appeared on my screen, magnified.

"What are you doing here?" I demanded, startled, and lowered my arms self-consciously.

"Today? Today I'm driving the parasailing boat. Grady's regular guy called in sick, and I was free, so here I am. What are you doing? I thought you were a lifeguard."

"I am. But I'm supposed to be a photographer. I mean, I am a photographer, it's just hard getting a new business off the ground."

West laughed. "Yeah, I hear you on that one. Start up's a bitch."

I looked at him, puzzled. "You're trying to break into the parasailing business? I thought the resort owned the boat and the sail?"

"They do, and I'm not. I owed Grady a favor though." He smirked.

"Okay," I said, taking a step away. "I'll let you get back to it then."

"Ever been up?" He took a step that mirrored mine, keeping even with me.

"On a parasail? Uh, no. And I don't plan on it."

"Why not? There's nothing to it. You just kind of . . . float. Only, on the end of a rope instead of in the water."

"Exactly."

"Exactly what?" His eyebrows dipped down.

"It's over the water."

He looked at me sideways, comprehension dawning. "That's right. You're scared of the water. Well, let's consider this step one in curing you of your phobia. You're not going *in* the water. You'll be going *over* the water. Way over."

"What if I fall?"

He turned back to face me and dropped his chin down to meet my wide eyes. "I won't let you fall. Sometimes, when I take the turn at the end of the island, your feet dip in for a second, but you're not going to fall."

"Don't you have paying customers you should be taking up?" I asked.

"We're in a lull. And it only takes fifteen minutes. Come on, let me help you. You live by the ocean now. This fear of yours is ridiculous."

I shifted my weight from side to side. Holding my hand up to my eyes, I scanned the water. The ocean looked calm right now. Non-threatening. Toddlers splashed where the waves rolled onto the beach. Even they weren't scared of getting their feet wet. "All right, fine," I said, giving in with reluctance.

I followed him to the border of the resort property, where the hut for the parasailing rides stood, and enormous butterflies took wing in my stomach—whether from my impending doom or West's presence, I wasn't sure. I handed off my camera and bag to Josie, the attendant, and then slipped off my shoes before trailing after West to the harness. Josie followed and helped hook me in to all the straps while West ran over the safety spiel. When he explained the emergency release, I looked at him with alarm. "I thought you said I couldn't fall!"

He sighed. "You are not going to fall. Trust me on this."

"How do you know?"

"You're strapped in." He reached down to where the webbed belts connected around my pelvis, sliding two fingers under the edges and tugging to show me they weren't loose. Catching my eye, he dragged his hand from one hip across my stomach to the other hip, his fingers brushing the top of my coral shorts. The butterflies ricocheted off my ribs. He tugged again. "See? All safe."

I took a deep breath and looked at where his fingers were still touching me. Heat seared through the cotton of my shirt, warming my skin and igniting my blood. The corded bracelets were hanging on his wrist, one blue and white, one green, and one shades of tan. Mixed in with those was a royal blue elastic band. My fingers circled my own wrist, where I usually wore my hair tie. I had a white one on today, but I was missing my blue one from my night at Grady's. I reached out and touched it. "Is that mine?"

He pulled his hand away. "Yeah. I found it in my bed after you left. I wanted to remember to give it back to you."

I looked at him expectantly.

"What?" He shrugged. "It looks like you've got another one." He turned and walked to the boat, leaving me watching after him in confusion. Did he not plan on giving it back then?

Minutes later, I was airborne.

He was right. It felt exactly like floating. Like I was a balloon and he was a little kid running as fast as he could, watching the balloon shadow his every move. I spotted my cottage and the Wreck. Hell, I could even see the next two islands from this height. It was beautiful. Freeing. A seagull flew by, and for a second, we soared side by side.

From here, the water looked benign. From here, it was hard to remember there were creatures with sharp teeth and poisonous barbs and strong jaws just waiting for their next victim. From here, West looked like a little toy Lego man in a bathtub, scooting over the surface.

Idly, I watched the boat make a wide U-turn.

The sail puffed and snapped once, hard, as we changed directions. The sail lost speed. I wasn't falling, but I was moving closer to the water at an alarming rate. My heart climbed into my throat, and my pulse doubled. Biting my lip in trepidation, I bent my legs and tucked my knees toward my chest, trying to escape the upward rush of the water.

The ocean no longer looked innocent. Angry, frothing waves reached up to snatch my feet and pull me in. A fish jumped to my left, and I shrieked. Why the fuck was it jumping? Was it trying to escape from a shark? I drifted closer and closer, and I closed my eyes, unwilling to watch any longer. The breakers roared as they rushed toward the shore, calling for my sacrifice. A fine spray misted my legs. I whimpered.

When my feet dipped in, I snapped my eyes back open.

This was it. I was going down. I clawed at the straps above

me, trying desperately to climb higher, to get away. The water swallowed my legs to just above my knees, and I felt my eyes burn with unshed tears. I opened my mouth to scream, but nothing came out. It was like one of those nightmares where you know you're not going to make it, and everything starts happening in slow motion.

I felt a tug from my hips, where the umbilical connected me to the boat. I wasn't sinking any farther. Another pull brought me a foot higher, until the water was only at my ankles. Something brushed the underside of my foot, and my whole body shuddered. And then I was soaring again, flying high like a human kite.

This time, I couldn't appreciate the view. Tears flowed from my eyes, and I just wanted this stupid ride to end. I sucked in huge lungfuls of air, trying to hold in the ugly sobs that threatened to erupt. The wind whipped tendrils of my hair against my face, small stinging lashes that seemed to mock me. Some strands clung stubbornly to the tears trailing down my cheeks.

As I came to a stop back on the beach, I grabbed at the harness around my middle, scrambling for the release. I sank to my knees, unable to figure out the clasp. Josie hurried to my side to assist me and looked at my face with concern.

"Hey," she whispered. "What's wrong? Did something pinch you or something?"

"Just get me out of here," I managed, gasping for control.

She worked me free of the straps, and I ran for the hut, tripping once on the soft sand. All I could think about was escape. I vaguely registered West's voice calling my name from a distance.

I snatched my shoes and hurried down the side path, taking a short cut back to the parking lot. No way I was waiting around and letting him see me like this.

I dragged the heel of my hand over my cheeks as I walked, feeling the grit from the sand sticking to the sea spray and my tears. I drew in a deep, shaky breath. It was over. I was fine. I dug my car keys out of my pocket.

Fuck, I needed alcohol.

I SLUNK INTO THE Wreck, hoping Wyatt wouldn't be there. I didn't want to see any reminders of West, nothing to remind me of my mid-air freak out. I just wanted a shot to settle my nerves. A petite, sandy-haired girl with freckles was refilling the red coolers by the front door with peanuts from a large bag. I looked around for a bartender, but the girl seemed to be the only other one here.

She wiped her hands on her jeans then walked behind the bar. "Hi. Can I help you?"

"A shot. Something strong."

Her gaze was curious, but she didn't say anything as she plucked a bottle from the top shelf and poured.

She slid the glass across the bar and waited while I tossed it back. I winced from the burn as I swallowed. The warmth pooled in my stomach, and I shook my head, working my mouth against the taste.

After snagging a bag of kiwis, the girl grabbed a cutting board and started chopping, dropping the pieces into another big red Coleman cooler. Fruit was spread out on the counter, and I guessed she was prepping the grog. She worked in silence for a few minutes, glancing up at me every so often like she wanted to ask me a question but was trying to hold back. What was her problem?

Then I remembered it was three-thirty on a Tuesday afternoon, and I was alone in a bar drinking. And that I was the one with a problem.

"I'm not normally like this," I felt the need to explain. "I just had a bad afternoon. There was this gu—"

"There's always a guy," she interrupted, rolling her eyes. "And it's always his fault."

I grinned. I liked her. "Well, of course it's his fault."

She finished with the kiwis and scooted a box of peaches closer. "Want to talk about it?"

I chewed my lip. I wanted to do anything but talk about it. I reached for my purse to pay and stopped short. My purse. It was still at the resort. Behind the parasailing hut. I swore under my breath.

"Ahhh . . ."

"Hailey."

"Right, Hailey. I seem to be having an extra bad day. That guy I mentioned earlier? I had to get away, and I left so quick I forgot my bag. And my wallet. Could I maybe help you chop fruit or something for awhile in exchange for that shot?" I shot her a beseeching look, hoping for some female solidarity.

She lifted an eyebrow. "You don't want to go get your purse? Do you have your phone?"

I was silent for a moment, embarrassment over my getaway creeping over me. "No. I guess I don't have that either. But I'm not going back there right now. I sort of had a breakdown over something stupid and humiliated the crap out of myself in front of this guy. I-I'll get it later."

"Where?" she asked curiously.

"The Edge," I said, looking at the dollar bill above my head. "It'll be fine. I work there. Josie'll probably stick it in my locker for me." *You be my Dairy Queen, and I'll be your Burger King: You treat me right, and I'll do it your way.* A small giggle escaped me, and Hailey turned to see what I was looking at.

"They're terrible, aren't they? Do guys really think we'll fall for that crap?"

I twisted my lips. "Some guys don't need a line."

She snorted. "Sounds like something my brother would say. West's ego knows no bounds."

I froze. "West is your brother? West Montgomery?"

She paused from peeling the peach in her hand and then removed another cutting board from behind the bar and placed it next to me. She grabbed two peaches and a knife and put them on top. "I take it you've already met him *and* his ego."

I picked up a peach and started peeling, ignoring the flush that crept up my neck. "You could say that."

"I'd apologize for him, but it probably wouldn't do much

good."

"Actually," I admitted, "Today he was trying to be nice. I just messed it all up." I told her the short version of my parasailing adventure.

"He dipped you in, even though he knew you were scared of the water?" She sounded outraged on my behalf.

I tipped my head to one side then the other. "He warned me that would happen. My legs just went in farther than I expected, and I freaked. It's not really his fault." I frowned. Wait, why was I defending him?

Hailey was watching me, her eyes assessing. She started on another peach. "What about the water scares you?"

I sliced the peach I had peeled into neat, even chunks, making a small pile. "I don't know. And it's not really the water. It's what might be in the water that I can't see. Like, some creature will try to attack me. It's stupid. I know it's stupid."

"Did something happen when you were younger? Something traumatic?"

I cut up the rest of the peach and started on the second. "Kind of. When I was five, I was running on the beach, looking for shells with my brother. We were just running and playing and having fun. Being kids. And I saw this big bubble thing, and I ran and jumped right on it, thinking I'd bounce up in the air or something. Only it was a jellyfish, and I ended up with a giant welt on both feet and my leg. My parents rushed me to the hospital, and I ended up having to spend the night. But I was fine once it healed. No lasting damage or anything crazy like that."

I cut a wedge of peach and popped it in my mouth. "It's dumb. People get stung all the time. And I was stung on the sand, not the water. But ever since then, I've had this phobia of the ocean."

"It's not dumb."

I looked up at her. "It is. And I know it is. I just can't seem to shake it."

"Well, West is still an ass for scaring you."

I gave her a halfhearted smile. "Maybe. He'll probably never talk to me again anyway. I'm sure he thinks I'm a head case now."

"He will not!" she protested. "And if he does, tough. It's his loss. You can be my friend instead."

I smiled. "I think that can be arranged." I handed over the cutting board piled with peach chunks. She dumped it, then handed the board back with a carton of strawberries on it.

"So what do you do at the Edge?" she asked.

"I lifeguard right now. I used to be a photographer though. I'm trying to be one again. How 'bout you?"

"I work here when I can. My brothers try to help me out. Mostly, I'm just a mom."

"A mom?" I looked up at her in surprise.

"I know, I'm young. Only twenty-two. My fiancé is a Marine. I met him right after he graduated from basic on Parris Island, and he totally swept me off my feet. Cody, my son, was an unexpected surprise. He'll be two next week. Adam's overseas right now, so he won't be here to see it." She blinked hard, and I could see tears fill her eyes.

Hmm. "What if he could?" I asked, wanting to help.

She took a deep breath and wiped her hand across her eyes. "What do you mean?"

"What if I came over this weekend, and we took a bunch of pictures and sent them to him?"

Hailey's eyes lit up, and she dropped her knife to clap her hands. "That would be so awesome! You would do that for me?"

"We're friends now, right? Plus, it'd be good for me. I haven't done a real shoot in awhile."

She squealed and came around the bar to hug me.

We discussed details for the weekend and then Hailey lent me her phone so I could text Josie to toss all my stuff in my locker at work.

Josie: Already handled, chica. Not a problem. FYI, West freaked when you vanished.

Me: Shit.

Josie: Don't worry, I covered for you. I told him you had gotten a little airsick and had to make a quick exit to the bathroom.

Me: Thanks! I owe you!

Josie: He seemed to buy it. Honestly, I thought it was sweet he was so concerned. You guys dating?

Me: NO!!

Josie: Do you want to be?

I stared at her words on the screen, my fingers hovering over the keys with uncertainty.

I never answered her.

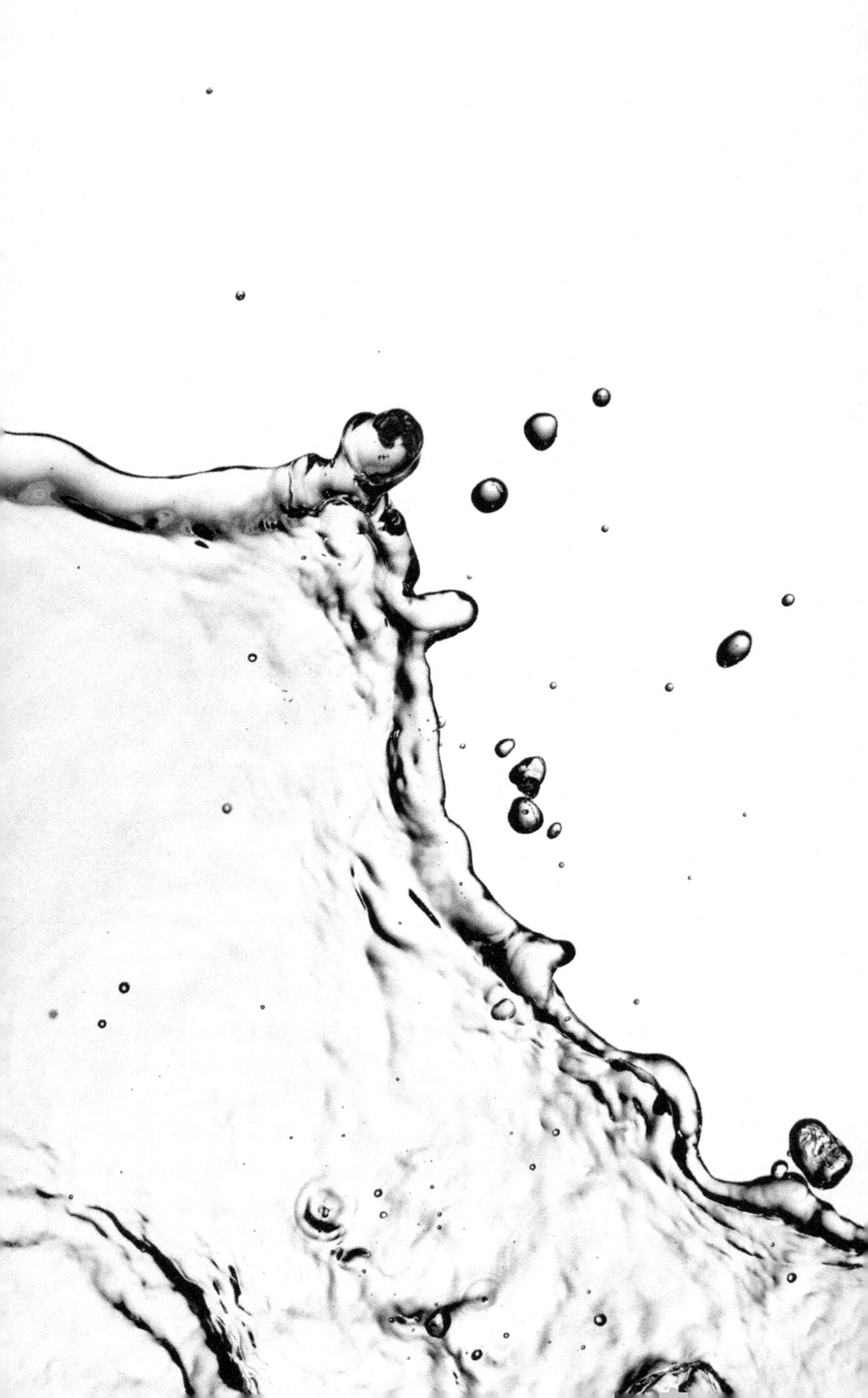

chapter seven

I LOOKED DOWN AT MY cell phone, then back up at the huge house in front of me. Hailey had texted me her address, but this couldn't be right. This house was huge. I bet it wasn't even called a house. It was probably called an estate or something. There's no way a barely employed twenty-two year old lived here. I double-checked the text then turned my Wrangler onto the huge circular driveway, parking next to a car that cost more than what most people made in a year.

I was second-guessing my wardrobe choice now. I'd thought I was meeting a broke young mom and had dressed down in a slate blue slub-knit tank and khaki shorts. My toenail polish was flaking, my cheap Old Navy flip flops had seen better days, and I wasn't wearing any makeup. Oh well, too late to do anything about it now. I texted Hailey that I was outside, then shouldered my camera bag and headed for the steps leading to the front door.

Before I could ring the bell, the door swung open, and Hailey appeared. A Jack Russell terrier flew around from behind her and jumped against my legs, demanding to be noticed. Bending down to pet the hyper dog, I spied a cute redheaded toddler peeking from the doorway. He was wearing a navy polo, plaid shorts, and a bucket hat, his thumb stuck firmly in his mouth. He was adorable.

"You're here!" Hailey cried, jumping up and down.

One side of my mouth tugged up. "I am." I stayed in my crouch and looked at Cody. "Hey, buddy. I'm here to take some pictures of you for Daddy. We're gonna have some fun today."

Cody took a few steps to Hailey and hid behind her legs.

Hailey laughed and scooped him up, balancing him on her hip. "He's always shy at first. Give him twenty minutes, and you won't be able to get him to hush. And the furball sniffing your toes is Edison."

Giving Edison one last pat, I stood up. "No problem. I don't have any other plans this morning except for you guys. In fact, Cody, I brought a present for you. Want to come with me to get it?"

He looked at me, then at his mom, then back to me. Finally, he unwrapped his chubby little arms from around Hailey and reached for my hand. Giggling, I took Cody, settling him on my own hip and handed Hailey my camera bag. "Come on, buddy, we have to go back to my car. I've got balloons!"

Cody's eyes lit up. "Bawoons?"

Hailey and the Jack Russell followed us down the steps, and

I grabbed the ribbons to the dozen blue helium balloons I had bought that morning. Motioning for Hailey to get the child-size white chair I had thrown in the back as well, we edged around the property to the backyard.

"So, Hailey, you live here?"

Hailey snorted. "Not what you were expecting, huh? This is my grandparents' house. My parents didn't want me living with them anymore because of the whole baby-before-marriage thing. They felt like it tarnished their perfect image or something. Whatever. I'd rather be here with my grandparents anyway. Plus, Wyatt and West are here. And Adam feels safer knowing Cody and I are surrounded by family while he's away."

"Where was home?"

"Chicago. But the three of us always spent our summers here, so this feels like home too. That's why Wyatt picked here to live after college—it felt like home, and it was far from Mom and Dad."

I raised my eyebrows. "You guys don't like your parents?"

"It's not that. They were fine as parents. Not spectacular, but not bad. They made sure we always had the best of everything. It's just that they required us to maintain a certain image, and Wyatt rebelled against that the most. He hated all the dinner parties and things we did because it was expected. He just wanted to be him. So as soon as he finished school, he came here and never looked back."

"So your parents cut him off?"

"No. We all have trusts. After college, we get yearly stipends as long as we're gainfully employed. So basically, as long as we're not sitting on our asses, we're golden. Wyatt used his money to open the bar. Figured he was there enough, he might as well own it."

"And West too, right?"

She hesitated. "Not quite. West is our half-brother. We have different dads. He *tried* to join the family business in Chicago. Went to Wharton, got his MBA. He played by the rules, jumped through all the hoops, was being molded into this perfect little clone of my Dad. I'm not sure what happened, but about a year ago he showed up here. Said he was sick of it all and was going to do his own thing his way. He runs a small charter fishing company."

"So he used the trust money for start up?"

Hailey shook her head. "He refuses to use his trust money for himself. Said he doesn't want it. So he dumps it all in Wyatt's bar. Wyatt wouldn't just take it though and made West a co-owner. West uses his half of the bar's profits to run his company. That's why he's living with Wyatt too—because he won't touch their money."

Well, that explained why Wyatt was in the kitchen when I woke up in West's bed. "And what about you?"

"I'm still in college, so I don't have any restrictions on my trust right now. I'm taking some business classes. Just a few each semester because of Cody, but I want to be like my brothers—independent. I'm trying to start up a jewelry company." She shyly held up her wrist so I could see the bracelets hanging there, braided cord with a nautical feel.

Wait a minute . . . "West wears some of your work, doesn't he?"

She blushed. "Yeah. He's sweet about it and tries to support me. He's trying to teach me about networking and commission sales. Maybe reaching out to some of the tourist shops on the nearby islands."

"That's a great idea, Hailey!"

She nodded. "I'm still working on product design and building up an inventory. We'll see."

We walked past a pool, a separate pool house, and a wide, curving stone patio with an outdoor fireplace before reaching an open spot. The grass was perfect—not one weed to be seen. Cody was climbing on the chair we had set in the middle of the yard, tugging on the balloon strings we tied to the back of it. I took out my camera and started snapping some candids while we talked. "So West fishes for a living?"

"Basically!" Hailey laughed. "He always says he has the best life now. He gets paid to take rich guys fishing. He does a bunch of those tournament things too, out of Charleston. You know, ten thousand dollars to the guy that catches the biggest mackerel or whatever."

I lowered my camera, stunned. "There are contests where people can earn five figures for catching a *fish?*"

"I know. Crazy, right? But some of these guys get super competitive about it. They think using a local guide with insider knowledge of the best spots will guarantee them a win. Too much money and too much free time, if you ask me."

I raised the camera again and went back to shooting Cody,

who was wrestling with Edison now. Edison was very tolerant. My mind was on West, though. He hadn't mentioned his business to me. He had let me think he was just a bartender. I wondered why.

Putting West out of my head, I focused on my photo shoot. We undressed Cody until he was just wearing his shorts and hat and then posed him with the balloons and the chair. I got a bunch of Hailey and Cody together. Them lying on the ground with their heads together but their feet going in opposite directions, so that one of them looked upside down. Some of Hailey throwing Cody up in the air, with Cody surrounded by the puffy clouds that were meandering across the sky. A few of them together with Edison, laughing and playing on the perfect lawn. Hailey had even made one of those cakes that looked like a giant cupcake, and we got a bunch of great shots of Cody diving into that, with Edison right there with him getting covered in blue frosting. Just sheer cuteness everywhere.

After cleaning up the worst of the cupcake mess, I showed Hailey some of the raw photos. I still had to edit everything, and they would look better when I was done, but it would give her an idea of what I'd captured that day. Cody was setting the balloons free one at a time, watching each one dance its way up to the clouds, getting smaller and smaller until he couldn't see it anymore, and then he'd let go of another one. "Bye bawoon," he called, waving as one twisted away on a breeze, pulled out over the water.

I was packing my camera away when two couples and a young

woman walked around the corner of the house, gesturing to the huge lawn spread between the mansion and the ocean. Hailey waved at them, and the older lady waved back. They were too far away for us to hear them as they stood at the corner, deep in discussion.

"The older couple is my grandparents," Hailey said. Hailey's grandmother was stylish in a summery dress with a wide-brimmed hat topping her gray hair. "And that's the Perottis with them. Aubrey is the same age as Wyatt."

Glancing over again, I studied Aubrey. She looked exotic, with olive skin and dark, glossy hair. She was dressed in white linen pants and a shiny high-necked navy top that left her arms bare. She looked like Yacht Club Barbie. Her parents looked like they had just stepped off the tennis court. I scanned my frosting-smeared tank and shorts and patted my haphazard bun, feeling inadequate.

The group was headed our way, and I stood, cursing myself again for not dressing nicer. As they got closer, Aubrey's tasteful gold jewelry flashed in the sunlight. Her hair was pulled back into a classic French twist, not one strand out of place, even with the ocean breeze. I wondered if perfect girls like her ever did normal things, like sweat or get a pimple. Probably not.

When Cody saw his great-grandma, he went running. She bent down and scooped him up, cuddling him close, heedless of the blue frosting still smeared in a few places. I instantly relaxed, that action alone telling me what kind of woman she was at heart. Separating herself from the group, she walked over to us, assessing our messy outfits and the two balloons still tied to the chair. "So I take it the photo shoot this morning was a success, dear?" she asked Hailey, warmth evident in her tone.

"Oh, Grandma, just wait until you see what Sadie's done! She's amazing!" Hailey gushed. "Sadie, this is my grandmother. Grandma, this is my new friend I was telling you about, Sadie Mullins."

The elegant gray-haired woman reached her hand out to me. "You can call me Margaret, dear." I took her soft hand in mine. She had a firmer grip than I expected.

So this was the grandma West kept mentioning.

I couldn't help but smile at her, genuinely pleased to meet her. She seemed like the type who would keep her grandkids in line.

"Your house is beautiful," I said.

She smiled. "You're welcome here anytime."

Hailey reached for Cody and nodded toward the others. "What are the Perottis here for?"

Margaret glanced back at the well-dressed group. "We're having an early meeting about the gala."

"What's the gala?" I asked.

Hailey rolled her eyes. "Every year Grandma and Grandpa host the annual Sailing Regatta Gala. It's where everyone on the island with money comes to see and be seen."

Margaret tsked. "It's not that bad, Hailey. You know we raise a lot of money for charity every year. Anyway, this year Aubrey is the event organizer. She wanted to come look over the space and start brainstorming."

Hailey snorted. "Sure. *That's* why she wanted to come over."

Margaret gave her a quelling look. "I expect you to behave."

"Always." Hailey batted her eyelashes.

After giving Hailey one last stern look, Margaret drifted back to the other group.

We picked up the rest of the props and then started herding Cody and Edison back around the other side of the house. We were just passing the pool when an unmistakable deep bay filled the air. We both paused and turned to see General Beauregard loping into the yard from the far side, announcing his arrival. Not far behind him were Wyatt and West. I glanced at Hailey. "Well, this should be interesting," she murmured.

Cody spotted his uncles. "Wy!" he called out, turning toward them. He started tottering in their direction, Edison dancing around him. As he rounded the pool, he picked up speed, startling Edison, who tried to dart in front of him. Edison yelped and tumbled, tripping Cody. As Cody pitched forward, his momentum carried him into the deep end of the pool with a small splash.

Hailey screamed, and the sound spurred me into action. Dropping the chair and my camera bag at my feet, I darted toward the pool, stepping out of my flip flops as I ran. Across the yard, I briefly registered West and Wyatt charging in our direction.

I reached the side of the pool and dove into the water, heading straight for the bottom where Cody's red hair waved at me. Kicking hard, I swam frantically to reach him, his little body putting up no resistance when I wrapped my arm around his chest. I pushed off the bottom, propelling us both to the surface. As soon as our heads popped up by the stone-lined border, strong arms were reaching down to pull first Cody, then me out of the water.

I gripped the lip of the coping, and my feet dangled in the water as I hunched over, pulling air into my lungs and trying to catch my breath. My pulse was racing from adrenaline and fear. Wyatt and West were both bent over Cody, their bodies blocking my view, but after a few heart-stopping moments, I heard the sweetest sound ever—Cody coughing. I lay back on the warm pool deck and closed my eyes in relief. Thank God he was okay.

A minute later, I heard Cody's weak voice. "Mama?"

Hailey, crying hysterically, gathered him in her arms and rushed inside.

From behind my eyelids, the sun turned to shadow, and I squinted up at it. West was hovering above me, concern etched across his face. "Are you okay?"

I rose up to my elbows and realized the rest of the group had crowded around. "I'm fine." West reached a hand down and pulled me to my feet. I stood there awkwardly, my bun flopped to one side and dripping down my shoulder, a puddle forming at my bare feet.

Margaret rushed forward and embraced me, soaking the front of her dress. "Sadie, my angel, you saved my baby!" Her voice caught on a sob, and her husband took her shoulders and drew her into his arms.

I shrugged. I hated this part of being a lifeguard. The overcome parents, thankful a crisis had been averted. I wasn't anything special, and I hated being the center of attention. I was just doing my job. I managed a relieved smile. "I'm just glad I was here."

A breeze whipped by us, and I shivered. Warm fingers tugged on my elbow, and West pulled me toward the pool house. "C'mon. Let's get you a towel and some dry clothes."

I followed him, grateful to escape. Inside, West dug around in a closet and came back with two thick towels. I wrapped one around my shoulders. "Why don't you jump in the shower and warm up?" he suggested. "I'll run inside and grab some clothes from Hailey for you." He pointed to a closed door that I assumed was a bathroom, and I nodded, moving toward it. "And Sadie?" I stopped and looked back over my shoulder at him, clutching the towel around me. He smiled. "Thanks for saving my favorite nephew."

"Anytime," I whispered. We looked at each other, and something seemed to pass in the air between us. Something electric and alive and shimmering. I shivered again, but not from cold this time.

Shutting myself in the bathroom, I leaned against the door. I took a slow, deep breath and closed my eyes. I had to be imagining things. All that adrenaline coursing through my system was making extra neurons fire, making me feel things that weren't real. Exaggerating gratitude into something more. After stripping off my wet clothes, I dumped them in the sink and then took the world's fastest shower, using whatever random toiletries were in there. I wrapped one towel around my head, the other around my body.

Opening the bathroom door, I peeked out. West was leaning against the wall just outside. He straightened and handed me an armful of clothing. "Here. These should work. And Hailey said thank you times a million." He gave a crooked grin.

I took the clothes and retreated into the bathroom again. "Thanks for getting these for me," I called through the door. "I wasn't looking forward to driving home in wet clothes."

West made a sound I couldn't interpret. Spreading out what he'd brought me, I surveyed it. An oversized Nike tee, matching shorts, bra, and underwear. I took one look at the bra and tossed it aside. It was way too big for my B cups. The rest looked like it would work. I dressed quickly and then towel dried my hair. I didn't see a brush and had to settle for finger combing the best I could. I checked my reflection. With my hair still damp, I was a bit chilled, and my hard nipples showed through the t-shirt. I hunched my shoulders. It sort of helped. I wrapped my wet clothes up in one of the towels and left the other hanging over the shower curtain rod. Upon opening the door, I stepped out and walked into West, who hadn't moved from his position. My arms holding their wet bundle pressed into his stomach, but he didn't move back. Instead, he reached for the towel and took it from me, setting it on a chair behind him.

"Tell Hailey thanks for the clothes. I'll wash them and get them back to her soon."

"I'm sure that's the last thing she's worried about right now."

"Oh, I left the bra in there. It was . . . not the right size."

His eyes dropped to my chest, and I hunched my shoulders

more when my nipples tightened in response. He lifted his heated gaze back to my face, and his lips quirked up on one side. "I have to admit, once I knew Cody was okay, I kinda liked the wet t-shirt look on you."

I took a step to the side. "I'm sure you did," I replied.

He took a step to match mine, and I was pinned between him and the wall. He leaned closer, and his breath fanned over me, sending small tingles up and down my spine. "Well, if I'm being truthful, I liked the way they looked naked the best. And, Sadie, they are definitely the right size."

His hands settled low on my hips, and I stopped breathing for a moment. "Were you spying on me in the shower?" I asked in confusion, my voice sounding breathy.

He leaned down until his lips were by my ear. "Not here. My house. The other night."

"I thought we didn't have sex that night."

"I might have been too much of a gentleman to take advantage of you when you were drunk, but I'm only human. I couldn't help sneaking a peek when I changed your shirt." His thumbs rubbed lazy circles against the points of my hip bones. He leaned back, his eyes sparkling with mischief.

Before I could come up with a response, his lips were on mine. It was just a gentle brush, an introduction. One soft sweep then back again. I sighed. His lips curled up in a grin and his fingers dug into the top of my ass. Settling his mouth more firmly against mine, he kissed me again. This time, he was thorough, learning the shape and contour of my lips, tracing the curve of my bottom one with his tongue before tugging on it with his teeth. He made a noise deep in his throat, and one of his hands coasted up my side to cup the back of my head, tilting me for better access.

Our lips clashed, and I twisted a handful of his shirt in my hand, using it to pull him closer. His hips pressed me against the wall, letting me feel how much the kiss affected him. Slowing the pace, his lips journeyed from my mouth, over my jawline, to the tender spot below my ear. I moaned and rocked against his hardness, dampness gathering between my legs. Desire made me dizzy. His breath was fast and harsh against the side of my neck, and his hand still gripped my hip, his fingers flexing. I tipped my head to the side, and his tongue had started a path down my neck when we heard the creak of the door opening.

West jerked away from me, stepping into the bathroom to grab the towel I had left hanging. I leaned against the wall, too unsteady to move. Aubrey poked her head in and saw me then turned to West as he emerged from the bathroom, holding the balled-up towel in front of him. Covering his anatomy, I noticed. I bit my lip to hide my grin.

"I better get back out there and help Wyatt. We're moving a sofa around for Grandma. Thanks again, Sadie. You're a lifesaver."

"Funny," I called out as he neared the door.

As he moved past her, Aubrey grabbed his arm and leaned close, talking to him in a hushed voice. West paused then shook his head. Aubrey spoke more adamantly, but I couldn't make out what she was saying. West's jaw hardened, and he glared at her before giving a stiff nod. As he moved out the door, Aubrey's hand trailed down from his elbow to his wrist. My stomach rolled. It seemed like an intimate gesture, yet he hadn't seemed happy to see her.

She walked across the room to me. "I just wanted to make sure you were all right. We haven't been introduced, but I'm Aubrey Perotti. And I would have been devastated if anything had happened to little Cody, so thank you again for, let's just say, being in the right place at the right time." Her husky voice had a slight accent. Of course it did.

"I'm just glad I could help," I said.

"And I'd like to return the favor, if I may."

I lifted my eyebrows. "And how do you plan on doing that?"

"You're a photographer, correct? I'd like to hire you. Hailey was singing your praises, and I trust her. Have you ever done . . . boudoir photography?" Her voice dropped at the end, like she was sharing a secret. "I've always wanted to have some shots made, you know, while I still have the body for it. And if I like your work, I'll be sure to whisper your praises in the right ears to make sure you have plenty more jobs headed your way."

"Why me?" I asked, cocking my head to the side.

She laughed. "Partly because I don't know you well. Somehow, stripping down seems easier in front of a stranger than with a friend, yes? You're a photographer, you must understand that. And, like I said, I want to do this now, while I'm young. While I still have the body and haven't lost my nerve. I'll pay you three grand. Is that enough?"

My eyes widened at that number, and I looked her over more

objectively as a possible subject. There was no denying she was beautiful. Her skin was flawless, her curves lush without being trashy. She would photograph well, as I'm sure she already knew. And, as coordinator of that gala thing Hailey was talking about, she was no doubt telling the truth about her connections and pull. Not a good enemy to make by refusing. Plus, three thousand dollars? Yeah, I could use the money.

I ground my teeth before forcing a smile. "When would be a good time for you?"

"Are you free tomorrow? Just after lunch? I'll text you the address."

I recited my number, and she programmed it into her phone, which was covered with pink crystals. "Well, I'm sure you want to get home and get . . . cleaned up." Her eyes raked over me with frank disapproval. "I'll see you tomorrow."

"Can't wait," I muttered under my breath to her retreating back.

I was almost done loading the Jeep when West snuck up behind me and boxed me against the driver's door with his arms. "Do you have plans for tonight? Have dinner with me."

I turned and found myself only inches away from him. He smelled slightly of sweat from whatever he'd been doing for his grandma, and he was short of breath, like he'd run to get to me. I liked it.

I put one finger over his chest. "I can't. I'm going out with Rue and Theo tonight." I drew my hand down, letting my finger trace over his abs. His shirt was damp and sticking to his skin, and his muscles tightened with my touch.

He growled. "Skip it."

"No." He stared at me like he couldn't believe I'd turned him down. "Look, you want to go out with me, give me some notice."

"I just did."

"Five hours is not notice."

"Fine. Where are you going?"

"Why?" I teased. "Planning on crashing?" His checks turned a bit red, and I laughed, a real laugh. "I don't know. It's Theo's turn to pick. Better luck next time." I patted him on the cheek and slipped out of his loose hold, opening the car door.

His hand grabbed the frame as I went to shut it. His eyes flashed as he looked at me, and he opened his mouth like he was going to say something, but then he shook his head.

Neither of us moved. Neither of us spoke. The air around us felt charged with heat and anticipation. Finally, he closed my door and backed away, watching me the whole time.

As much as I felt drawn to him, a part of it scared me. It felt like too much too soon, like a firework, all bright and shiny and exciting, but with no staying power. If I was smart, I'd remember it wasn't safe to play with matches.

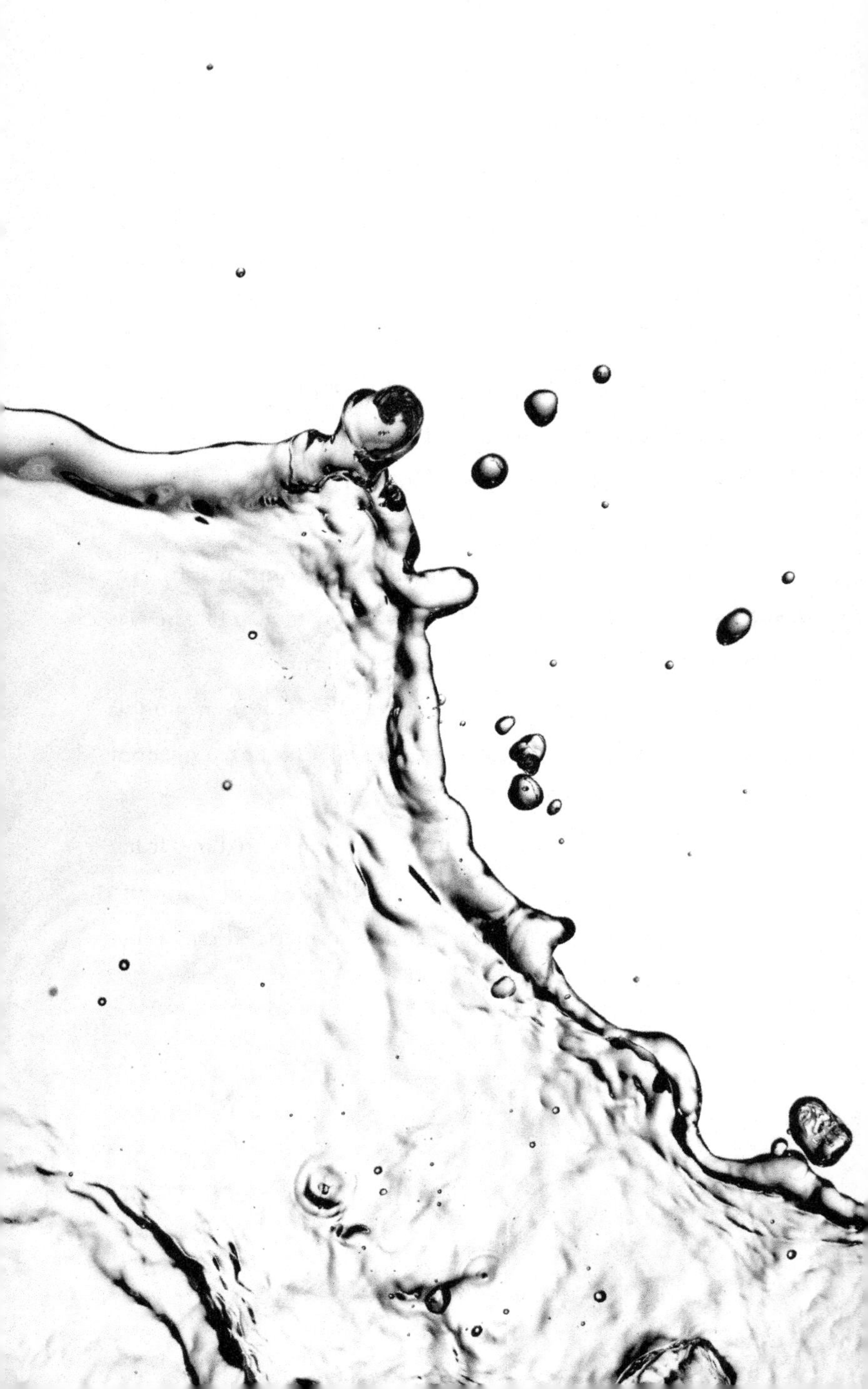

chapter eight

DINNER WAS AWESOME. We'd driven over to this tiny pin dot on the map called Frogmore and eaten at The Foolish Frog. We sat outside, listening to live music and catching up with each other in between stuffing our faces. I was tired of red meat, and they had chicken piccata, my favorite, so I ordered that, but I was also stealing bites from Rue's shrimp and grits and Theo's Frogmore stew, a delicious mix of sausage, shrimp, potatoes, corn, and spices.

And I was drinking. Theo was DD for the night, so Rue and I were indulging. A lot. In fact, I may have already been partially drunk when we piled out of the restaurant and into Theo's old beater.

"Ugh, take me home," I said, moaning. It had been a long day, and the thought of dealing with Aubrey tomorrow was so depressing that I hadn't even mentioned the whole episode at dinner.

"Nuh-uh," Rue said, shaking her hair and making the pink tips swirl. "*We* are going out!"

Theo looked over his shoulder at her as she sprawled in the backseat. I had shotgun. "Where are we going?"

"To get laid!" Rue cried, throwing her arms up in the air. Theo and I laughed. Rue always wanted to get laid. "Let's hit up Anchor for some tourist booty!" She pulled out her phone and started texting furiously. "And I may have told Boone we were headed there. You can thank me later, Sadie."

I stopped laughing. Boone. I had kind of forgotten about him after Grady's party. Boone with his floppy hair and his laid-back vibe. Boone could be fun. And then West's face skittered through my mind, and I got butterflies. I frowned and tried thinking about Boone with his skateboarder's body again. No tingles. I remembered West crowding me against my Jeep. Goose bumps.

Well, maybe I just hadn't given Boone enough of a chance yet. Besides, I didn't think I'd be in over my head with him. He didn't strike me as particularly . . . deep. I could already tell West was going to be trouble for me. And I wasn't sure I was ready for something that strong. I needed something lighter, easier. I needed a Boone.

"To Anchor!" I yelled through my open window, flinging my arm out to feel the sticky humidity blowing through my fingers.

Theo grinned and shook his head. "You guys are going to be crazy tonight, aren't you? Just text me if you find another way home."

When we pulled up to Anchor, the parking lot was almost full. Theo found an unopened bottle of water on his floorboards and made me and Rue each drink half, trying to pace us for the night ahead. Rue rubbed some pink lipstick across her lips that matched her hair and straightened her white eyelet dress. She was playing up the whole I-may-look-innocent-but-trust-me-I'm-not thing. I bet she wasn't even wearing underwear, knowing her. I was buzzed enough I didn't care anymore. I halfheartedly smoothed my dress down as I climbed out of the car. It was soft and short and red, and Rue had made my eyes all dark and smoky and lent me some crazy heels. I felt sultry, and that was good enough for me.

Theo shook his head at me as I stumbled over the crushed oysters in the parking lot. "Sadie, do you at least have your phone with you, so you can call me if you need me?"

I waved my phone at his face. "Yes, sir." I did a mock salute and smashed the phone into my forehead and dissolved into giggles.

Theo sighed. "I swear, the only reason you guys invite me along is so you have a babysitter."

Rue snorted. "We don't need a babysitter. We just take pity on you and your love life. You should be thanking us for dragging your preppy ass out here for some action."

Theo glared at her. "I don't need help."

"Of course not," she mocked.

"Shut up."

"Oh, Theo, you know we love you!" She kissed him on the

cheek, leaving behind her pink lipstick.

"Aargh," he muttered, rubbing at his cheek. "I feel sorry for whatever guy picks you up for the night. Does he know what he's in for?"

She winked. "Not yet." Rue linked her arm with mine, and we sashayed into the club.

I looked around. Jason, the bald, stubbly bartender was working again tonight. I was pretty proud of myself for remembering his name. Maybe I wasn't as wasted as I thought I was. "Let's get drinks!" I yelled at Rue, trying to be heard over the loud music, and she nodded. We wedged ourselves into a small open spot on the bar. Rue got a mojito, and I debated between a rum and Coke and a margarita. I decided on the rum and Coke.

I was just taking my first sip when a warm hand ran up my back and rested on my shoulder. It was Boone. I swallowed fast. Damn, he got here quick. Or maybe he'd been here waiting? He was wearing a surf company tee and cargos, and a beanie over his floppy hair. And I kind of liked it. It looked cute on him. I set my drink down and grabbed his hand. "Let's dance!"

He made an *after you* gesture with his arms, and I led us out onto the dance floor, ready to shake it. Boone was a pretty good dancer. His moves were a little awkward at times, but it was counteracted by his complete lack of concern over it. I laughed and moved with him through three songs before Rue and Theo joined us. Katy Perry came over the speakers, and Rue grabbed me. She loved Katy. She loved every girl power anthem for that matter. So when the chorus started, Rue and I ignored all the guys around us and got our groove on, dancing dirty with each other, which, of course, attracted that many more guys. Somehow in the mix, Boone disappeared. But that was okay, because there was Rue and a bunch of other guys, and we were all just dancing, twisting, and swaying to the beat.

I lost track of time as I stayed on the floor, my hips in constant motion. My buzz was wearing off, but I didn't want to leave the dance floor. Rue drifted away at some point, tucked tight to a dark-haired guy with a full sleeve of tattoos on display. Taking her place, a guy with a sexy British accent and nerdy-chic glasses scooted over to me and complimented me over the music, and we started working it together, totally getting into it. By our second song, we had a feel for each other's rhythm and were really starting to rock. I was beginning to think I had found my lucky guy for the night. Especially if he planned on whispering to me with that amazing accent of his.

I held my hair off my face with one hand as I spun in a circle and then dropped it low. As I came back up, a pair of hands grabbed my hips and pulled me back against a hard chest, dragging me away from the British hottie. Indignant, I grabbed the hands holding me and tried to remove them, but I stiffened when I recognized the bracelets—and my royal blue hair tie—on one of them. *West.* My breath hissed out.

Without turning around, I let my muscles relax, softening against him. He pressed his head to the side of mine, and his lips feathered over my ear. "Mind if I cut in?"

I should have said yes. I should wriggle back through the

crowd until I found my British guy and stick with the tourist. Or figure out where the hell Boone escaped to. Either option was safer. Smarter.

Instead, I arched my back, letting my ass press against his front. His hands slipped down my hips and over the tops of my thighs before tracing a path back up to my waist as he moved us to the bass, our bodies sliding against each other, my hands still holding his wrists. The nerve endings where he'd stroked me shot to life, burning for more of his touch. I bit my lip and forced myself to release him and put a little more distance between us, trying to keep things light. The song changed, and the opening notes to Pitbull's latest hit reverberated through the club. I loved this song. The beat was playful and flirty. It was just what I needed.

Spinning around to face him, I let the music move me. I raised my arms above my head and swiveled my hips, letting my hair fly around me in a wild tangle. I twisted and turned, and partway through the second chorus, I ran one hand down his neck, needing to feel the heat from his skin in that moment. His eyes darkened at the contact, and he hooked an arm around my back, forcing one knee between my legs and pulling me closer. My breath hitched as the feel went from fun to foreplay in an instant. He snugged us together from hip to thigh, and I allowed my hands to roam over his shoulders, not sure where to settle them.

Touching his forehead to mine, he did a slow, dirty grind against me with his hips, and my eyes drifted shut. I couldn't help but compare this moment to the one with Theo a few weeks ago on my doorstep. Then, I'd felt nothing. But with West, even though we were pressed like sardines in the middle of the crowded bar, it wasn't just a spark. It was the whole damn stick of dynamite. And every warning I'd ever heard about not playing with fire went right out the window.

With one hand, he brushed my hair away from my neck and then slid his lips down my exposed skin to where my shoulder started. I tilted my head to the side, giving him more room as he blazed a path back up to just below my ear, nibbling gently. Taking a shaky breath, I leaned back and looked at him. His lust-filled eyes locked with mine, and his mouth tipped up on one side. The little patterns he was drawing with his thumbs on the small of my back were robbing me of rational thought. Licking my lips, I leaned closer to his ear. "Wanna get out of here?" I asked, just loud enough for him to hear before catching his earlobe between my teeth.

Without saying a word, he grabbed my hand and headed straight for the door.

We got to his truck and he yanked the door open, the metal creaking in protest. He tossed me up on the seat and then stepped between my legs, wrapping his strong arms around me. My heart pounded beneath my ribs, and I ran my fingers through his hair, tugging impatiently. Groaning, he pressed his lips to mine in a hot open-mouthed kiss. There was nothing tentative or gentle about it. His mouth branded me as his fingers tangled in my hair, and I hooked my legs around his waist, digging into him with my heels. He nipped at my lips in response.

"You want to play rough, huh?" His voice was ragged.

I kissed my way up his jawline. "I just want to play. Naked."

After one last taste, he drew away and then jogged around the front of the cab to hop inside. As he pulled out of the lot, steering with one hand, he used the other to slide me to the middle of the bench seat, and I rubbed my palm down his thigh. He brought my hand back up and farther into his lap, and I let my hand hover above his crotch, rubbing him with just one finger, up and down, as he drove. "Any nicknames I need to know about before we get started?" I teased.

He slanted me a glance, his mouth curving up. "For my cock? No. But I might be open to suggestions later."

He grabbed my hand and stroked himself with it once, then twice, before raising it to his mouth and sucking one of my fingers all the way to the knuckle, biting the tip before releasing it. I closed my eyes and tried to remember if the condoms were in the nightstand or if they were in the bathroom medicine cabinet. Now was not the time to be searching, and the bar was less than a mile from the cottage.

Rolling my head on the back of the seat, I stared at West's neck. The tan skin stretched over chords of muscle. He had those muscles that ran between his neck and shoulders that made some guys look bulky. Traps? Is that what they were called? His hand gripped my thigh, his thumb stroking my bare skin, and my mind whirled. The truck lurched as he yanked it to a stop. He'd read my mind and gone to my place. Rue would kill me later, but it was two blocks closer and, right now, I just wanted to find a flat surface. West swung open the driver's side door and dragged me out through his side, too impatient to come around.

Lips fused, we stumbled up the steps to the cottage. I unlocked the door, and we stepped through. He closed it behind us and locked it. He tore his lips from mine long enough to ask, "Which way?" Ripping my dress over my head, I started walking, leading him down the hall to my room.

We didn't turn the lights on. Didn't even pull the covers back. I launched myself at him, and he grabbed my ass, lifting me up, and we tumbled back onto the bed. He turned us as we fell so he landed on the bottom, and I splayed across him, wearing only a strapless bra and panties. I braced my arms against his shoulders, shrouding him in my hair.

For several heartbeats we stared at each other, lingering, savoring the anticipation. His hand cupped my face, his thumb smoothing my cheekbone, and I leaned into the caress. Then his mouth opened, and that one tiny movement set me off. I became a whirlwind of motion, eager to feel his skin against mine. I tore at his clothes, and he tried to help, twisting and pulling until his shirt was over his head and his jeans and boxer briefs were around his ankles. After sliding from the bed, I yanked his pants off and tossed them in the corner, leaving him bare to my view. I paused, kneeling on the floor at the foot of my bed, between his thighs, looking him over as he leaned up on his elbows. His erection rose proudly in front of me, impossible to ignore. He was bigger than I'd expected, and my stomach clenched with desire. Leaning forward, I ran the tip of my tongue up his hard length from base to tip, pausing to swirl the velvety tip. I pulled back and blew softly against the head of his cock and watched as it jumped, his balls tightening. I was just getting ready to take him in my mouth when he grabbed my upper arms and hauled me up his body.

"No," he ground out. "I won't last, and I've waited too damn long for this to be over that quick." He brushed my hair from my face and grabbed a loose fistful of it at the back of my neck, using it to bring me to him.

I wrapped my arms around his shoulders and crushed my mouth to his, eager for more of his kisses. Parting my lips, I licked into his mouth, dueling with his tongue and learning his taste. We kissed fiercely, both of us straining, trying to get closer. My tongue felt the rough edges of his teeth and his explored the inside of my lower lip. It was like I couldn't get close enough, any molecule between us was one too many. I framed his face with my hands, holding him still so I could take what I wanted. Our lips tangled hungrily, too impatient for nuance.

With his arms, he pushed us up until he was sitting and I was straddling his lap, his cock pulsing against me. Breaking off the kiss, he dragged his mouth down my neck to nuzzle my chest, rubbing his face against the mounds of my breasts. He used his tongue to trace my skin where the black lace edged my nude bra. "I like this," he murmured against me, nipping lightly. "It's pretty. Sweet, but a little naughty." His finger touched the center where the two cups were held together with black corset-style laces.

Slipping his other arm around my back, he made short work of the clasp, tossing my bra toward the dresser. His big hands cupped my breasts, squeezing gently. Freed, they seemed to swell, growing to fill his fingers. Arching, I pushed my breasts closer to him, wanting more. I closed my eyes and bit my lip at the feel of his rough palms against my tender flesh, his calluses thrilling me. I loved the slight abrasion of his touch, the contrast of our bodies heightening my arousal.

Ducking his head, he latched on to one of my hard nipples with a greedy mouth. An answering pull echoed deep in my core. I moaned, running my fingers into his hair and scraping his scalp with my nails. He gave my other breast equal attention, laving it with his tongue before taking the nipple into his mouth. I tipped my head back as I held him against me, all my focus on his touch, his lips, his tongue, his urgency.

He raced his hands up my thighs and around to cup my ass, bringing me tighter against him. The heat of him throbbed through my thin panties, and I undulated against him. With a groan, he twisted us on the bed until I was on my back, and he was half on top, half beside me, one of his heavy thighs thrown over mine. He rained kisses over my face—my eyelids, my nose, my cheeks, the tip of my chin. His hand crept down the plane of my stomach and dipped under the edge of my underwear, teasing the skin there and sending my nerve endings into overdrive. *Oh, dear Lord, yes.*

I sucked in a breath, letting it out in shaky pants. He rubbed his nose across my jaw and buried it in the crook of my neck, pressing his face against me, and then he lowered one finger to delve into my folds. I knew he could feel how wet I was for him. He growled my name and sucked at the bottom of my neck near my collarbone.

A raw sound of need escaped my throat, and I ran my hand from his shoulder down his chest and over his hard abs, feeling his muscles contract in my path. I followed that sexy muscle that ran from his hip to his erection, wrapping my fingers around his hardness and stroking him, loving the way he felt like silk over steel. He covered my fingers with his own, guiding me, showing me how he liked it.

"Sadie. Condom. My wallet." The words were a soft staccato against my neck.

Letting go of him, I rolled across the bed and opened my nightstand drawer. Groping blindly, I felt the crinkle of foil and tossed the packet on his chest. He made short work of the wrapper and, with one hand, yanked my panties down my legs, throwing them somewhere beyond the bed. Returning his hand to my center, he pushed a finger inside of me. "Jesus, Sadie, the way you feel against my hand—" His voice was husky with need. He added another finger, and I lifted my hips to meet his thrusts.

I ran my hands over his torso, following his contours, unable to settle on one spot. He was all heat and lean muscle, and I couldn't get enough, couldn't stop moving. I opened my legs wider, trying to get him where I wanted him most. Taking the hint, he rose over me and braced himself on his forearms while he nuzzled my ear.

Unable to wait any longer, I reached between us and guided him to my opening, and he pressed the first inch of himself inside me. I put my feet flat on the bed and lifted up, impatient to feel him deeper, stretching me, filling me. He withdrew except for the tip and then thrust again, wrenching a soft moan from my throat. I whispered his name. "More," I demanded.

He moved his hands down to my hips to hold me still, and with his next plunge, he entered me fully, staying deep while I adjusted to the size of him, my muscles tensed. He swore under his breath. "You ready?" His question was a harsh exhale against my ear. "Because I want it hard and fast, and I think you do too."

I dropped my hands to his tight ass and squeezed. "Waitin' on you," I managed to get out.

He laughed once and then started to move, setting a pace that had me clinging to him. I clutched his shoulders, his arms, his neck, whatever I could reach, and matched his rhythm, the force of his hips pushing me into the mattress. He groaned, pinning me beneath him, his weight forcing me to take in shallow breaths. A light sheen of sweat slicked our skin, and our movements became jerkier, less coordinated, our primal instinct to chase release overtaking finesse.

Heat, friction, need, desperation—everything was magnified, and all I wanted was more. I lost control, abandoning myself to the moment knowing he was as close as I was.

My heels dug into his ass, and he ground deep against me, rubbing his pelvic bone against my clit. I flew apart, tightening before shattering beneath him and calling out his name as I came. He wrapped an arm under my lower back as his movements became a blur, his hips plunging over and over until he gave two hard thrusts and shuddered against me, rocking slowly as he rode out his own orgasm. He held his breath as he flexed one last time, and then he pulled his arm out and collapsed, his cock still throbbing faintly inside of me.

I rubbed my hands up and down his back, relishing the way his body pinned me to the bed, anchoring me, as I gradually recovered from his onslaught. My body felt boneless, like putty to be molded by his hands. Our heartbeats eased in unison, and his breath slowed against my neck. He pressed soft kisses there, tickling me a little. My skin felt oversensitive and raw now that we were done.

Lifting off of me, he slipped from the room for a moment. I heard a rustle in the bathroom, and then he was back, pulling the covers down and gathering me to him until I lay on top of him, my head pillowed on his shoulder. He drew the quilt up to our waists, and I snuggled closer, utterly content. His fingers sketched an abstract pattern over my back, and he pressed his lips to the top of my head before rubbing his cheek against me.

"That was almost as good as I imagined." His chest rumbled against my ear as he spoke, and it took a minute for his words to register.

I reared back. "Excuse me?"

"We skipped a step." His tone was soft, almost sad, and it was the only thing saving him from a slap in the face.

What the fuck did he mean, we skipped a step? My brows knitted in confusion. I came, and I sure as hell felt him finish.

Smiling, he smoothed my wrinkled brow, ran his finger down the length of my nose, and then traced my lips. I made a sound in the back of my throat and jerked my face away from him, and he dropped his hand.

"It's okay." He leaned up and pecked my lips. "We can fix it."

I narrowed my eyes at him. "Look, maybe I'm not as experienced or flexible or—"

He pressed his finger against my lips, silencing me. "You were great. Fucking mind blowing. But in my fantasies," he paused to tuck a strand of hair behind my ear, and his words echoed in my head—*you've had fantasies about me?*—"I always fall asleep with the taste of you in my mouth."

I blinked at him, and he traced my sex until I understood what he was implying.

"Oh. Well." I licked my lips. "What are you waiting for?"

He gave a wolfish grin before flipping me on my back. Pinning my arms next to my head, he slid down my body until he was nestled between my thighs. He let go of my arms and drew my legs over his shoulders, shifting until he had me how he wanted me. Reaching back up, he took hold of my breasts, caressing them.

He placed soft kisses all around my folds, taking his time, teasing me, but not touching me where I wanted it most. I squirmed, restless, and rotated my hips. He pinched my nipples in reproach and then soothed them with his palms. I stilled. Finally, he took the flat of his tongue and slowly, oh, so slowly, licked all the way up my center.

Yes.

My hands gripped his short hair, and I released a breath I hadn't realized I was holding. His lips and tongue explored every inch of my slit, licking and sucking, but always keeping the pressure light to tease and torment me. I tugged his hair and lifted my hips, needing more friction.

His fingers converged from my breasts to just my nipples, rolling and tugging them. I moaned, burrowing deeper into the bed. Finally, his mouth zeroed in on my clit. Taking that sensitive nub between his lips, he sucked, stroking it with tongue. When he hit that perfect spot, the one that made every nerve in my body fire simultaneously, I couldn't help bucking against him, and his lips stretched into a smile before he did it again. And again. He increased his speed and pressure, sucking me harder until I was writhing beneath him, my head digging into my pillow. His fingers tightened on my nipples, and he stroked me with his tongue until I was crying out, "Right there . . . right there . . . oh God, yes . . . now . . . *now! West!*"

Light splintered behind my eyelids, and I bowed my back, pressing my hips upward, desperate for more of him. I clutched his head to me with my hands and my thighs until it was just too much, and when I relaxed my death grip, he slowed, kissing me as the aftershocks rocked through me. When I could do nothing but lay there in a helpless puddle of satisfaction, he climbed back up next to me.

His eyes glittered as he took in my slack features. "*That's* what I dreamed about. That look right there. And knowing that I put it there."

I tried to come up with a snappy retort to keep his ego in check, but really, what could I say? The man had a golden tongue.

So I'd let him have this one.

Smiling, I rolled over onto my stomach, snuggling into my pillow and closing my eyes. Who needed sweet dreams with sex like that? He gathered me in his arms and pulled me up against him. His thigh worked its way between mine and his hand reached under me until he cupped my breast. His nose brushed against my hair, and he inhaled, breathing me in. He kissed the back of my head softly. Almost tenderly.

I was more asleep than awake as I tried to figure out what was happening. He was snuggling me. Granted, I loved to snuggle. It was the one thing I missed the most about being in a relationship. But West? He didn't strike me as the staying-to-cuddle-afterwards type.

So why wasn't he leaving? It was the last thought I had before sleep claimed me.

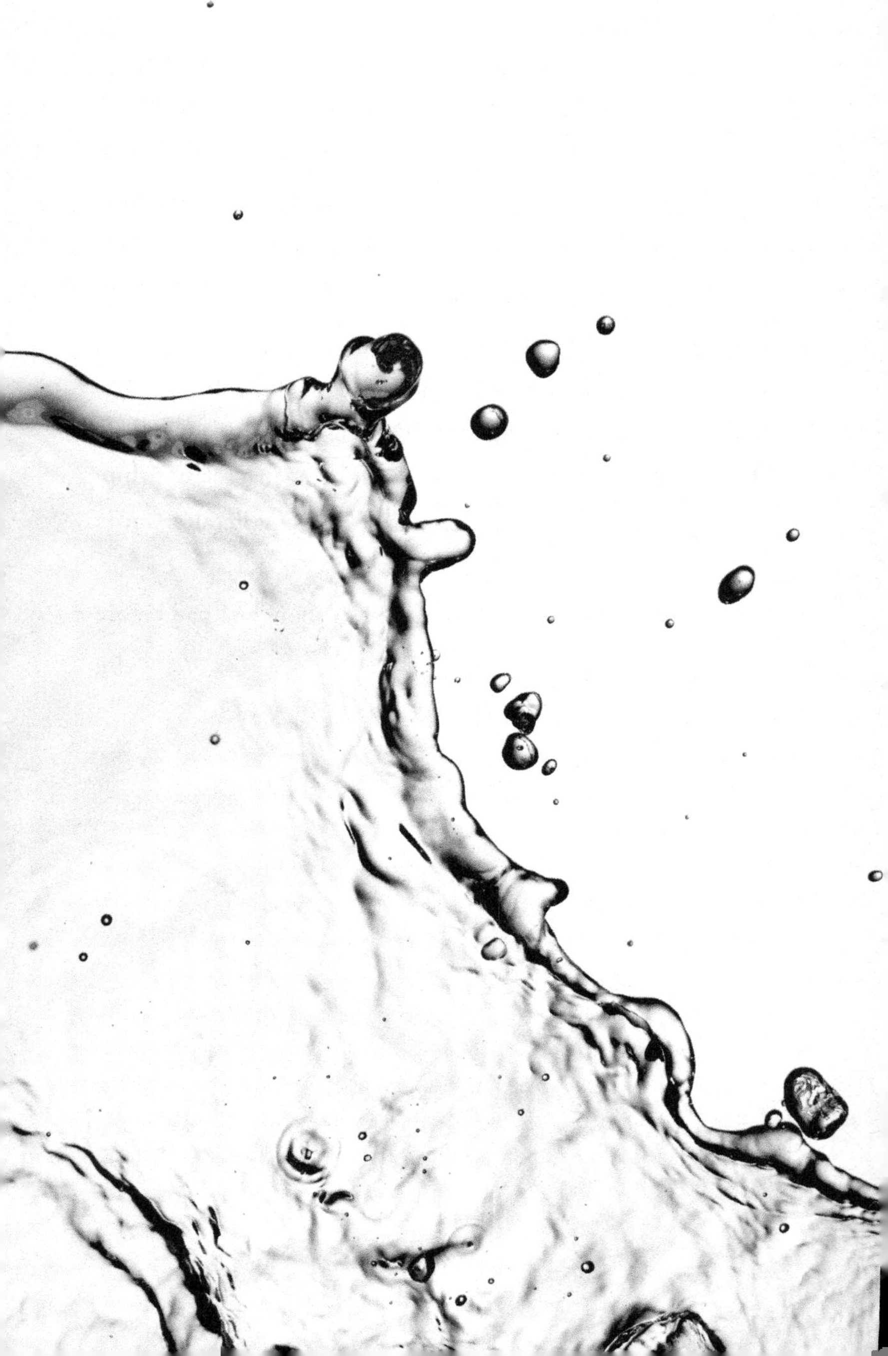

chapter *nine*

I WOKE UP TO THE INSISTENT beeping of my cell chirping at me from some far corner of the room. Still groggy, I followed the noise to behind the rocking chair and located the damn thing under the lobster pillow that had been chucked the night before. I punched at it, silencing it, and crawled back under the covers. I stretched, yawning, feeling a well-used achiness in certain muscles, and then I froze with realization.

I was alone.

I looked around. His clothes were missing. Water wasn't running in the bathroom. Puzzled, I crept over to the window and pulled the curtain aside to peek. No truck. He was gone.

I collapsed back on the bed again, not sure how I felt about that. Had I really expected him to stick around for the awkward morning after? He was doing us both a favor by disappearing.

That way, when we bumped into each other next time, we could both kind of pretend this little one-night stand never happened and keep things casual. Easy.

Just like I wanted.

And yet, I couldn't help the little frisson of disappointment I felt at not waking up in his arms. Getting one last kiss.

Especially after last night's epic orgasms.

Turning, I buried my head in the pillow and inhaled. I could still smell him. I wondered how long it would last if I didn't clean my sheets. One night? A week? I could see now why Rue always went back to the guy's place. My bed was awash with memories of West and me tangled together. There was no way I wouldn't be thinking about it when I went to bed tonight. Alone.

I pulled my phone out and checked it. One text from Theo, reminding me of our gym date at ten. I groaned in annoyance. I'd forgotten about that. Granted, we'd moved the time back from seven to ten, but still. I just wanted to lay here and do nothing for a couple hours.

Except maybe daydream about last night.

Dragging myself out of bed, I took a shower and brushed my teeth, moving sluggishly through my morning routine. Throwing on some gym clothes, I glared at my phone when it told me I didn't have enough time to make coffee or I'd be late. Theo was just going to have to take me *au naturale* this morning. Poor guy.

Peeking into Rue's room and finding the bed empty, I sent her a quick text to make sure she was okay as I ran down the front steps. She texted me back as I buckled in.

Rue: Weird tattoo on his thigh—Popeye, really?—but he found my g-spot, so I'll try to ignore it. I'll be home later. I may let him find it again first.

I couldn't help but laugh. Rue sure knew how to pick 'em. At least she'd remembered the rule and gone back to, well, wherever he was staying so she wouldn't be haunted by spinach-eating sailors tonight.

I parked next to Theo's beater at the gym and trudged inside with zero enthusiasm. He was already plodding away on an elliptical, so I grabbed the one next to him. I matched my pace to his, grateful that he was going more snail than rabbit this morning, and squinted over at him. He gave a tired nod, and I dipped my chin in return. Thank God he wasn't feeling chatty.

Thirty minutes later, Theo called time. We both looked over at the weight area and back at each other.

"Nope. Not today." I shook my head. "Not without caffeine in me."

He looked relieved. "Krispy Kreme?"

"God, yes," I agreed, desperate for some coffee and sugar.

Twenty minutes later, we were settled on the beach with a box of glazed nestled between us, and each of us clutching the largest coffee Krispy Kreme sold. Holding my coffee in one hand, I pried loose a doughnut with the other, taking a huge bite and closing my eyes in absolute bliss.

He polished off his own in record time and sipped his coffee. "You know, today's workout won't even burn off one of these bad boys."

I shot him a devilish smile. "Last night's will."

Theo choked on his coffee. "You realize I saw you leave with West, right?"

I faltered for a moment and then shrugged. "And?"

"*And* I totally distracted Boone for you while you slipped out."

I froze. "What did you say?"

"I didn't say anything. Just that I hadn't seen you in awhile and that you were probably still dancing."

I twisted my lips. I didn't want to lead Boone on, but I guess I wouldn't have wanted it rubbed in his face that I had left with someone else. I nodded in thanks.

"Yeah, you're welcome. Do you feel better at least? You've been uptight for the last two weeks." Theo regarded me steadily.

I rolled my shoulders. The sugar and coffee were beginning to seep into my system, perking me up. And I did feel better. Looser. More relaxed. I tried to hide my smile. My voice was softer this time. "Yeah. I do." Turning to Theo, I pinned him with an assessing look. "What about you? Did you have any luck last night?"

Theo's eyes sparkled, and he turned to look back at the waves. He took a long, slow drag of coffee before he answered, gloating. "Yup. A redhead. A real redhead." He held up his fist, and I bumped it.

"Wait. What do you mean, a real redhead? How do you—" I shut up when I figured out what he'd been implying. I shook my head, trying to rid my mind of the image. "So, you going to see her again?"

"Why? I've already had first, seconds, and thirds."

I rolled my eyes. "Boys." When I turned to scowl at him on behalf of womankind, he shoved a doughnut in my mouth and effectively silenced anything else I had to say.

Before I could finish chewing, Theo grabbed one last pastry and jumped up. "All right, I gotta get back to the gym for a client. I'll see you Tuesday, usual time. Next time, we are not skipping weights. Be ready." He pointed at me for emphasis.

"Wait! I can't eat all these!" I gestured at the box still sitting next to me as he jogged away.

"Feed the gulls!" he suggested, halfway back to the boardwalk.

Uh, no. I was not giving those pesky creatures perfectly good doughnuts. After nibbling my way through one more and draining my coffee, I headed back to my Jeep, taking the box with me. If Rue didn't want them, maybe I could look up recipes online. I'd heard there was a good bread pudding recipe that called for day old Krispy Kremes.

After dawdling at the cottage as long as I could, I headed out to Aubrey's. This time, I'd dressed in head-to-toe black, trying to look the part of a professional photographer. My hair was twisted into a low bun, and I wore light makeup, a silky black top, and cigarette pants. Not real exciting, but then, I already knew today's shoot was going to be all about Aubrey Perotti.

Her family's old, plantation-style house with its large, white columns in the front didn't faze me. The fact that Aubrey opened the door wearing only a short, silky robe over lingerie didn't surprise me either. But the genuine smile of delight Aubrey greeted me with threw me for a loop. I'd expected her to be more cool, more calculating, the whole afternoon more of a business transaction.

"You came!" she exclaimed, reaching out to clasp both my hands in both of hers.

I raised my eyebrows. Of course I came. I'd been half-threatened, half-blackmailed about the consequences if I didn't. I forced a smile back, unsure of how to react. Had I misjudged her the other day? "For you, of course I did."

If she caught my slight sarcasm, she didn't let on. Instead, she hurried me through the showpiece of a house and up to the third floor. By elevator. I tried not to be impressed, but damn it, who has an elevator in their beach house? Her room, well, her suite of rooms, was in a rounded part of the house, kind of like a lighthouse, or a turret. Aubrey literally lived like a freaking princess in a tower. Her bedroom was light and gauzy with antique furniture, authentic I was sure, and heavy moldings.

Aubrey drew me to a little alcove off to the side. "I've got some ideas. I mean, I'm sure you know what you're doing and all, but I wanted to make sure we were on the same page." She was as excited as a little girl playing dress up. I started to feel guilty for judging her so quickly.

She pulled up a Pinterest board she'd made, and I reviewed the photos. They were all sultry without crossing over into sleazy, and I got the feel for the general vibe she was going for. She'd done her eye makeup dark and dramatic, and her hair was in big, sexy, loose curls. She was styled perfectly for what I had in mind.

"We'll shoot it so it's all about the tease. For you, I'm thinking black and white. Make it more classic and sophisticated. High-end editorial style." I saw her eyes light up at the end. Bingo! Nailed it. "Let me see what you were thinking of for clothes."

Nine outfits were displayed in her dressing room. Yes, her dressing room. As in, a separate room from her closet with a settee and a big, round ottoman and even a little mini fridge, all done in pale Parisian pink and black. "You like?"

I looked over the ensembles with a critical eye. Classic men's white dress shirt, yes. Oversized, chunky v-neck fisherman's sweater, yes. The other choices all consisted of lace, satin, mesh, and feathers.

Feathers?

"There's too much going on in some of these lingerie sets," I said. "The focus needs to be on you. Your skin, your curves, and maybe even your hair, but not so much on the clothes. They're more background. You're the main attraction."

She nodded, digesting my words. "I like the way you think." She moved through the lingerie options and tossed all but two in a pile. She kept one black and one white. "We'll use these. Angel and devil."

I had to force myself not to comment on that last part. It was just too easy. "All right, so let's get down to the details. How much do you want to show? What are you comfortable with?"

She'd clearly already thought this all through. "From the back, everything is fine. From the front, underwear down below, and as long as no nipples show up top, I'm good."

I set my bag down and pulled out my camera, all business now. "Let's start with the men's white button down. Nothing underneath. And I want you to pin your hair up high, so we can see your neck for these first shots. Just pin it up quick so it's messy and haphazard. And throw on whatever music makes you feel sexy. I need you to be as relaxed as possible for this."

Aubrey smiled, seemingly delighted, and clapped her hands together in glee. "This is going to be so fun!" While she sat at her dressing table to fix her hair, she nodded at the mini fridge. "It's fully stocked, so feel free to help yourself."

I went over to see what she had. Soda, fresh fruit juice, water, even tiny bottles of liquor. I chose a bottle of orange juice. "Can I get you anything?" I offered.

She crossed over to me, grabbed the tiny bottle of Bacardi, and tossed it back. "You wanted me loose, right? This should help." She lifted one shoulder in a shrug, and the robe slipped down her arm.

While she changed, I moved around her bedroom, checking the lighting from various angles. In front of the windows would be good for these first shots. With the light shining through the shirt, her curves would be visible as shadows beneath. I dragged a chair out of the way. Better.

The bass thumped loudly, and I jumped, startled by the volume. Ray J's "Sexy Can I" blared from a hidden sound system, filling the air with its playful vibe and talk about a Kodak moment. I grinned at Aubrey as she shimmied her way into the room, holding the shirt closed at her breasts. "Perfect song, right?" She smiled back.

"It is," I agreed, pulling the camera up to my eye. "Just dance around there for a bit, if you want. Do what feels natural. Let's just see what happens before we start doing actual poses."

She moved to the small open space beside the window and kept the beat with her hips. She faced away from me and raised her hands above her head, causing the shirt to rise up, allowing a glimpse of her butt cheek. I snapped off a few shots and tried to direct her a little. "Look over your shoulder at the camera every once in a while. Keep it flirty. Pretend I'm the hottest guy you've ever seen."

She danced around a little more until the song ended. Then I started working her through some specific poses: Facing away from me and letting the shirt fall to her elbows, exposing her upper back. Extending her arms out and holding the window frame, so the shirt fell around her and the sunlight shone through, leaving her silhouette outlined underneath. Profile shots looking out the window. Some sitting on the window frame, one long, shapely leg propped up opposite her.

She changed into the fisherman's sweater, and Shaggy's "Boombastic" kicked in. I lowered the camera, feeling lulled into a sense of camaraderie. So far, Aubrey had been nothing but cooperative and enthusiastic. Now I just felt like a bitch for my earlier misgivings. "Shaggy's awesome. I wonder what ever happened to him? Do you have any more of his stuff?" I was surprised to find myself enjoying the shoot.

Aubrey nodded and adjusted her playlist so a few more Shaggy songs would play next. For this look, I had her unpin her hair so the curls hid most of her face. Letting the sweater droop off one shoulder, baring it and the top curve of her breast, she tugged the sweater down between her legs, as if trying to modestly hide herself. I took shots of that pose from several angles, knowing the contrast of her shiny hair and smooth skin against the rough weave of the sweater was going to look great on film. I had her crawl across the bed toward me, with the sweater still hanging off one shoulder, and from the angle in front of her, the low v-neck allowed a view of her cleavage and flat stomach, depending how she moved.

We took a short break after that, and I showed Aubrey some of my raw footage so far, just to make sure we were still on the same wavelength. She looked at each picture critically, as if she were viewing a stranger and not herself. A sense of uneasiness crept over me as I waited for her verdict. "You look beautiful," I said truthfully. "What we've got so far is fantastic. Is this what you were thinking of when we started?"

She looked at me, her eyes big and guileless. "No. It's so much better. You've somehow made it so erotic and yet, sweet."

"Wait 'til I get it all edited. It'll look even better. Softer, more intimate." I was pleased with my work so far and knew it would be some of the best I'd done in awhile. The stuff I'd done of Cody was adorable, but kid's shoots were easier in the sense that every parent already thought their kid was the cutest thing ever. Making a grown woman like photos of herself was a whole different bag of tricks.

Aubrey went to change again while I hummed along to Shaggy's "Luv Me, Luv Me," and I couldn't help but giggle when Aubrey reentered the room to the opening bars of Akon's "Smack That." She'd put on the black lingerie. "All right, for this next section, I just want you to roll around the bed looking sexy, and I'll move around you and shoot it. Move through some poses slowly, and try to keep your movements soft and feline. Slinky. And remember to keep your face either innocent or like you're thinking really, really dirty thoughts. Try not to let it go blank. You'll just come across as looking bored, which is not what we're going for here."

Aubrey lolled against a mountain of white, frilly pillows and sucked on her fingertip while looking at me out of the side of her eyes. Perfect. She tangled her hands up in her hair then ran them down the side of her body, eyeing the camera. Next, she rolled until she lay on her back across the bed, propped up on her elbows with her knees bent, arching her back upwards. She let her head drop back until her neck was stretched and exposed, and I said, "Hold that," as I moved to shoot her from both head on and at a forty-five degree angle. Then, I kicked off my shoes and climbed up on a chair off to the side and captured the same pose from overhead, careful to keep my shadow from entering the picture.

As I got down, Aubrey looked at my foot. "Nice tattoo. What's it for?"

I glanced at my tattoo, the little paper airplane with the dotted line behind it indicating it had done a loop. "You know, it was supposed to be a metaphor. Life's about the journey, not the destination, some crap like that. I thought it was deep and philosophical when I got it." Another lie. The truth was private.

Aubrey smiled and nodded like she understood and then shifted her body again, showing off her hourglass figure.

After I gave her the signal that I'd gotten those shots, Aubrey sat up straight. I had her tilt her head forward so her hair cascaded over her breasts, and I shot some close-ups of just her torso showcased by her black lace balconette bra.

"Okay, now, if you feel comfortable, I'd suggest removing your bra, and I'll get some of your bare back and of you from the front with your arms covering your chest."

She hesitated. "You're sure this isn't going to start looking . . ."

"Trashy? No, not if I do my job right. But it's up to you. What we've got so far is great if you want to stop there."

She bit her lip and went to unfasten the bra.

"Wait! Do it slowly and let me shoot that too."

I stood behind her and clicked a quick succession of photos as her hands twisted behind her and unclasped the hooks. She flung the bra to the floor out of sight and leaned her back one way and then the other, peeking over her shoulder at the camera coquettishly. I wouldn't have been surprised if she'd fluttered her eyelashes. She seemed to be getting into the role. I could imagine her fitting the whole cliché of lady-in-the-streets-and-a-freak-in-the-bed. Somehow, I didn't think Aubrey had a problem with kinky. Without any cues at all, she laid on her back, one arm across her chest, her hips twisted to the side so it wasn't a full on frontal shot, and, of course, her hair fell in perfect disarray above her head. She lifted her other arm above her, letting it settle in her hair. I did my job, capturing the tableau before me of a curvy young woman inviting someone to join her in bed, her face conveying her utter confidence, as if she knew—and expected the person viewing her to know—exactly what would happen next. As an Usher song faded out, I put down my camera.

"I think that's a wrap. I know you still have the white outfit left to go, but I think we've already got everything you'll need. We ran through most of the poses you tagged on your Pinterest board, and I know I've got pictures of you ranging the whole gamut from demure to seductive."

Aubrey walked over to the ottoman that dominated her dressing room and started to slip on a robe, when I had a flash of inspiration.

"Hold on one minute," I called out, grabbing my camera and hurrying over. "Let's get a few of you on this thing." I nudged the ottoman with my foot.

Surprised, Aubrey looked at it and considered the prop, then draped herself suggestively across it. "Like this?"

I nodded, snapped a few shots and then walked around to get some from the back. "Perfect." Aubrey twisted a few different ways, even lying on her back and stretching her legs straight up in the air, crossed at the ankles, before we quit.

As she slipped on her robe, I finished off my orange juice from earlier. "How soon were you hoping to have prints of these?"

"Initially, I was going to say a week would be fine, but now I'm so excited to see the final results that I'll throw in an extra thousand dollars if you can have them for me tomorrow."

My eyes widened, and I tried not to let my shock show. Damn, I could do a lot with four thousand dollars for a day's work. I glanced at my watch. It was already three-thirty. If I hustled, I could probably finish tonight. She wouldn't need that much retouching. "I'll have the prints here at noon tomorrow. Will that work for you?"

She reached over and squished me in a hug, catching me off guard. I patted her shoulder awkwardly. "I can't wait! I can't wait, I can't wait, I can't wait!" she squealed, bouncing on her toes. I could feel her bare breasts under her robe pressing against me, and I eased back from her, trying to put a little distance between us. It was one thing to photograph those bad boys but it was quite another to have them all up on me.

Shouldering my bag, I headed for the door. "I can let myself out, if you want to stay here and finish getting dressed. I'll text you when I'm on my way tomorrow."

"Thanks! I can't wait to show them to my boyfriend!"

I paused on the threshold to her room. "Oh yeah? Text me and let me know what he thinks."

"You can ask him yourself," Aubrey said, her voice dripping sweetness.

"Oh? Will I get to meet him?" My brow furrowed in confusion.

"You already have. West Montgomery."

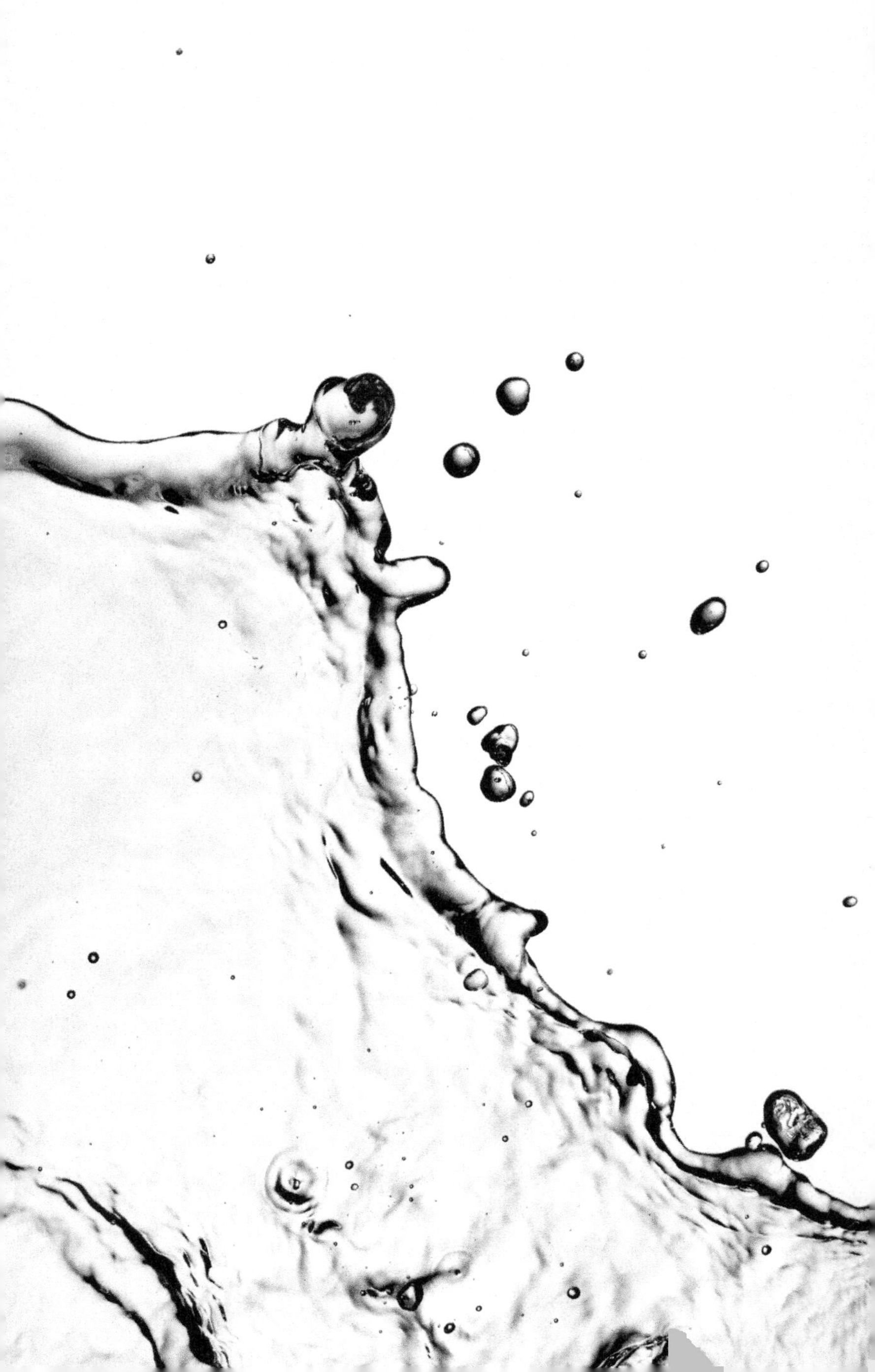

chapter ten

I DON'T REMEMBER LEAVING Aubrey's house. Don't remember the drive home. I had no clue how long I had been sitting in the driveway, white-knuckling the steering wheel and gritting my teeth so no emotion could escape. Holding myself on lockdown. Aubrey's announcement felt like a sucker punch right in the stomach.

West had a girlfriend.

West had a *fucking* girlfriend.

The words played on repeat in my head.

Of course, he did. He looked like he could be Poseidon's bastard son. It would be against the laws of nature for him not to be paired up. The man was made to procreate.

My phone chimed, the sound muffled by the detritus in my oversized purse. I reached for it and dug to the bottom of the bag, where my phone usually ended up hiding. I frowned at the unknown number.

You looked beautiful this morning. I hope I didn't wake you when I left.

My fingers tightened around the phone. It was from *him*.

How did he even get my number?

I punched delete and then threw my phone down like it was diseased. It bounced off the passenger seat and settled somewhere in the foot well, the action not enough to calm my temper.

Blinking, I looked out my windshield and focused on the sky. The sun was just starting its descent. Dinnertime had long since passed, but I wasn't hungry.

I tapped the steering wheel as I contemplated my camera bag. The memory card with Aubrey's photos was stored safely inside. I could accidentally-on-purpose delete the whole session. Photoshop some zits onto her flawless skin. Maybe some wrinkles too. I could even make her ass and her boobs look saggy. An evil grin brightened my mood at the thought.

But I couldn't do any of those things. I needed the cash too damn bad. And, if I was being logical, my real beef wasn't even with Aubrey. It was with fucking West. And more than feeling hurt and angry, I just felt . . . stupid.

Stupid for not listening to Rue and her brilliant rules. Stupid for not leaving with that British guy instead. Stupid for thinking West felt those same crazy sparks I did when we touched. Stupid for secretly hoping that maybe, *maybe* it would turn into more than just a one-night stand.

Stupid for contemplating for even one minute that West would pick someone who looked like me over someone that looked like Aubrey.

With a drawn-out sigh of self-disgust, I grabbed my bag and trudged up the stairs to the cottage, ready to admit defeat.

Before heading toward my bedroom and the inevitable editing session, I made a pit stop in the kitchen, pausing to glance between the stainless steel, French-door fridge and the smaller wine fridge. Did the situation call for ice cream or wine? I tipped my head in contemplation. Nabbing a bottle of white and deciding I didn't need a glass, I made it to my bedroom and tossed my purse and camera bag on my bed.

And stopped.

I couldn't do this in here. I couldn't edit photos of West's girlfriend on the same surface I had fucked him less than twenty-four hours ago.

Closing my eyes, I replayed our night together. I could still feel his callused hands dragging across my skin. His lips tasting and teasing all of me. His cock hard against my hip as we pressed together.

And the whole time, he was cheating on his girlfriend.

This wasn't the same situation as Asshole and me. I was the other woman this time. Suddenly, my skin crawled, and I felt dirty.

Leaving my stuff on the bed, I stripped down, snagged the bottle of wine, and headed to the shower. Turning the knob as hot as it would go, I drank straight from the bottle while I waited for the water to heat. When steam rose from behind the curtain, I took one last gulp, left the bottle on the back of the toilet tank for easy access, and slipped inside. Grabbing some gritty body scrub, I scoured every inch of my body, every part that West had touched. I repeated the process until my skin was pink and raw, and I no longer felt contaminated.

The water was starting to run cool by the time I finally stepped out, wrapping myself in a towel and retrieving the wine bottle. I'd drunk most of it over the course of my shower. Leaning my head back, I drained the last of it and then abandoned the bottle on my sink as I returned to my room.

Pulling on a soft tank top and some flannel pants, I left my hair wrapped in a towel turban and grabbed my laptop and camera bag. Settling on the couch, I dug the memory card out of my camera and loaded the pictures onto my computer.

Rows of thumbnails appeared, pieces and parts of Aubrey filling my screen. I started the process of culling the shots, deleting the ones where the focus was off or the lighting unflattering. Gritting my teeth, I went through the images one by one, picking the best of each pose for additional editing.

I swallowed painfully as I scrolled through them. I had very little actual editing to do. Aubrey was just that gorgeous. The contrast of her dark hair, olive skin, and white bed linens was classically striking. She was petite, curvaceous, and the embodiment of everything a guy could want. Dirty Barbie brought to life. Of course, West was with someone like her.

Finishing before midnight, I emailed the files to a twenty-four hour print shop in Beaufort. The fee for the rush job would be more than covered by what Aubrey was paying me. I'd drive over in the morning to pick them up, deliver them, and forget about West.

Resolutely, I shut down my laptop. After blow drying my hair, I climbed in bed with my phone. I sent a text to Rue, telling her I missed her, and that I needed a girl's night *pronto* when she got back tomorrow. I was checking Facebook when I got a text back. I opened it, thinking it was Rue, but then I recognized the same number from before.

West.

Narrowing my eyes, I deleted it without reading it and then powered my phone all the way off.

THE NEXT MORNING, I got up before my alarm even went off. Throwing on workout clothes, I drove straight to Krispy Kreme, ordered two coffees and two chocolate-covered cream-filled doughnuts. All for myself. I slid my sunglasses on, cranked the radio volume, and focused on the check this little field trip was going to net me. I'd finally be able to get that new camera lens I'd been wanting forever.

I picked up the prints, gave them a cursory glance to make sure they looked okay, and then I reversed directions, heading back to Reynolds Island. I'd make it to Aubrey's early at this point, but I was fine with that. The sooner this was over, the better, as far as I was concerned.

It was just past ten when I dropped the envelope of prints off on her doorstep, not bothering to ring the bell or even turn the car off. I hightailed it out of her driveway and down the block. Stopping at the stop sign at the end of the road, I shot off a quick text.

Me: Aubrey, prints are at the front door.
I didn't want to wake you if you were sleeping in.
I left my address. Feel free to mail the check.

Then I revved the engine, heading for the public beach access halfway down the island.

Parking the car in the mostly empty lot, I pulled out my phone again. I held it at arm's length, like it was a coiled snake about to strike, and waited for a response. Just when I was about to give up, it beeped.

Aubrey: *Squeal!* I LOVE THEM! He'll love them! Worth every penny!

My stomach lurched, the coffee and doughnuts threatening to reemerge at the thought of West with the pictures. Would he get off to them? Isn't that what photos like those were for? I dashed to the public restroom at the end of the lot and puked.

After washing my hands and splashing my face with cool

water, I gripped the edges of the sink and stared at the mirror. He was just a guy. It was just one night. Nothing to get this worked up over. And if he was a cheating scumbag, better I learn it now. Better it be her problem than mine.

Feeling resolved, I went back to my Wrangler and gathered my phone, ear buds, a visor, and my water bottle. I scooped my hair up into a tight bun and pulled the visor on. Not the most attractive accessory, but with my long hair, it worked better than a baseball hat.

Scrolling through my playlists, I searched for something with more edge than my normal stuff. I stopped on S. Seether, Stone Sour, Avenged Sevenfold, Eminem. Okay, so Eminem was a stretch, but he was the real Slim Shady, so I put him on the S list with the others. I queued up his "Monsters" and took off down the beach, setting a punishing pace.

I wanted this run to hurt. I wanted my muscles to burn and ache so badly by the end that I wouldn't feel the twinge in my chest when I thought of West or when I looked at my bed.

I wanted to pound his memory into the sand with my shoes and leave it behind in my footprints, to be washed away at the next high tide, erased forever.

The thing about running, though, is even though your body's busy, your mind is free. And if I was honest with myself, I didn't regret my night with West. I might feel bad about the aftermath, but that was more of a problem for West and Aubrey to deal with, not me. If the lying piece of shit even came clean to her. I wouldn't be telling.

My night with West was a wake-up call. Sex with Asshole had been pretty good, if I was telling the truth. Annoying to admit now, but true nonetheless. West was on a whole other level. Tepid words like *pretty* and *good* would never apply to him. He made me feel wanton, greedy, primal. I wouldn't settle again. If West could do all that to me in one night, who knew how many other guys were out there, just waiting to rock my world?

Rue had the right idea. Quantity was probably the best approach. Try enough flavors until you found the one you couldn't live without. Guys did it by default, it seemed. No reason it wouldn't work for me too.

When I spotted a Weimaraner up ahead that made me think of General Beauregard, I took stock of my surroundings and slowed my pace. I didn't want to risk seeing West, so I turned around early, before I passed his house, and headed back the way I came, increasing my intensity to make up for the shortened distance. The sun was in my eyes going this direction, and I'd forgotten my sunglasses again. I pulled the visor lower and dipped my chin, watching the ground. I headed higher up the beach, to the looser, dry sand, forcing my legs to work harder. My calves burned, but I relished it.

I had a plan now, one that didn't include West. Intent on shutting my brain down, I dug into the sand harder and focused on the driving beat of the music in my ears. I pressed the button on the side of my phone, raising the volume until I couldn't hear anything else, especially my own thoughts.

When I reached my Jeep, I was gasping for breath and

drenched in sweat. I chugged what was left in my water bottle and bent over at the waist with my hands on my knees, trying to slow my racing heart. I took my time stretching and felt the protest in every single muscle in my legs.

Exhausted, I hobbled around to the driver's side, climbed up, and buckled in. I was about to turn the key when something white caught my eye. I frowned. Something was stuck under my windshield wiper.

My quads almost buckled as I got back out of my Jeep. Groaning, I snatched the paper and reentered the car with as few movements as possible.

I stared at the paper in my palm in confusion. It was shaped like an airplane. What the hell?

I unfolded it carefully. It was made from cheap, lined notebook paper, one side ragged, like it had been torn from a spiral-bound notebook. Turning it so it was right side up, I read the message written in bold, black Sharpie. *Playing hard to get? It's working. Quit playing games and call me. West.* His phone number was scrawled after his name.

I snorted and wadded up the paper in my fist. Arrogant bastard didn't like being ignored? Well, I didn't like being lied to.

I started to toss the paper into my Krispy Kreme bag when I hesitated. I'd let the situation with Asshole get the better of me and run me off, and I didn't want to be that same pathetic girl anymore. I wanted to be a strong, take-no-prisoners woman who stood her ground. Time to call West out on his shit. Then we'd see what he had to say for himself.

Smoothing out the paper as best I could, I added West's number to my phone and then sent him a text.

Me: I just left your girlfriend's house.

I smirked at my phone. Yeah, West, what do you have to say about that?

West: What girlfriend?

My eyebrows lifted. Was he really going to try to play dumb with me?

Me: Aubrey.
West: Aubrey's not my girlfriend.
Me: She thinks she is.
West: She is most DEFINITELY not.

I hesitated, thrown off by his continued denial. Maybe it was semantics.

Me: Did she used to be?

There was a definite pause before he answered this time.

West: No. Last I heard, she was with some NFL player.
Me: Have you hooked up with her though?
West: Yeah, but not in a long time.

His quick response surprised me. I'd expected him to deny it, since he'd denied their relationship.

West: You were better.

I rolled my eyes but couldn't stop my smug smile or the feeling of victory those three little words gave me. The catty side of me bitch-slapped Aubrey with that juicy tidbit and then rubbed it in her face for good measure.

West: Meet me tonight.

I wavered. Could I have the situation all wrong? I mean, Aubrey had seemed pretty genuine yesterday, but my gut didn't trust her motives. Maybe West was being honest, and Aubrey was a lying skank. I preferred that scenario. It meant another serving of West in my future, and God knew, I had an appetite for that man. My resolve began to evaporate like raindrops on a hot sidewalk, disappearing like it had never been there to begin with. The truth was, I *wanted* to see him again.

My mind screamed a warning at me to slow down and think this through, but my body hollered at me to give in and enjoy the feast. I had to buy myself some time, regain my equilibrium.

Me: I can't. Girl's night.
West: Fine. Tomorrow. 7 @ the Wreck. K?
Me: I don't know.

Yeah, so I admit, I wanted to meet him. I just wasn't sure I should. I needed a day to try and figure out what the hell was really going on with those two and then I could confront him in person if it came to that.

Not wanting to be a liar myself, I quickly texted Rue.

Me: Dinner tonight? Girl talk?
Rue: Can't. Business dinner. After?
Me: Sure. Ice cream and doughnuts?
Rue: Absolutely!

Later than night, while waiting for Rue to get home, I watched bad reality TV, which seemed to reinforce the likelihood that West was a dirtbag who only thought with his dick and that I was probably being played, along with Aubrey, and whoever he'd done at the hotel the night he gave me a ride home. My anger was rising when my phone buzzed.

Rue: Sorry, girl. Saw this Adonis as I was leaving and am having drinks.

Quelling my frustration, I turned the television off and picked up a book instead. Two hours later, I was convinced West had to be some poor, misunderstood prince-in-disguise who just needed the right girl to open his heart of stone. Someone like me.

My phone buzzed again.

Rue: I'm sorry, but I can't resist! He says he's pierced! You know how long I've been waiting to try that. I'll bring Krispy Kreme for breakfast, I promise!

Me: Be safe and have fun. Forget about the doughnuts, meeting Theo at the gym, then work.

Rue: Ok! Sorry! Later this week?
Me: Sure. And I want details!
Rue: ;-)

I wanted to be mad at Rue for flaking on me, but it was hard to hold onto it when I pictured her following a hardware-sporting Adonis with her tongue hanging out and a zombie-like expression on her face. In my mind, zombie-Rue was under Adonis's spell, blindly trailing him and whimpering, "Must see piercing!" while she clutched at his shirt.

Happy for Rue, but annoyed with myself for letting West consume my thoughts, I tossed the book aside and booted up my laptop. I had one last backup method to take my mind off him. Calling up Pinterest, I typed "male model" in the search bar and daydreamed. The girly side of me enjoyed the eye candy for what it was, reminding myself that there were plenty of hot guys out there besides West. The photographer side of me took notes, paying attention to camera angles, lighting, poses, props, and staging. I tried not to compare the guys I was ogling to West, and was only partially successful.

My flimsy resolve annoyed me. I was turning into the kind of girl other girls mocked on those reality TV shows I was watching earlier. I like him. No, I don't. Yes, I do. No, I really don't. Yes, I do. Barf. It made me think of that bug from the cartoon movie, the one that was mesmerized by the bug zapper and kept drifting toward it, crooning, "I can't help it. It's soooo beautiful."

Zap!

I did not want to be just another West Montgomery casualty.

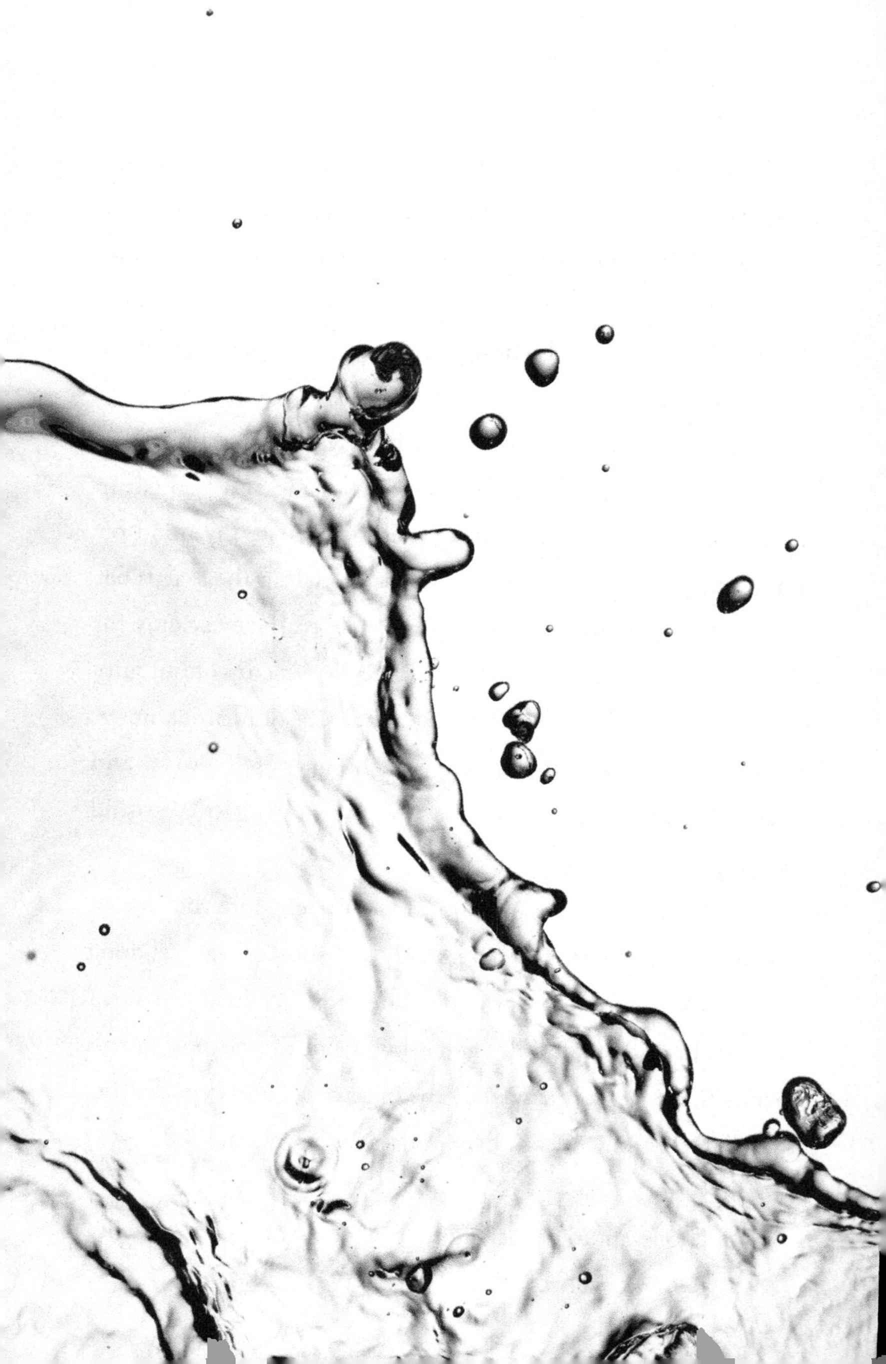

chapter eleven

"REMEMBER THAT REDHEAD I mentioned the other day?" Theo watched me work my triceps on one of the machines. "I think she's stalking me. She was supposed to leave after the weekend, but it's been another week, and she's still here. And I keep seeing her everywhere."

"Are you really complaining?" My voice was laced with skepticism.

"Yeah. It's weird. She's obsessed or something."

"Obsessed?"

"I dunno. Maybe? I've seen her at work, at Starbucks, the drugstore, the freaking gas station."

"It's a small island," I pointed out. "Maybe it's coincidence?"

"I think this is the only place she hasn't tracked me yet," he said, muscling through a set of chin-ups on the machine next to me. "And that's only because I parked two blocks away, in front of the Starbucks."

"So, will she be at the resort today? And does she have a name? I feel bad calling her 'the redhead.'"

"Probably. And it's Chelsea."

"Well, that should be easy enough to deal with. Just tell her that you and I started seeing each other in the meantime, and that I'm the jealous type. If she shows up, we can flirt like crazy until she gets the message."

"You think that'll work?" Theo sounded dubious.

"What? I'm not good enough for you?" I teased.

"No, no, it's not that. I just don't want her going after you or anything. It's bad enough that I keep bumping into her everywhere."

I wrinkled my nose. "Do I need to be worried?"

Theo shrugged. "Maybe. She even knows what kind of shampoo and deodorant I use. She followed me around the grocery store the other day and bought some so I'd have it 'at her place.' Who does that after a one-night stand?"

"Was it really only one night?" I crossed my arms and stared him down.

Theo face reddened. "Well, I mean, she was willing . . . and she followed me home."

"Theo!" I said, groaning.

"What?"

"Just on principle, I should refuse to help you."

"Okay, then just on principle, these sessions cost fifty bucks each from now on. So you owe me roughly . . ."

I narrowed my eyes at him. "Fine. But drinks are on you this week."

Theo grunted and threw a medicine ball at me. "Crunches. Two sets of thirty. Then we're done."

After our workout, we headed back to the cottage in my Wrangler for breakfast, leaving Theo's clunker abandoned at Starbucks. He made us egg white omelets with cheese and tomatoes, while I blended up some mango, pineapple, and spinach smoothies. As yummy as the food was, I barely tasted it. Being back at home reminded me of West all over again.

On the way to the Edge, I worked up the nerve to ask him for insight. "So, Theo, if I ask you something, can you keep it just between us?"

"Yeah, what's up?"

"It's about West, and I know the guy code, bros before hoes, and all that."

"Nah, I wouldn't do that to you."

Hesitating, I drummed my fingers on the steering wheel. "What's the story with him and Aubrey?"

Theo hesitated. "I'm not sure I know the whole story. I know his parents and her parents are close, like, really close. And they always hoped Aubrey and West would end up together. I think Aubrey did too. And West just kind of seemed to go along with the whole thing. Like, he was usually her date for the gala at the end of the summer, or if there was some big social event. But I haven't seen them together since he moved down here from

Chicago last year. So who knows? Plus, I heard she was dating some football player."

I swallowed uncomfortably. Aubrey and West had a history together. A pretty long history, it sounded like. And Aubrey didn't strike me as the type to not get what she wanted. West's story about the football player seemed to check out, but maybe Aubrey was hoping to rekindle things with West on the rebound?

Theo watched me. "Does that mean there's something going on with you two? Did *you* hook up with *him* more than once?"

"No! But I worked with Aubrey on . . . a little project, and she threw out that West was hers."

"Bitch was marking her territory, huh?"

"Theo!"

"Well, wasn't she?" Theo sounded unrepentant. "She's manipulative, so be careful around her."

"She do something to you?" His anger sounded a little personal.

"I don't want to talk about it," he muttered, looking out the window.

"Did you and her. . . . ever?"

"What? Hell, no. I wouldn't touch her if my life depended on it."

Curious about his strong reaction, I studied him. There was a story there, but I'd respect his privacy for now. Besides, we were almost at work. I didn't have time to pry it out of him. "You know I'm here if you ever need to talk."

He nodded.

"What's the deal with West? When I asked who was a good hook-up the other night, you didn't mention him."

"'Cause he's not a good choice. Girls fall for him. Often and hard. And he's nice enough about it, doesn't lead anyone on or anything, but something about him makes girls go nuts. They chase him until it's just embarrassing. I've heard the bathroom at the Wreck is a shrine to him. Not that I've investigated that particular claim."

I wrinkled my nose.

Theo glanced at me. "No one would be surprised if you went for him again. Like I said, lots of girls do. It's ridiculous. I just don't want to see the aftermath. It's never pretty."

Taking a deep breath, I nodded. Note to self—no turning into a West zombie.

Pulling into the employee lot, we grabbed our bags and headed toward the locker rooms. "Hey, Theo, when we get out there, make me an iced coffee, will ya? I need some caffeine."

He grinned. "I'll make it a double."

Work sucked. Kendra called in sick, and the pool was packed. The only time I had a spare second to even think about anything other than lifeguarding duties was during the adult swim break every hour, when I blew the whistle and everyone under sixteen had to clear the pool for ten minutes. And during those breaks, I was trying to help poor Theo.

Chelsea had shown up, all right, and hadn't budged from her stool by Theo's hut the whole morning. It was like she was chaperoning him or something. I came over every chance I got, but at this point, I was about to float away from all the drinks he kept making me. We were acting like a flirty couple, but Chelsea did not seem to be taking the hint. Or maybe she just didn't care. It was hard to tell.

Around one, I was trying to quickly eat the turkey sandwich Theo handed me during my break. "Thanks, babe," I said, leaning over to brush his hair off his forehead. I could hear Chelsea hiss on the other side of the bar.

Theo pressed his lips together and leaned over the bar toward me. "Why isn't she leaving? I've done my best to ignore her and flirt with you. What am I doing wrong?"

I peeked around him. Chelsea's eyes were glued to us. "She's stubborn, isn't she? We'll just have to up our game." Speaking louder, I arched my spine. "Sweetie, my back has a knot in it. Could you help me out?"

Theo rolled his eyes, since Chelsea couldn't see his face, but managed to make his answer sound suggestive. "Sure thing, Sadie."

Coming around from behind the bar, he slid up close to me and dug his thumbs into the tender flesh along my spine, rubbing in circles. I arched more and groaned, trying to play it up. "Oh yeah, right there. Your hands are amazing."

Theo ducked his head and whispered in my ear. "I can't take much more. I'm going to bend you over the bar and shove my tongue down your throat in a minute if she doesn't leave soon. Think that'll get the point across?"

Chelsea fumed at me, the flames from her eyes almost searing me with their intensity. "Theo!" I squealed, swatting his hip. "Not at work." I giggled and pressed my hands to my cheeks, like he had said something naughty.

With a huff, Chelsea slid off her stool and marched away, shooting one last glare in my direction.

Theo froze behind me, his hands still on my back. "It worked, didn't it?"

I smiled at him smugly. "What'd I tell you?"

Giving me a quick hug, Theo resumed his position behind the bar. "You're the best. I owe you."

Nodding my emphatic agreement, I wadded up the wax paper with the remains of my lunch.

As I walked to the trash can, I almost ran smack into Aubrey, who was rounding the corner with three other perfectly-coiffed clones of hers. I stepped back, indicating for them to go ahead.

Aubrey stopped and removed her sunglasses, looking me over. I crossed my arms self-consciously, well aware that her chic resort-wear looked a lot more polished than my modest red two-piece bikini, messy bun, and bare feet. Her friends stopped behind her.

"Girls," Aubrey started, tipping her head to one side. "This is Sadie. The photographer I told you about."

"Sadie? I had a dog named Sadie once," one of them sniffed. She had on mirrored sunglasses, so I couldn't see her eyes.

My blood boiled, but I bit my tongue and waited, curious what this was all about.

"Those photos of Aubrey came out really nice," another one said, elbowing the other girl in the side.

Aubrey smiled. "Of course they did. She might be rather plain-looking herself, but she knows how to capture real beauty with a camera. It's truly a gift. And I told her I'd help spread the word so she could expand her business. I'm sure she'd like to have a real job by now, instead of just playing lifeguard at her age. You ladies will help me with that, won't you?"

Reaching out, she patted my arm. "Good to see you again, Sadie." As she pulled her arm back, she rubbed her fingers together like I'd soiled her. Slipping her sunglasses back on, she sailed past without waiting for a response, her friends following dutifully in her wake.

I stood there, dumbfounded.

What. A. Bitch.

She'd just insulted me to my face. Yeah, she sort of wrapped it in a compliment, but, *damn.* And I hadn't even tried to speak up for myself, which pissed me off just as much. Not that there was anything I could say with the way she worded it without sounding ungrateful. Plus, she was a hotel guest, and I was an employee. I was here to serve her weasily little ass. I forced my fingers to relax from the tight fists I had made and took a deep breath, letting it out slowly. She wanted to get a rise out of me, and I didn't plan on giving her the satisfaction.

Aubrey could go to hell. And if West wanted me, he could

have me, regardless of his status with Aubrey. It would serve her right either way. Pushing her from my mind, I dumped my trash and got back to work, spending the rest of the afternoon being the bad guy to a bunch of kids intent on playing water volleyball without a net.

By the time my last break of the day rolled around, Chelsea had reappeared and was once again fixated on all things Theo. I rested my elbows on the counter, watching Theo make me yet another lemonade. Chelsea eyed me and then turned back to Theo, reaching out to touch his hand. "Doesn't this place close soon, baby?"

Theo shot me a desperate look. "Yeah, but—"

"But we have plans," I interrupted, adjusting my bikini straps and batting my eyes at Theo. "Don't we, baby?" I mimicked Chelsea's tone on the last word. She scowled at me.

"Right! So, as much as I'd like to, I can't hang with you tonight." Theo tried to let her down easy.

I was annoyed. It had been a freaking long day, and she wasn't one for subtlety. He'd ignored her most of the day, giving her one-word answers to her questions, and she seemed oblivious to all the times he and I had flirted and touched. Chelsea was alone in her own little Theo bubble, and he needed to pop it, stat. From what I had gathered during my breaks, she had about as much substance as her fake boobs, and he was going to have to spell it out for her, or this would never end.

"Where are y'all going?" she purred, leaning forward so most of her chest spilled out of her bikini top.

I shook my head at him, trying to warn him off, but he answered, "The Wreck," before I could stop him. Fuck! I hadn't told him I was planning to go to the Wreck tonight to meet West, and I didn't want him showing up there too. This day just kept getting better.

"Where's that?" Chelsea asked, looking puzzled.

"It's kind of a far drive," I interrupted, shooting Theo a hard look. "Back roads with no names, things like that."

He finally seemed to pick up on my clues. "Yeah, it's just this hole in the wall. Not your style at all."

She looked thrilled that Theo knew *her style*. I wanted to bang my head on the countertop. Taking my lemonade from him, I headed back to my lifeguard stand. "See you in an hour, honey!" I called back over my shoulder, blowing him a kiss for good measure. He so owed me.

By the time I dropped Theo back at Starbucks and got home after work, it was six-thirty. Taking a quick shower, I debated the wisdom of even meeting West. My gut warned me that he wasn't going to be easy to forget when this was over, regardless of his baggage with Aubrey. Should I risk it? Maybe I was better off just sticking with tourists for the summer, like Rue did. But then I looked at my bed and remembered our night together. Who wouldn't want more of that?

Besides, it would be rude to cancel at the last minute.

Ugh. I wasn't normally like this. Indecisive. Unsure. Questioning my own motives. West just stirred me up inside, like shaking a soda bottle and opening it up too soon. I was a soggy mess, and it was all his fault.

Wishing I had time to do my hair and makeup up right, I ended up going super casual, knowing I was already running late. It was better this way, anyway. I didn't want to seem desperate. After throwing on a skinny olive green tank, an oversized white v-neck t-shirt that fell off one shoulder, cutoffs, and leather flip flops, I sprayed my hair with a massive amount of my favorite sea spray and hoped it didn't look horrible when I arrived. I swiped on a quick coat of mascara, grabbed my bag, and ran out the door.

The clock on the dash read seven twenty-six as I pulled into the Wreck's parking lot. I glanced in my rearview mirror and cringed. Yeah, my hair had seen better days. Sighing, I twisted it up into a loose bun, so at least the mess would look like it was on purpose.

When I walked in, I spotted West immediately. He was sitting at one of the picnic tables between the door and the pool tables, a small mountain of peanut shells in front of him. He looked up as I slid onto the bench across from him.

He looked at his watch. "I was starting to think you weren't gonna show."

"I thought about it."

His eyes roamed my face. "I'm glad you did."

I shrugged. I still wasn't sure if this whole thing was a smart idea. But West looked good tonight, relaxed in a faded tee and dark jeans, his nose a little sunburned.

He stood and gestured toward the bar. "Can I get you something to drink?"

I shook my head. "I didn't come here for drinks. This isn't a date."

West looked wounded. "Why did you come then?"

"I'm . . . not sure. Why did you leave the note? I figured I wouldn't hear from you again after our . . . one-night stand." My voice trailed off at the end to an embarrassed whisper.

"Who said anything about a one-night stand?" He growled.

I scrunched my eyebrows, confused. What would he have called it? I picked a peanut from the bucket and cracked it open to give my hands something to do. "I just didn't expect to hear from you again, that's all."

Didn't expect to, but had crossed my fingers and toes and wished on a star for good measure. Until Aubrey had ruined my fantasy.

"So, you were just using me?" He sounded amused by the idea.

I almost choked on my peanut. "Not any more than you were using me!"

His eyes darkened, the gray more prevalent than the blue. "I'd like to use you again." His eyes dropped to my lips. "And again and again."

I forgot to breathe for a long moment, the look in his eyes so similar to the way they'd looked the other night. But I reminded myself who I was dealing with—and Theo's warning—and steeled my resolve. I cocked my head at him and pretended to consider his offer. "You got any tricks left up your sleeve?"

"Not my sleeve. Lower." He gave a wicked grin. "Go out with me this weekend."

I was annoyed that he didn't make it a question. "I'm not sure that's a good idea. What about Aubrey?"

"You want her to come too?"

"No!"

He smirked. "But you do want to go."

Again, it wasn't a request. "You seem like trouble," I told him. "Maybe more trouble than you're worth. I'm just looking to chill and have fun this summer."

"I'm fun," he countered. "Let me prove it to you. This weekend."

"You could try asking, you know." I was exasperated.

"I am."

"No. You're telling me. I don't like to be told what to do."

He leaned back, crossing his arms across his chest. "How 'bout this? We play for it. If I win, I get to take you out this weekend. If I lose, I can just be your back-up booty call, and we'll leave it at that."

I copied his stance. "What game?"

"Lady's choice."

I sucked at pool. "How are you at air hockey?"

"Hopefully better than you."

"Doubt it." Losing to Boone the other day had been a fluke. I had mad air hockey skills. "And I'll take that drink now."

"What can I get you?"

So he did know what a question was. "Rum and coke . . . and cherries."

He groaned and looked at my mouth before standing up. "Be right back."

While West was at the bar getting our drinks, Theo showed up and made a beeline for me.

"You came! I wasn't sure if you would." He plopped down next to me and grabbed a handful of peanuts.

"I came to meet West, not you." I pointed to the bar.

Theo did a quick scan of the room. "That's fine, I don't see Chelsea anyway." He cracked a peanut and popped it in his mouth. "So, you and West? Things are over for sure between him and Aubrey?"

"Either that or he's blatantly cheating on her with me. I'm not sure I care if he is. Aubrey's a piece of—"

"Shit," Theo finished for me. "And West wouldn't cheat."

"How do you know?"

"West doesn't do girlfriends. Can't cheat if you're not together."

Before I could reply, West returned and handed me my drink.

"Theo. What's up, man?" West and Theo bumped fists.

"Not much. Listen, if this redheaded chick shows up later, I might have to borrow Sadie."

"As long as you give her back at the end of the night." West took a drink from his longneck.

I glared at both of them. "I'm not a library book! You can't just pass me around."

West cocked an eyebrow. "No? 'Cause there sure are a lot of guys here checking you out."

"Did you steal that off one of the dollar bills? That was bad, man." Theo shook his head.

"It wasn't that bad. It was funny."

"It was *that* bad," I confirmed. I picked up the stem of one of the maraschino cherries and put the fruit in my mouth, tugging on the stem until it broke free.

West paused in the act of lifting his beer again. "If they weren't watching before, they sure as hell are now."

I flushed and took a quick peek around. There were a few guys looking my way.

"We're up next." West nodded toward the air hockey table.

"Any stakes?" Theo asked.

"She has to go out with me if I win." West smiled.

"And if you lose?"

"I won't lose."

"You sure?" I appreciated Theo having faith in me at least.

"Yeah. Sadie doesn't really *want* to win this one." West winked, infuriating me.

Oh, hell no. He did not just challenge me like that. "You don't think I can beat you?"

"I didn't say you couldn't. I'm saying you won't."

"Finish your beer, West. I'm taking you down."

"Oh yeah? Right here?" West's arm swept across the table, clearing it of peanut shells. "I'm not usually one for exhibitionism, but I'm willing to try anything once." He patted the picnic table.

"Not here," I said. "On the air hockey table."

"I can work with that too. It's just about the right height, if I took you and laid you back, for me to—"

"I think I'll leave you two alone," Theo cut in, hopping to his feet.

I couldn't look at him as he left. West took one last swallow and set his bottle down. "Ready when you are."

I picked up my other cherry and looked right at West. I put it into my mouth and pulled it back out, licking off the rum and Coke. Lifting the cherry high, I extended my tongue and sucked the cherry back in, twirling the stem a few times before popping it off. When I finished, I licked my lips. "Sure you're ready?"

He cursed under his breath and glanced at his lap. "Well, if I wasn't before, I damn sure am now. Why don't you go ahead? I'll be there in a minute."

Smiling victoriously, I sauntered over to the air hockey table, picking the same side I had played on last time. Sliding the puck across the table, I got a feel for how much resistance there was. I'd bent over to retrieve it when I sensed West lean over behind me, pressing his chest to my back, and letting me feel his hard length against my ass.

"Sure you don't just want to forfeit?" he whispered against my ear.

I was not going to fall all over his feet like every other girl did. If he wanted me, he was going to have to work for it.

I pushed against him as I stood up. "I'm sure. I got this."

He stayed plastered to my back. "I have no problem with the

woman coming out on top, just so you know." He squeezed my hip before moving around to the opposite side of the table and gripped the other mallet. "Game on, Sadie."

I hit the puck with a sharp snap, bouncing it off the side and toward his goal. With a lightning fast flick of his wrist, he slammed it back my direction, straight into my goal. He glanced up from the table, a smirk on his face. "I think I just scored."

Taking a deep breath, I placed the puck on the table and decided this was serious. My pride was at stake, if nothing else. I narrowed my eyes and sent the puck flying his way.

The score was tied six to six. A big hand settled on the small of my back. Startled, I twisted to the side and heard the distinctive *thunk* as the puck slid into my goal. Damn it! I glared at Theo and got the puck out of the tray. "Sorry, sweetheart," Theo said, stepping close. "She showed up a few minutes ago."

Closing my eyes and praying for patience, I counted to ten. When I opened them, Chelsea was standing next to Theo wearing what might generously be described as a dress. It looked more like a partially buttoned long shirt she forgot to wear pants with. Noticing West eyeing the newcomer, I took the opportunity to power the puck straight down the table, right into his goal. West looked surprised at the noise.

"I think I just scored," I mocked, batting my eyes at him.

Chelsea looked from me to West and then back again. "I thought you were with Theo."

"I am," I said. "West is . . . an ex. I get a kick out of taunting him."

"Oh." Chelsea looked West over. "So, Theo's taken, but he's available?"

"Yeah, Sadie, am I available?" West stood up straight, pausing our game.

I scowled at Theo, shooting daggers at him with my eyes. "He's not with me."

Chelsea scooted closer to West.

"But he's gay," I added. "I ruined him for women. Now he's only into dicks. I don't take it personally, though."

I bit my lip to keep from smiling as West shot me a look of pure disbelief.

I pointed across the room. "See that big guy playing pool over there? The one covered in tats? That's his boyfriend. What's it been now, West, two years?"

West looked down and shook his head before grinning at me. "Yup. And I thank my stars every day that the good Lord brought him into my life. I am so, so blessed."

I could barely hold back my giggle at the disappointment on Chelsea's face.

"Oh, and Sadie? You better believe the stakes just went higher." West's face was pure innocence.

Chelsea looked at him. "What are y'all playing for?"

Theo cleared his throat. "Who has to pay for the next round. Me or him. I guess the next two rounds, now."

West didn't take his eyes off me. "Because someone will have to pay for this, you know."

I tried to hide my laugh, and turned into Theo's side to

compose myself, wrapping my arm around his waist. "Honey, I could use another rum and coke. Would you mind . . . ?"

Grateful to escape, Theo started for the bar. West called after him, "Sweet cheeks, I'll take another beer!"

After he made sure Chelsea wasn't watching, Theo flipped West off as he walked away.

West turned back to me. "Seven to seven. You ready for this?"

"I've been taking it easy on you," I scoffed.

"That's nice and all, but I'm *gay*. Don't you know I like it hard and rough?"

Dampness pooled in my core. I shifted my weight to rub my thighs together, trying to find some relief. West noticed the movement and smiled broadly.

Ten minutes later, it was match point in his favor, and West was running the table, the puck flying so fast I couldn't connect with it at all. I settled for blocking my goal, trying to keep my puck centered over the opening to protect as much of it as I could. The puck ricocheted so quick it was hard to keep up with it, until suddenly it disappeared. Confused, I looked at the table and then at my goal. He had scored.

West had won.

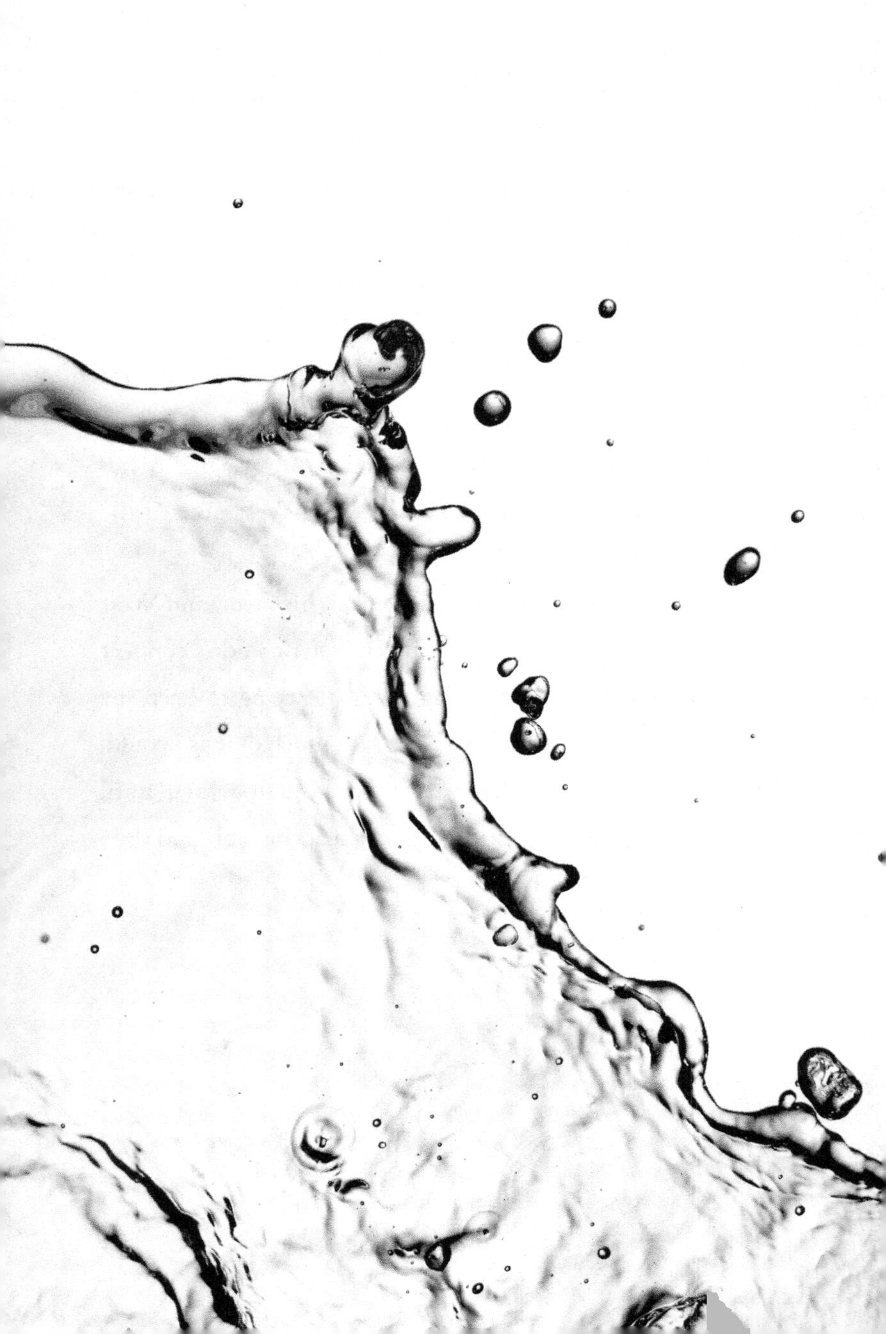

chapter twelve

I took a deep breath, my head still tipped down at my goal.

A twinge of excitement battled with annoyance. I'd lost at *my* game. Again.

I peeked up at West from under my lashes. "Double or nothing?" I offered.

West shook his head, keeping eye contact. "I don't think you can afford those stakes."

Chelsea cocked her head. "Yeah, 'cause, like, lifeguards don't make that much, do they?"

"I make enough to afford a whole outfit." My voice was like syrup.

Chelsea looked confused, and Theo choked on his beer.

Trevor and Dylan were walking by to the pool tables and West snagged Dylan's arm as he passed. "Chelsea, have you met our *single* friends Dylan and Trevor?"

Chelsea put her palms against the air hockey table, straightened her arms, and leaned forward, pressing her breasts up between her stiffened elbows. Right on cue, both boys looked down and changed directions. "Nice to meet you," she cooed.

Dylan sauntered around to her side. "I believe the pleasure will be all mine." Trevor chuckled behind him. Hooking his arm around her waist, Dylan tugged her in his direction. "Why don't you come with me and be my lucky charm while I beat this asswipe at pool? I bet you're magically delicious."

"What?" I heard her ask as they moved off. I rolled my eyes. The line was wasted on her. I wondered if that one had come off a dollar bill too or if he'd thought it up on his own.

"That one's above the bar," West said, reading my mind and moving closer. "Come on, sweetheart, dance with your ex, for old time's sake." He took my hand and pulled me toward the dance floor. "I'll bring her back soon, Theo."

As I followed him, I gazed down at our hands. He'd laced our individual fingers together and seeing those digits all tangled up suddenly brought back some very intimate memories. I swallowed hard and tried to channel Rue's casual love-'em-and-leave-'em attitude.

Once we were swallowed up by the crowd in the middle of the dance floor, West spun back toward me, yanking me into his arms. The unexpected move had me tripping over my flip flop and threw me right up against his chest. He tightened his arms, keeping me there. The song was a fast one, but only our lower bodies were moving to the beat. My arms slid hesitantly up his and settled into a loose loop around his neck. Our hips moved together, rubbing, and through the friction, I felt him grow and lengthen. He glanced down between us and then back up at me.

"So, this weekend—"

"Will be a date, not a hook up," I interrupted, before he got the wrong idea about me. Hell, the wrong idea? I'd slept with him *before* our first date. I couldn't get much easier than that.

"I was thinking a picnic. Close to the water. We're going to get you over this fear of yours." He continued like I hadn't interrupted him, and heat invaded my face. Okay, so maybe I was the only one already thinking about sleeping together again. "Wear a swimsuit under your clothes."

"Why?"

He shrugged, and his eyes dropped down to our hips again. "In case we decide to get wet." One side of his mouth quirked.

Heat flared in my core, and I dipped my hips a little lower, coming back up against him. He made a rough sound of pleasure in the back of his throat and tugged my head closer. Leaning down to my ear, he said, "I like you like this. Not all done up like last time. Your shirt falling off you shoulder." He tugged my sagging sleeve. "Makes me want to finish the job." He pressed his lips under my ear, letting his tongue touch the side of my neck.

The song changed, and I made myself pull away before I made an utter fool of myself by dissolving into Jell-O right there on the dance floor. "Saturday? Noon?"

He nodded and let me make my escape, his eyes watching me

as I backed away. He had a crooked grin on his face, like he knew exactly what I was doing and why.

Later that night, I lay in my bed, tossing and turning, unable to fall asleep. Unable to stop thinking about West. His hands holding my hips on the dance floor. His eyes laughing at me across the air hockey table. His ab muscles contracting against my stomach. And his tongue barely touching my neck but promising to do so much more.

I groaned and flipped over onto my back, staring at the ceiling. It was going to be a long night. Biting my lower lip, I slid my hand down my stomach, my fingertips toying with the lace trim of my panties. Maybe this would help me get to sleep. Raising my knees up to get more comfortable, I traced a line down my center, reveling in the silky whisper of my panties pressing against my folds. I lifted my hips to slip my underwear off when I heard a soft tapping sound.

I froze and turned toward the window, straining my ears, my hips still raised in the air. The hum of the air conditioner kicking in startled me, and I rolled my eyes at my own paranoia, my body relaxing back against the bed. I hooked my thumb under the material at my hip and tugged. The tapping sounded again, louder this time.

Definitely coming from my window.

Easing from under my covers, I grabbed the metal baseball bat I kept under the bed and moved closer to the window. Carefully lifting one of the slats of the wooden blinds up, I peered out onto the front porch, squinting into the faint light emitted from the streetlight. A large, shadowy shape was just visible, and I jumped back, shoving my fist into my mouth to smother my shriek.

"I know you're awake in there. Might as well come out and talk to me." West's voice floated to me from the other side of the window.

I sagged in relief and twisted the blinds so I could see out. West lounged against the wall, one leg bent at the knee with his foot against the house. I opened my window a couple of inches.

"What are you doing here?" I hissed.

He shrugged, the muscles in his arm contracting with the movement. "Couldn't sleep. Thought you might want to go for a walk."

I looked back at my clock. "At midnight-thirty?"

"Midnight-thirty?" he repeated, amused.

"Twelve-thirty. Whatever. It's late!"

"So?"

"So . . ." I sputtered, unable to come up with a good response.

"The beach is deserted and beautiful this time of night. Come walk with me."

"I thought we had a date for Saturday?"

He laughed. "Does that mean you're off-limits until then?"

I opened my mouth and then closed it again. *Well, no, not exactly.* I let the silence drag out for a long minute before a grin teased the corner of my mouth. "Give me a minute to change."

Closing the blinds again, I quickly added gym shorts, a bra, and a lightweight, long sleeved Vanderbilt shirt to the tank and panties ensemble I had been sleeping in. Stepping into a pair of flip flops, I slipped out the front door and closed it behind me.

West was still dressed in the same clothes he wore earlier—jeans and a tee. I walked over to him, hands on my hips. "How'd you know I would still be awake?" I cocked my head to one side and regarded him.

He smiled. "I couldn't stop thinking about you. I hoped the feeling would be mutual."

"I *was* asleep until you knocked and woke me up," I lied, unwilling to feed his ego.

"No, you weren't. I could hear you moving around from out here." He raised his eyebrows, daring me to lie again.

I was glad the streetlight didn't provide much illumination so he couldn't see the blush staining my cheeks. Dear God, he could hear me getting ready to get myself off? Thank goodness I hadn't been five minutes further into it.

Ignoring his comment, I started down the steps. "Where are we going?"

He followed me and pointed to his beat-up truck parked on the street. I hadn't even heard his engine when he'd pulled up. "Back by my house. The beach is perfect right now."

"I didn't hear your truck," I said as I hopped in the passenger side.

He climbed in and looked at me, the dome light between us

lighting up his face. He held the steering wheel with his hand but made no move to start the car. His thumb tapped against the steering wheel and turned back toward the windshield. "I've been out here awhile," he admitted.

"Creeper, much?"

His cheeks reddened, and seeing him embarrassed made my lips stretch into a huge smile. He faced me again and pinned me with a more serious look than I was expecting. My smile faded. He reached his hand out and captured a lock of my hair, running his fingers down it until his hand dropped back to his lap. "There's just something about you," he said. His lips lifted and then he started the truck, and the moment was broken.

We didn't speak on the ride back to his place. Once he parked between the stilts holding his and Wyatt's house up, he came around to my side and opened my door, taking my hand and helping me down.

Without releasing my hand, he tugged me around the house and stopped by the stairs leading to the small deck off his room. I narrowed my eyes at him. "I didn't come over here to—"

Squatting, he tugged my flip flops off before kicking off his own shoes and continuing to walk down to the beach. "To what?" he called back over his shoulder.

Biting back a sharp retort, I shook my head and trailed after him. When I started walking along the hard, packed sand midway between the foamy licks of the ocean and the soft, sinking sand near the dunes, he snagged my hand again, redirecting me closer to the water. I resisted, trying to maintain my current path. He was undeterred, his grip solid, and I had no choice but to follow him, losing our silent battle of wills.

"Where are you taking me?"

"I told you, we're going to get you over this fear of yours. Starting with a walk in ankle-deep water. Ankle deep, Sadie. You can handle it."

I tried to free my hand from his grasp. It didn't work. "I can't see though. It's dark. What if there's something there?"

"What if there is?"

"You're wearing jeans," I pointed out, trying a different tactic.

"And they can get wet."

I looked at him helplessly, and he stared back at me, a mischievous grin softening his features. He pulled me closer to where the waves began lapping at our feet as they rushed up to reclaim the beach for themselves. I squealed and jumped when a larger wave splashed over my ankles.

West laughed and kept walking, keeping my hand tight in his. "You're enjoying this too much," I said, grumbling.

"Walking in the moonlight on an empty beach with a beautiful girl? Yeah, I am."

His words melted my lingering resistance. I probably would have followed him anywhere at that moment.

He started rubbing his thumb against the sensitive skin above my wrist as we walked, and I didn't even notice the tickle of the waves against my ankles for several minutes.

I didn't notice much of anything except for the nerve endings prickling up and down my arm in response to his slow caresses.

I relaxed by degrees, listening to the soft slurping sound of the wet sand trying to trap our feet with every step and the lullaby of the waves rushing up the shore and then retreating. My arm rubbed against West's as we meandered up the beach. The silence between us felt comfortable, and my mind wasn't racing with ways to fill it. I let the calm seep through me. Trusting West to lead me, I tilted my head back to gaze up at the stars. You could see so many from here, away from the city lights.

It was beautiful.

When I looked over at West, his eyes were locked on the curve of my neck, and I stumbled. His

hand tightened around mine until I regained my footing. "Don't worry," he whispered. "I got you."

I bit my lip. I liked the sound of that far too much.

Six steps later, my foot landed on something slimy. I squealed and started hopping on my tiptoes, whimpering.

West raised his eyebrows and continued his steady pace up the beach, pulling me with him. "You gonna live over there?"

My fear mixed with irritation. Who knew what my foot had come in contact with? I turned back to investigate, but West just kept tugging me forward.

"You're fine. Get over it. Keep walking." I could hear the laughter in his voice, and I glared at him.

I kept up with him, but now I was on hyperalert, trying to peer through the sudsy water in the dark at the sand where my feet were about to step each time.

West jiggled my arm. "Stop that. Just walk."

"But what if—?"

"What if what? You step on something? Then you step on something."

"But what if it . . . hurts me?" My voice cracked on the last words, and I realized how stupid I sounded, but I couldn't help it.

"Then I'll save you from whatever evil ocean crap might wash up on the exact speck of beach you plant your perfect, dainty foot on."

"It's not funny." I half-whimpered, half-laughed.

"Yeah." He glanced at me. "It kinda is."

Just then my other foot landed on something decidedly squishy. Slimy was one thing, but squishy? Oh, hell no.

I squeaked and ran a few steps like a chicken on a hot plate until our arms were stretched to their max between us and then I stopped, yanking my hand from his. "I think that's enough for tonight." Yeah, I was trembling like a baby, but I was done.

West stopped next to me, nonplussed. "So, now what? You just going to stand here all night? The tide's coming in."

I started to hightail it higher up the beach, but West caught me by the wrist before I could get more than three steps away. Sighing, he said. "Are you really that scared?"

Hot, embarrassed tears pricked the backs of my eyes, but I refused to cry in front of West. Willpower alone held them back as I nodded.

Turning his back to me, he faced the water, his shoulders drooping with resignation. "Well, I promised." He crouched down and patted the top of his back. "Come on."

I looked at him blankly. "Come on, what?"

"Hop on. I told you we're taking a walk in the water, and I meant it. If you're that scared, I'll do the walking for the both of us. You can ride piggyback."

I rolled my eyes and wiped away the one traitorous tear that had escaped. "You're not carrying me. We're almost a mile from your house."

He glanced back over his shoulder at me. "Are you trying to get me to flex? Prove my strength? 'Cause I can do that for you."

I snorted and crossed my arms over my chest. "I'm not doubting your strength per se. But, West, I'm not exactly tiny, and we're almost a mile from home." I said the last words slowly, emphasizing them in case he didn't hear me the first time.

He remained crouched over. "Two choices. Hop on or walk through the water."

A slightly larger wave rushed us, reaching mid-calf, and I leapt at him, scrambling up his broad back. West teetered and then wrapped my legs around his waist before reaching up to tug at my arms. "Sadie?" he croaked. "You're choking me."

I readjusted and looped my arms more across his shoulders than his windpipe. My chin settled into the slope where his neck and shoulder met, and I couldn't stop myself from inhaling him. His scent was drugging. They should make candles that smelled like that.

Gripping me under my knees, he started back the way we came. I shifted from side to side as he walked, my open legs pressed against his back, my breasts plastered against him, my nipples hardening from the friction. My breath caught and then began to speed up.

The muscles in his arms and torso and flexed, moving sinuously under me. I exhaled and couldn't resist trying to press my pelvis a little firmer against him, trying to get some pressure where I wanted it most. West bounced me up higher on his back and picked up his pace. Oh, dear God, yes. Somehow that motion bunched up his tee between my thighs a little more, giving just enough pressure to drive me crazy. I buried my nose against his skin and breathed in his citrusy, sweaty scent.

We were halfway back, and I was halfway to release.

There was just something about West that my body craved.

His voice floated across the salty air, his tone conversational. "I know I'm good, but I've never gotten a girl off before with a piggyback ride. If you finish back there before we get home, I'm writing 'I'll give you a piggyback ride' on a dollar bill and posting that baby at the bar tomorrow. Is faster better?"

I stiffened, trying not to move at all, trying not to even breathe as the mortification washed over me. West tried to jog, but I bounced against him roughly, and his steps slowed, my rigidness hindering his stride. "Hey, babe, relax back there. I'm not complaining. Trust me. I am not complaining one bit." Amusement radiated off of him.

All of a sudden, I tipped hard to the right. West's leg seemed to just sink into the sand, and I gripped him desperately. He tried to yank his leg free, but stumbled with my extra weight, and we both fell over, splashing sideways into the waves.

Caught by surprise, my hair covered my face when I first surfaced, and I couldn't see anything. I was lying on my side with West's shoulder pinning me down. The water wasn't deep, but I was practically horizontal, and when the next wave rolled through, my head went under, and I sucked in a burning lungful of seawater. While I hacked and choked, West yanked me up and dragged me higher to the edge of the waterline. He scooped the wet strands off my face and rubbed my back as I coughed and spit into the sand.

"Sorry, babe. I didn't mean to land on you."

I nodded, trying to slow my breathing back to normal. Jesus, that saltwater burned.

When I raised my face to his, West looked at me apologetically. "I feel like we've done this before," he tried to joke.

I tried for a smile. "You can't blame this one on me."

"Really? Because I was pretty distracted with you pressing and rubbing against me, all but moaning."

My face flushed, and I was glad yet again it was night and he couldn't see.

He lowered his head and put his mouth right up to my ear. "It was so damn unexpected, it's no wonder I couldn't walk right." His hot breath burned the side of my neck, and I couldn't help but close my eyes and bite my lip. I leaned toward him, and his lips brushed my ear, his tongue tracing the rim. I let out a shaky breath. "Sadie? As much as I want to rip your wet clothes off right here, right now, I've learned that sex on the beach is a little overrated. Sand gets in places it shouldn't, and, yeah, it doesn't always end well."

I jerked away from him. I was such a slut. I was all but panting because a hot guy was touching me. Oh Lord, what was wrong with me? I braced my arms on my bent knees and stared down between them at the sand.

West stood next to me and hauled me up by the armpits. I wavered for a second, and he grabbed my waist to steady me. "You gonna be okay there, babe?"

I took a step away from him, causing his hands to drop. "I'm fine." I didn't know what to feel. The dunk in the ocean was exactly what I needed. My body seemed to catch fire whenever I got to close to West, but from what I'd heard, that kind of thing happened all the time to him. I didn't want to be just another mindless fuck.

That made me pause.

What did I want to be to him?

We slogged back toward his house. My shirt hung heavily on me, clinging to my body, water dripping in a steady rhythm down my legs as we walked.

West walked awkwardly next to me, holding his jeans at the waistband.

"Problem?" I asked, watching him clutch at his pants and take wide, stiff-legged steps.

He quirked a brow at me. "You ever try walking in wet jeans with a raging hard-on? Not that easy."

A small, satisfied smile crept across my face. At least I wasn't the only one affected tonight.

We walked a little farther before West cursed and stopped. "I give up." He turned away from me, and the next thing I knew, his jeans were slipping downward, before getting hung up at his knees. He tried to get one leg free, but the wet denim was uncooperative, and he lost his balance, falling on his ass in the hard sand. Laughing, he wrestled with his jeans until they were off and then picked them up, tossed them over his arm, and started walking again.

I was a step or two behind him, choosing to stay there so I could sneak a peek at his sand-encrusted, wet boxer briefs. Catching up to him, I rubbed my hand over his ass, brushing the sand off. "I think you have something here." West stopped mid-step and looked over at me, his eyelids closing partway. "There. That's better."

West shook his head at me. "Yeah, I think I have something here too." Grabbing my hand, he pressed it against his erection. "Now, *that's* better."

I cupped him and ran my hand up his length once before I lost my nerve and pulled away. Wrapping his arm around my wet shoulders, West pulled me into his side and kissed the top of my head. "Oh, Sadie. What am I going to do with you?"

I have a few ideas. But I couldn't bring myself to speak up. I wanted to be more than a quick lay, more than a convenient fuck.

I wanted to be . . . more.

When we got back to the steps where we left our shoes, West started up to his room. "C'mon. Let me get you some dry clothes."

I followed behind him. When I stepped through the sliding

glass doors, West was rustling through his dresser. Snagging some drawstring gym shorts and a shirt that would come to my knees, he herded me to the bathroom. "Here. I know you have to be freezing. Take a hot shower and warm up and then you can put these on. I'm going to run over to Wyatt's bathroom and do the same."

I was tempted to ask him to stay, to share this shower, but before I could work up the courage, he was gone, pulling the door shut behind him. Jumping in his shower, I quickly cleaned myself, washing my hair as best I could without conditioner. It was still tangled in places, especially by the nape of my neck. When I got out, I pulled his shirt over my head and took a deep inhale. Between wearing his shirt and using his shower products, the smell of West surrounded me. I liked it. After wrapping my hair up turban style, I slipped back into his bedroom.

He was already waiting for me, perched on the side of the bed. A hairbrush lay next to him. He saw me looking at it and held it out to me. "I found this in Wyatt's bathroom. Not sure what chick left it here, but I thought you might need it. It looks clean enough."

I was oddly touched by his thoughtfulness. I pulled the towel off my head and sat next to him, wincing when I tried to pull the brush through my snarled strands. West's hands took the brush from me.

"Here, let me. It's my fault your hair got all messed up in the first place." West grabbed my hips and moved me until I was positioned sideways on the bed between his outstretched legs.

Pushing me forward at the waist so he could reach the ends of my hair, he started working the brush through the tangles, gently tugging the knots free.

My scalp tingled as he worked, and I relaxed, slumping forward and letting him do as he pleased. By the time he finished, I was almost asleep. He dropped the brush and ran his hands through my damp hair, the locks sliding smoothly between his fingers.

I sighed in utter contentment and leaned back against his chest. "You ready to take me home?"

His hands tightened around my upper arms. "What if you stayed here tonight? We could have a sleepover. Old-school style. No sex, just two people sharing a bed."

I arched an eyebrow. "No sex?"

"No sex. But if you ask nicely, I might go for a cuddle."

"Why no sex?"

He hesitated and ran his hands down my arms and back up again. "You're different. You make me want to do things the right way with you." He leaned his forehead against the back of my head. "But I'm also a selfish bastard, and I want to go to sleep knowing you're in my arms. Knowing I get to wake up to you."

I melted farther back into his chest, nuzzling against him. "A sleepover sounds good."

He smiled against the back of my head.

"You know you're too good for me, right? That I don't deserve you."

My answer was muffled against his pectoral muscle.

Hugging me to him, he scooped me up in his arms and lifted me off the bed before yanking the covers back with one hand and depositing me on the mattress. "Lady's choice. Which side do you want?"

Picking the same side I woke up on before, the one closest to the door, I settled stomach down onto the bed and flipped my wet hair up onto the pillow while he went around to the other side. "Hey, West?" I whispered. "Pretty please, with a cherry on top, can I have a snuggle?"

"Fuck, yes," he breathed, spooning against my back. He wrapped an arm around my waist, slipping his hand under my borrowed shirt to rest against my bare skin, and wedged one of his thighs between mine.

His warmth and scent surrounded me. His breath pulsed against the back of my neck. I'd never been more comfortable than I was at that moment, tucked tight against his body. It felt right, like I belonged there.

I was just drifting off to sleep when I thought I heard him whisper, "Damn, I could get used to this."

So could I.

chapter thirteen

On Saturday morning, Rue and I relaxed in our sunroom, sipping mango smoothies and eating our way through a mountain of strawberry-topped French toast triangles. She was home after the successful social media launch of a new bike rental company based in Charleston and Savannah, and I was flying high from the revival of my photography company. I'd gotten three jobs scheduled in the last two days, all referred by Aubrey.

The last one, a wedding, made me a little nervous. I usually needed a photography assistant for a job that size, but after my last assistant had turned up naked under Asshole, I wasn't keen on the idea of hiring another. The frantic bride had explained it was a small, intimate wedding, only sixty guests, and her scheduled photographer had backed out last minute due to a medical emergency. The wedding was next weekend, and the amount she offered to pay me made me forget any lingering doubts I had. A sixty-guest wedding was doable for a single photographer. I'd be busy, but I could make it work.

And I'd make some serious bank while I was at it.

The other two jobs were pretty standard. One was an engagement photo shoot and the other was new headshots for the agents of a nearby real estate company. I'd asked for more money than I normally would, and neither party balked in the slightest at the price. There were definite perks to working in a wealthier town.

The fact that all the jobs came from Aubrey . . . Well, I still wasn't sure what to think about that. I wanted her to be the bad guy. She kept trying to blur the lines.

Rue stretched and patted her stomach. "God, I'm such a heifer," she said, groaning. "I'm going to end up like you and have to *run*." She said the last word with a shudder and made a face.

I rolled my eyes. "Yeah, you're massive."

"Whatever. What's up with you and West? Anything going on there?"

"Maybe. What's the story with him and Aubrey? I've been meaning to ask you." I was curious if she knew anything more than Theo.

Rue rolled her eyes. "Aubrey's been trying to land him for years. Ain't gonna happen. You know my parents are friends with both of their parents, right? Anyway, her parents keep pushing for a match, and West kind of humored them or some shit for awhile to keep his parents happy. Took her to high-profile events or whatever. I'm sure they screwed around some too. I mean, come on, they're both freaking gorgeous! But I don't think it ever meant anything to him. I do know Aubrey was super humiliated when he broke it off with her. The football player thing was an attempt to show him she could do better." Rue waved her hand dismissively.

God, I was so attracted to West, but I did not want to deal with Aubrey. I snagged another piece of toast.

"Anyway, tell me about the pierced dude," I said, redirecting the conversation.

Rue closed her eyes and purred. "Yeah, that totally lived up to the hype. I might be ruined for regular cocks now."

I raised my eyebrows. "Seriously?"

Rue nodded. "Yeah, it was ... *mmm, mmm, good.*" She shivered at the memory, her lips curved into a satisfied smirk.

"Did you see him again?"

"Nah. He snores. Like a fucking freight train."

I shook my head. It was always something.

When West picked me up at noon, it wasn't in the banged-up pickup truck he'd been driving before. It was in a shiny, white extended cab dually with a company logo on the side, and his bloodhound was sticking his head out the window, drool dripping down the door.

"What's all this?" I waved at the massive truck. Thank God it had chrome running boards to help me climb up.

"*This* is what I drive when I want to impress a girl. Size matters." West wiggled his eyebrows as he opened my door.

I was almost in the front seat when I paused, looking back at him. "You weren't trying to impress me before?"

"Nope. Before you were just, just . . ." His voice trailed off, and he left the sentence hanging. "Today, I'm taking you on a date."

I arched an eyebrow but refrained from commenting.

As I settled my bag onto the floor of the front seat, General Beauregard scrambled around the back, trying to climb over the center console to greet me. I reached back to rub his floppy ears and ended up covered in puppy kisses. A small flock—a herd? a pack?—of butterflies took flight in my stomach, and I took a deep breath to calm myself, but I couldn't stop a small grin from escaping.

Slipping my sunglasses on, I waited for West to climb in next to me, and I fiddled with the air conditioning vents. "Yeah, I'm impressed with the chaperone. And you never told me where we were going. Am I dressed okay?"

West's eyes darted over me, from my flat-ironed hair to my aviators, past my racerback sundress with my bikini straps peeking out, and down to my seafoam-green painted toenails.

His lips twitched. "It'll work."

West turned the radio station to the same one I had picked the day he drove me home from the hotel—coincidence?—and headed toward the main parkway that ran the length of the island.

"Where are we going?" I tried again, since subtlety hadn't

gotten me very far.

"Picnic. Don't you pay attention?"

I took a deep breath. "You're going to be difficult, aren't you?"

"We've already done easy. Thought I'd try something new."

Smiling and shaking my head, I turned the radio up and looked out the window, content to wait him out. The road was lined with oak trees draped with Spanish moss that arched over the road, forming a canopy and cocooning us in dappled shade. Stripes of cirrus clouds lined the sky, and the humidity was only moderately suffocating. It was a beautiful day to hang out with a hot guy and his cute dog. The truck took a left, but I didn't recognize the street we turned down. We passed a bait shop and a gas station, and eased into a . . . marina.

"We're going on a boat?"

A huge grin split West's cheeks.

"Not *a* boat. *My* boat. There's a difference."

I took a deep breath.

"West, you know I'm scared of the water."

"I do. Which is why you'll be on a boat."

I stared at him, wondering about his intelligence level.

He sighed. "You'll be on a boat. The boat will be in the water. *You* will *not* be in the water. See what's happening here?"

I swallowed, uncomfortable. I could do this. I would be safe on the boat. I'm sure it had life jackets or those lifesaving rings or something. And it had West. I'd be fine.

Perfectly fine.

Pinning an apprehensive smile on my face, I jumped out of

the truck, hitching my tote with my towel and things over my shoulder. West directed me to hold General Beauregard's leash while he balanced one of the giant Coleman coolers from the bar on his shoulder and carried a large beach bag in the other hand.

As soon as I slipped my hand through the loop on the end of the leash, General Beauregard took off, pulling me through the parking lot toward the dock. "Whoa, boy," I said, trying not to trip as we raced down the main walkway.

When we got almost to the end of the dock, General Beauregard suddenly swerved, then took a flying leap and jumped into a long white-hulled boat. Running behind him with my wrist stuck in the leash and unable to stop the momentum, my eyes grew wide as I launched myself after him, Superman-style.

I kind of made it.

My upper body cleared the side of the boat, but my hip and shin slammed into the fiberglass hull. General Beauregard was trying to get to the bow of the boat, and his continued tugging pulled me the rest of the way onboard.

Damn, that was going to bruise. Sex-*ay*.

Mortified, I just laid there, slumped against the sidewall, prying the leash off my wrist so that crazy ass pony that masqueraded as a dog wouldn't drag me like a bobsled across the snowy white deck. My shin throbbed. Yeah, this is why dates were a bad idea.

West's footsteps echoed off the aluminum dock as he approached.

"Sadie!" he called out, dropping the gear and hurdling over

the side of the boat like a track star, landing gracefully on his feet.

Show off.

"Are you okay?"

He scooped me up and set me down on a large orange bean bag. I looked down. A bean bag? Yup, there were two bean bags in a big open area behind the hardtop-covered center console. He ran his hands down my legs, and I winced and hissed out a breath when he brushed over my shin. He swore and jammed his hand through his hair before jumping back to his feet.

After retrieving the rest of the supplies from the dock, he rustled around in them before returning with ice wrapped in a beach towel. He sat down next to me, pulled my leg into his lap, and placed the ice pack against my tender shin. I was mesmerized by West's fingers as he held the cold towel against me, one hand massaging the back of my calf.

Thank God I had shaved my legs this morning.

General Beauregard walked over, tucked his tail, and looked at me with sad eyes. He whined and snuggled up next to me, nudging my hand with his nose and giving me his best doggy apology. I patted him once, forgiving him, mostly because he looked so darn remorseful with those droopy eyes and ears.

"Fuck, Sadie, I'm sorry. If you want me to just take you home, I understand." Frustration colored West's voice. "Wyatt was meeting with the bank guy, and I told him I'd take the dog. Dumb hound loves the boat. I didn't think about how strong he was for someone as small as you."

A giggle bubbled from my lips, growing until I was full on

belly laughing. I fell back against the bean bag and shook my head in defeat. "Seriously, I'm not a clumsy person. But, somehow, every time I'm around you, something happens. You sure you don't plan this shit, just so you can swoop in and play hero?"

West squeezed my calf. "I'm fucking this all up. This is why I don't date. I don't know how to do this right."

General Beauregard licked my hand. I glared at him. "You're lucky you're cute." Peeking at West out of the corner of my eye, I added, "You too."

West looked at me, his eyes blazing with intensity.

Reaching out, he captured a lock of my hair and ran his fingers down the length. He tugged the end. "Want to try this again? I'm going to motor us out a little ways, and then we'll have a floating picnic like I promised you. You can stay right here and relax. The bean bags are the best seats on the boat."

I took a second to look around. The boat was long, easily forty feet, but was mostly empty deck. The tall bench behind the center console was embroidered with the same logo I'd seen on his truck. *Vitamin Sea.* A fishing pole underlined the words.

My lips quirked, and I nodded at the graphic. "Who named the boat?"

"Hailey named her."

"Her?"

"Yep. Anything I spend that much time riding on had better be a female."

I pointed around me at the expanse. "Is she big enough?"

He shrugged. "Depends. Are you impressed?"

"I've been told size matters."

"It's true. Want to see her flex her muscles?"

General Beauregard bayed in excitement, his tail thwacking my arm.

"Sure. Show me how your fancy toy works."

West's lips twitched, whether from annoyance or amusement I couldn't tell. "This *toy* is my livelihood, babe. Be nice."

As he made his way to the center console, I called after him, "Or else, what?"

"Or else I'll make fun of your little Polaroids."

I snapped my mouth shut. Was that a reference to Aubrey's pictures? I had no idea if Aubrey had given him copies or not, and I sure as hell wasn't going to ask. I brooded as West untied the lines from the dock, and we puttered out of the marina until we reached the end of the no-wake zone. Cranking the four outboard engines, West sped up, and the boat skimmed over the water, practically flying. My hair flew everywhere, and I abandoned the ice on my leg to try to salvage my tangling strands. Catching as much of it as I could, I made a messy side braid and wrapped the hair tie from my wrist around the end, securing it.

We were going so fast it was making my eyes water, even behind my Ray-Bans. Struggling to my feet, I made my way up to the center console, where the windshield provided some protection. I leaned back against the tall bench seat, keeping my knees bent to absorb the bounce of the boat as we scooted across the rolling waves.

West grinned over at me, clearly in his element. Snaking his arm around my waist, he pulled me to his side, keeping his other hand relaxed on the steering wheel.

Turning his head toward me to be heard over the roar of the wind and the engines, he yelled, "Want to drive?"

Surprised at his question, I shook my head no. "I have no idea how to drive a boat!"

Laughing, he took my hand and put it on the steering wheel under his, maneuvering me so I was standing in front of him. "There. Now you're driving a boat. This screen here is your depth finder. We need at least five feet." The display showed thirty-four feet of water under us. Plenty deep.

Uneasy, I gripped the wheel, my body stiffening with anxiety. We hit a wave, and I smashed back against West's chest, my head popping him in the chin and my bruised leg throbbing. Grasping my hip harder, he nudged the back of my knees with his, forcing them to unlock. "Relax. Look around. There are no other boats in sight. What are you worried about? There's nothing to hit. We're going to go up the coast a ways and then we'll eat. Just keep her pointed that way." He raised an arm and pointed straight ahead.

I licked my lips and nodded. Widening my stance, I held the wheel at two and ten, concentrating on the horizon.

The warmth from West's hand disappeared from my side, and he moved from behind me and headed to the side of the boat.

"Where are you going?" I asked, panicking.

"You're fine. I'm just packing away the buoys from earlier. Keep going straight."

I didn't like him not being within reach of the controls. "Can we go slower?"

He shrugged. "Sure. Just ease back on the throttle next to you."

I pointed at a black lever, and he nodded. I curled my fingers around it and pulled it halfway down.

We lurched forward with the sudden loss of speed, my stomach slamming into the console and West tumbling to the deck, catching himself on his hands and knees. Near the front, General Beauregard yelped as he slid into the bow of the boat.

Swearing, West picked himself up and came over to stand next to me. "Easy with my girl there, Sadie. She can handle a rough ride with the best of them, but she prefers a gentle touch." He put my hand on the throttle and showed me how to change speed smoothly.

I tugged my hand out from underneath. "Maybe you should drive."

"Nope. You got this. You're going to earn your lunch."

Leaving me again, he walked to the front of the boat and stood next to the floppy-eared dog as we hurtled over the water. The muscles in his forearms stood out as he braced himself against the rail, and I was transfixed by the strong lines of his back as the rushing wind molded his gray shirt to his ribs. His muscled thighs flexed and adjusted to the oscillation of the waves, reminding me of our night together, his hips pumping against mine.

And, yeah, I stared at his ass too.

It was a *very* nice ass.

After awhile, West came back and took over the wheel. "Why

don't you go back to the bean bag and put some more ice on that leg? We still have about thirty minutes to go."

I was grateful to give up captain duty. I dug another handful of ice cubes out of the cooler and plopped back down on the squishy seat. Just as I nestled into a comfy position with the makeshift icepack secure around my shin, General Beauregard snuggled up next to me, putting his head in my lap. "Oh, now you want to play nice," I said.

The hound whined and covered one of his eyes with his paw before burrowing closer.

At least the ocean was pretty calm today. The waves were slow, gentle rollers and the hull sliced through the tops of them, rocking us softly.

Closing my eyes against the bright sun, I rubbed the dog's long ears and let my mind drift.

The next thing I knew, I was startled awake by West's fingers brushing wayward strands of hair off my forehead.

"I'm botching this whole date thing, aren't I?" he said, looking adorably disgruntled. "Now I've literally bored you to sleep."

I yawned and removed my arm from under the dog, stretching my arms high above my head to get the kinks out.

Yuck. My entire left hand was covered in puppy drool.

Casting a devious glance at West, I reached out and wiped my wet hand all over his shirt and tried to get some in his hair, but he dodged my fingers and snagged my wrist in a firm grip. He held it until I raised my eyes to his, our gazes locking. Twisting his lips into a sexy smirk, he dragged my hand down his chest.

"Better?"

I nodded, feeling the definition of each hard ab muscle as my fingers passed over them.

He laughed. "Now you've gotten me all dirty."

"I'm sure you were plenty dirty before you ever met me."

My hand fell to my lap as West backed away from me and stripped his damp shirt over his head. I breathed out and forgot to inhale.

Dear Lord, the man was beautiful. His tan skin stretched over taut muscles that I ached to trace, to explore, to taste. From his broad shoulders and defined chest, down the ruggedness of his abs and those delicious obliques that angled past his hips, I was in serious danger of imitating General Beauregard and drooling on sight.

I swiped a quick finger across my chin just in case.

West laid his shirt across the bench seat to dry, and I tried to redirect my focus away from the onboard scenery.

I gulped and got to my feet, twisting to look in all directions.

Water, all around us, as far as I could see.

I squinted at it, raising my sunglasses to the top of my head to get a clearer view. The water looked different out here, the color softer. The translucent green was clearer than I'd expected. Closer to shore, it mixed with a deeper blue and became impenetrable, frothing with agitation. But this—this expanse of ocean looked less sinister. The undulations seemed gentle, almost welcoming. It was hard to explain.

I looked at West, bewildered.

"We're a couple miles offshore." He grinned, reading my mind. "Once you hit the Gulf Stream, the ocean changes personalities. Isn't she gorgeous?" He swept his arm out, like he was presenting me with a gift.

For a few minutes, I studied the ocean around us, taking in the differences. I could see down at least twenty feet. It wasn't crystal clear, like you see in photos of the Caribbean, but it wasn't what I was used to either. I watched a pelican circle before diving, hitting the water at an awkward angle before floating and shaking its head.

"Why is the water so much calmer out here?" I asked, perplexed.

"The water's a lot deeper. Waves tend to be more pronounced in shallower water."

General Beauregard let out a long exaggerated bay from the other side of the boat as he propped his feet up on the side, his tail beating with excitement. We both turned and scanned the ocean, trying to see what had him worked up.

West pointed. "Look! A sea turtle."

Indeed, the graceful creature was swimming about twenty feet away from us, its shell bigger than West's oversized truck tire. "It's huge!" I said, turning to West in surprise.

He smirked. "That's what they all say."

I rolled my eyes and shook my head in mock disgust. "Your modesty is by far your best quality."

"No, I'm pretty sure that's my—" I slapped my hand over his mouth, muffling the rest of his words.

"Don't ruin such a nice moment by talking. Just don't," I admonished, giving him the side eye.

The laughter left his gaze, and he brought his long fingers up to my arm, holding my hand against his lips. He kissed my palm and then my inner wrist, leaving the sensitive flesh tingling. Then he laced our fingers together and wrapped our conjoined hands behind my lower back, forcing me against his warm, bare chest.

"Wouldn't want to do that," he murmured, his lips just grazing mine as he spoke.

He pulled me closer, raising me up on my tiptoes, and I braced my free hand on his shoulder. His lips brushed mine, a mere tease of a kiss. Humming deep in his throat, he cupped the side of my neck, holding me in place as he deepened the contact. His mouth settled over mine with lazy intent, molding my lips with his. The tip of his tongue traced the seam of my lips, and I smiled beneath him, but he didn't push for more. He dropped hot kisses across my jawline until his breath warmed my ear as he nuzzled my neck with his nose.

"Hungry?"

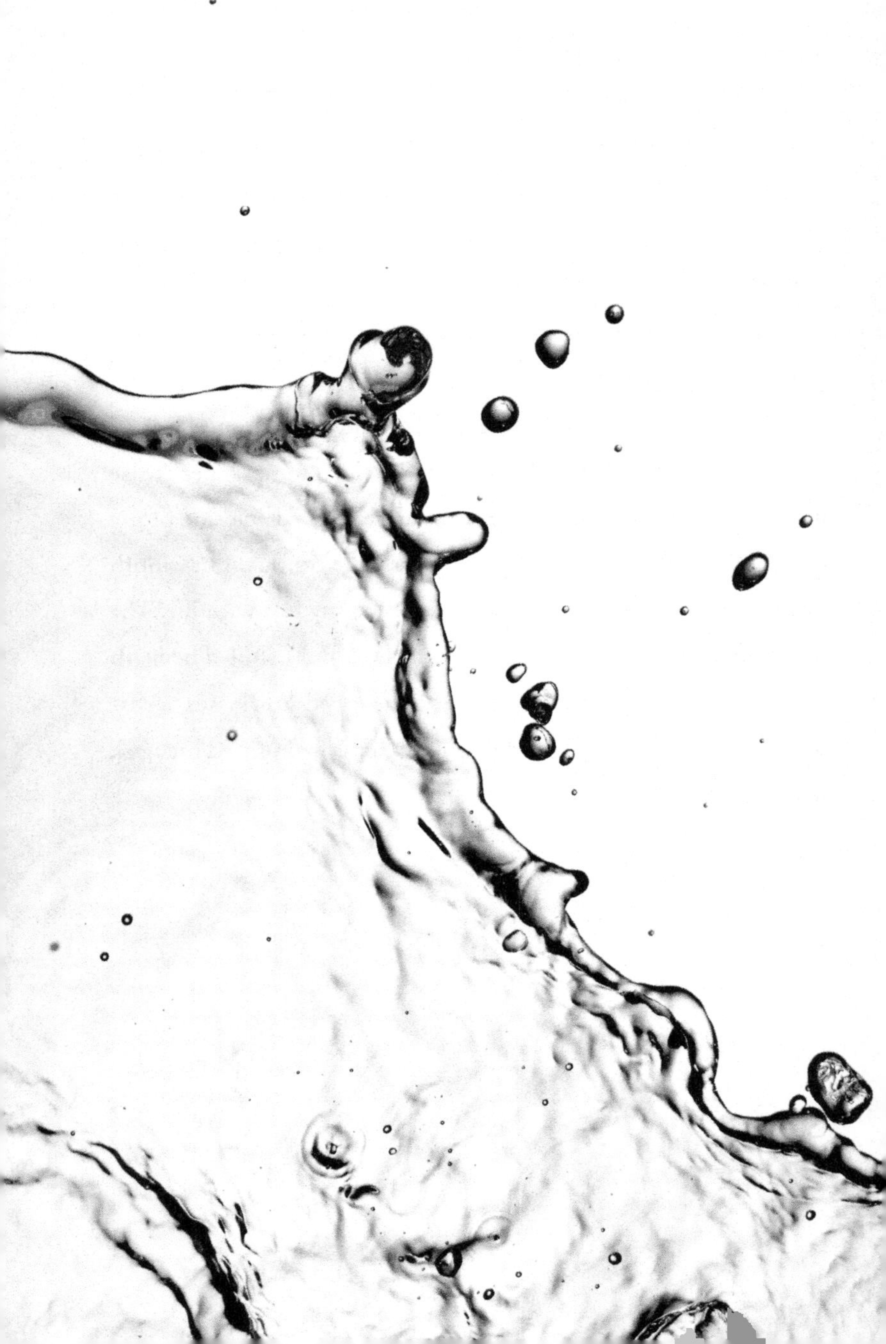

chapter fourteen

I nodded, exposing my neck to his warm lips.

He let go of the hand behind my back, his fingers biting into my hips instead. My lips were a bare inch from his shoulder. I closed my eyes and just absorbed his nearness, the intensity of the moment building as he nipped a path down my neck to my collarbone. When he drew back and I felt his eyes on me, I forced my own heavy lids to open partway. He lifted a hand to trace my lips before his fingers blazed a path back to my waist, skimming the side of my breast in the process. My nipples beaded in response. I exhaled, not realizing I had been holding my breath.

His fingers flexed, and his mouth brushed the shell of my ear as he leaned down and whispered my name.

"Ready to eat?"

Disoriented, I blinked at him.

"Our picnic?" His eyes sparkled with mischief. "You know, the whole reason we came out here?"

I took a step back and ran my tongue across my teeth in annoyance. He was playing with me. And it was working.

"Sure. Let's eat." I marched over to the cooler and beach bag. Finding an oversized beach towel inside, I spread it out near the bean bags and sat down on one side of it, wrapping my arms around my bent knees. "What's for lunch?"

West grinned. "I wasn't sure what you liked, so I got a little of everything."

Reaching into the cooler, he started pulling out small plastic containers, subdivided into sections holding crackers, cheese, and circles of meat.

My eyebrows shot up. "You brought Lunchables?"

"Hey, don't laugh. I love these things. I have turkey, ham, bologna, and pepperoni, your choice."

"You brought Lunchables," I repeated, this time a statement instead of a question. "For our picnic."

"Not just Lunchables. I packed apples and watermelon too."

I nodded at him, dumbfounded. I'm not sure what I expected when he invited me on a picnic, but somehow, this wasn't it. Shaking one of the plastic sealed containers at him, I said, "I thought size mattered! These are for kids!"

"Babe, I got us covered. I have three of each kind."

I tipped my head, not sure how to even reply to that kind of logic.

"Plus, I brought us dessert. Hold on, you'll like this." Rising up on his knees to dig through the cooler, West put the fruit and Lunchables between us, tossing one of the apples to General Beauregard, who happily set to gnawing on it a few feet away from us. After placing some bottles of water on the striped towel, he extracted a familiar looking green-and-white box from the cooler, and my breath caught. "Krispy Kreme original glazed. Bought fresh this morning."

My eyes crinkled in the corners, and I bit my lip, trying to contain my laughter. He displayed the box like a model on The Price is Right.

"Come on, admit it. I did good."

"The doughnuts might make up for the Lunchables," I conceded.

"Hey, when was the last time you had one? I'm telling you, whoever invented these things was a fucking genius. Meat, cheese, *and* crackers, all packaged together. What's not to love?"

He seemed genuinely thrilled. I poked my tongue in my cheek and picked up a package, staring at it. "They make pepperoni ones now?"

He waggled his eyebrows. "Yup, with mozzarella. Fancy, right?"

I blew out a breath and gave in to the laughter. "Very."

Peeling back the plastic wrapper, I assembled my mini cracker stacks. I would never admit it to him, but they were a lot better than I remembered. West worked his way through one of each variety and then pointed to the apples. He'd bought two of each color. I picked up a Golden Delicious and took a bite.

After snagging the other red one, he whistled. General Beauregard perked his ears in our direction, his tongue lolling out of his mouth and his original apple long gone. Panting, the dog lay next to West and wagged his tail. West pulled his arm back, and General Beauregard leapt to his feet, instantly alert. Throwing the apple high in the air, West yelled "Catch!" as the hound crouched low. As the apple began its descent, the dog jumped, the fruit easily snatched out of the air, his ears spread like wings steering him in for the landing. Regaining his footing, he adjusted his grip on the prize, working his jaw, and shook his head with the fruit clenched between his jowls. Then he settled onto the edge of the oversized towel, holding the apple between his paws, and began crunching on it.

"He likes the red ones the best."

I wrinkled my brow. "How in the world do you know that?"

"I know. Me and General Beauregard, we talk about these things, man-to-man. I take care of him, and he's a chick magnet for me. We have this partnership all worked out. He gets paid in food, I get paid in pu—" West broke off in a coughing fit.

"Right," I said.

West ducked his head and smiled, a dimple showing in his cheek. "He caught your attention, didn't he?"

"Yeah, 'cause I thought he was abandoned. And he looked sad."

"He always looks sad. It's the big ears. I told you, size matters. And looks are deceiving. That dog has the best life ever."

"I figured that was you."

"Me? Why would you think I have the best life ever?"

"You live at the beach—"

"So do you," West interrupted.

"You fish and bartend for a living."

"Okay, yeah, that part's pretty awesome."

"You live with your brother."

"I live with my best friend, just like you. He just happens to be my brother too, the fortunate bastard."

I rolled my eyes. "You're close with your family."

"Mm, you're partly right. I'm close with my siblings and my grandparents."

"Not your parents?"

West hesitated, tilting his head. "You really want to hear about this?"

I shrugged. "Isn't this what people do on dates? Get to know each other? You were the one who insisted on taking me out today. So talk."

West sighed and shifted on the towel, lying back until his head was in my lap. "If we're going to have a therapy session, I'm going to get in the proper position," he joked, looking up.

I followed his gaze. Wispy cirrus clouds painted the sky with their pale brushstrokes.

I reclined back onto one of my hands and ran my fingers through his hair with the other. He leaned into my touch, and I repeated the motion, lightly scraping my nails against his scalp. He groaned.

"Keep that up, and I'll tell you anything you want to know.

Family history. Social security number. Where I hid the body."

I paused, stilling my hand, and he squinted up at me. "Kidding."

"You better be."

Settling back against me again and closing his eyes, West took a deep breath before he started. "Okay, so, my parents. There's not much to tell. Appearances are everything to them because they have money. And I wanted to please them, so I tried to fit the mold. Went to the right school, followed my stepdad into the family business—do you know who my parents are?"

I shook my head.

"Montgomery Golf? No? The company has a couple of different sides to it. From golf course design and management to golf clubs and golf accessories. It's a rich man's game, and my parents like to look the part. Picture catered parties and symphony halls and charity balls and—really, just about any excuse to gossip about the other rich assholes, but with better food and better clothes than most people. Don't get me wrong, some of the men run companies, but a lot of them, like my father, are the heads of boards, and it's the managers who do the real work."

My mouth twisted. "So you grew up with money, and your parents liked nice things. I'm not seeing the problem here, West."

He let out a dark chuckle. "I didn't at first, either. I spent years going to pointless meetings, shaking the right hands, networking with the power players. And why? I hated it. It just took me awhile to realize that was okay. I didn't have to take over the company one day. I could be myself, and that was enough."

"What made you figure it out?" My fingers were still sifting through West's short hair.

"Wyatt," he said, a smile drifting over his face. "Every time I'd come down to visit him and his stupid beach bar, it was obvious how happy he was. Like, he loved getting up every morning and living his life here. I wanted that. That simple fucking everyday happiness."

"So . . . what happened?"

"I figured he had the right idea and followed him. Told my parents, packed up my shit, and left Chicago and all that phony ass kissing behind. Decided to grow up and be a man and make my own money, not live off my parents' hand-outs. Bought a boat. Figured out a way to make money with it. End of story."

I studied him. The relaxed lines of his body as he sprawled across the towel. His strong jawline. His long fingers resting on his sculpted abs. His citrus and salt scent.

"It's that simple?"

He nodded. "Yeah, it is. I love being on the water and the challenge of trying to catch the biggest fish. Finding a way to make other dudes pay for the gas and bait was genius. My friends are here. I own part of a fucking bar. Life's pretty damn perfect if you ask me."

"Do you miss it? The wealth and the perks that came with it?"

He dropped his head back to study me. Reaching up, he pulled my sunglasses off my face, looking me right in the eyes. "Nothing was genuine. How can you appreciate something—I mean, really, truly appreciate something you've never had to work for—something that's just handed to you—something you don't create or build or earn yourself?" He paused, and his blue-gray eyes moved over my face before locking on mine again, his gaze intense. "I wanted something that's mine. Mine and nobody else's."

The air crackled between us, the slap of the water against the side of the boat sharply staccato. The humidity was tangible, pulled away by an errant breeze before settling back around our shoulders, urging us to give in to the heat building between us. A seagull floated overhead before diving into the water in search of its own lunch.

I let out a shaky breath and swallowed hard.

"Is that such a crazy dream?" he asked, his voice rough.

I traced his eyebrows, smoothing the furrows from his forehead. "No. It doesn't sound crazy at all."

West's lips twitched, and he shifted off my lap to sit up and face me. "Enough of this serious bullshit. You want any of this watermelon before I eat it? I could only fit three slices."

I rolled my eyes at the subject change. "Yeah, I'll take one."

West split the seedless fruit between us and took a big bite of one of his slices, a dribble of juice snaking a path down his chin.

"Know why I packed watermelon?"

I swallowed a mouthful, feeling some drip down my own chin. "Why?"

"'Cause of your shampoo. I looked in your shower.

You always smell like watermelon, and now I find myself buying one every time I'm at the damn grocery store."

I bit my lip to keep my smile contained. "You don't like

watermelon?"

He waited until I met his eyes. "It's quickly becoming my favorite."

I flushed and tried to change the subject. "Favorite color?"

"Blue. Really? You want to know this shit?"

I shrugged. "You said you wanted to get to know each other better."

"Fine. Morning or night person?"

"Night. Pancakes or waffles?"

"Pancakes. Chocolate or vanilla?"

"Chocolate. Chinese takeout or Mexican?"

"Mexican. Dress up or dress down?"

"Dress down, most of the time anyway." He nodded in agreement with my choice. "Batman or Superman?"

"Batman. Favorite position?" He looked at me with an innocent expression and took a big bite of melon.

I stared at him for a moment and put my rind in an empty Lunchable container. "Offense."

West tossed his rind next to mine and wiped his mouth with a paper napkin. "So you like to be in charge?"

I didn't pretend to misunderstand. "If the guy doesn't know what he's doing, then yes."

"And if he does?" West leaned closer.

"Then wouldn't he be choosing the position?" I cocked one eyebrow, challenging him.

"Probably. Unless he wants to see what kind of moves you've got."

I licked my lips. "I've got moves."

"I know. And I can't wait to see them again but not here. General Beauregard is underage. We need to keep it G-rated, PG tops." West winked. "Wouldn't want to traumatize the audience."

I blinked at his comment. Suddenly, I was back in Nashville, back in my loft, listening to Asshole and Jameson talk about videos of me. Footage of Rebecca. Sex tapes. I gasped and turned away, shoving my sunglasses on top of my head and rubbing my eyes with the heels of my hands, trying to erase the memories. Even though I had destroyed all the evidence, I still felt dirtied from the experience, like I wore a scarlet P for porn. I was anything but an ideal match for a guy like West, where image mattered to his parents. Maybe he didn't want to be a part of the family business, but his love for them was clear from his actions. I had a past as an inadvertent adult film star, and I took boudoir photos for a living. What was I thinking?

A warm hand rubbed my back. "Hey, you okay?"

"Yeah," I muttered. "Something in my eyes. It's better now." Forcing myself to lower my hands, I dropped my sunglasses back over my eyes and smiled at him. "I'm ready for a doughnut, aren't you?"

Moving away from him, I popped open the hinged top of my favorite green-and-white box, snagging one and taking a big bite. Yeah, I might have been eating my feelings just a little.

"How'd you know about the doughnuts?" I asked between bites.

"I'm just that good." He lifted one shoulder in an arrogant

shrug.

I snorted.

"Fine," he admitted. "I asked Rue what your culinary weakness was. Fair warning—I plan on finding out all of your weaknesses and fully exploiting them."

He looked at me, his eyes dark with promise, daring me to disagree.

I was starting to think West was my biggest weakness.

And I wasn't ready for him to know that.

Breaking his gaze, I finished off my doughnut, holding my sticky hand in the air as I looked for another clean napkin. Not finding one right off, I licked the sugary remnants off my thumb. I heard a soft groan and peeked up to see West focused on my mouth. Eyes half-lidded, he pulled my hand to him and drew the tip of my first finger into his mouth, his lips wrapping around my sensitive skin. The rough scrape of his tongue as he licked and sucked each finger set me on fire, my eyes closing and lips parting. By the time he finished, my breathing was ragged, my thighs were clenched, and I wanted to feel that hot mouth moving on a different part of me altogether.

"You taste sweet," he murmured. "Like you did the other night."

I bit my lip to keep my moan contained.

Adjusting himself, West let out a slow breath. "Yeah, it's time to cool off. C'mon, we're going for a quick swim before we head back."

I opened one eye and gave him my best *are you crazy* look.

West stood above me and reached down to help me up.

I remained firmly ensconced in the bean bag and crossed my arms over my chest.

"I just ate," I pointed out. "We can't swim for at least two hours. I'm a lifeguard. I know these things."

He stared at me for a beat. "Then you know that's bullshit."

I squirmed. "West, I told you, I don't like getting in the water."

"I drove you miles offshore so the water would be clearer. So you could see what you were getting into. I thought this would help."

I shrugged, undeterred. We were in deep water. I had no doubt there were some big ass sea animals out there. That sea turtle had been cool and all, but he didn't live alone.

West crouched in front of me, putting his hands on my knees. "Care to explain it to me?"

I made a face.

He chuckled. "Please? With doughnuts on top?"

I rolled my eyes. "It's stupid."

"Nothing about you is stupid."

Sighing in defeat, I told him my lame story. I expected annoyance or dismissal or irritation. Instead, he listened quietly and didn't interrupt my woeful tale of childhood jellyfish trauma.

Rising to his feet again, he held out his hand. "Will you take a quick dip with me?"

I lowered my eyes, embarrassed and frustrated, but at the same time, pleased he'd worded it as a request instead of an order for a change. "I can't," I whispered, agitated.

"Okay." West didn't press me further. "General Beauregard and I are going to cool off for a few minutes. You can stay on the boat and enjoy the view."

I grinned and made a point of focusing anywhere but him. "Yeah, the scenery is pretty amazing out here."

He put a finger under my chin and lifted my face to his. He made a show of looking me over and then winked. "It's fucking beautiful."

I sucked in a breath as he turned and walked to the back of the boat and whistled for the dog, the eager puppy immediately on his heels. West opened some kind of hatchway that separated the back of the boat from a swim platform, and both he and the dog jumped overboard, uncaring of what might be waiting for them.

My heart leapt to my throat, and I raced to the rear of the boat, scanning the water for any signs of sea life, vicious or otherwise. Really, I considered all sea life malicious until proven innocent.

West splashed the hound, who whined and swam in happy circles around him, before switching to float on his back, his muscular body on full display. He seemed carefree and relaxed, his eyes closed against the sun's glare and his arms splayed wide at his sides.

It was like a damn Greek tragedy; the land-bound mortal maiden drawn to the unreachable sea god. Well, I wasn't quite a maiden anymore, but still.

I spotted a small jellyfish—a damn *jellyfish*—but it was far enough away from them I didn't sound an alarm yet, although I resolved to keep a close eye on it as West relaxed, and the dog paddled nearby.

But when a small torpedo suddenly launched out of the water not ten feet from General Beauregard and flew, fucking *flew*, past the boat, I screamed like the scared little girl I was. The thing skimmed across the top of the water for about thirty feet before it dove back in. West shot up in the water and swam back to the boat when he heard my piercing cry.

Pushing the dog onboard ahead of him, West rushed to my side. He grabbed my shoulders and gave me a quick once-over before scanning the horizon. "What's wrong?!"

Two more torpedoes took off on the left side of the boat. Starboard? Port? Who the fuck knew? I gasped and pointed. West whipped his head around in time to see the things before they slipped back into the ocean.

Turning back to me, he dropped his hands from my shoulders and clutched his stomach, laughing uncontrollably.

I turned wide, disturbed eyes in his direction.

"I take it you've never seen a flying fish before?"

I blinked at him. "That's a real thing? Flying fish?"

He nodded, trying to reign in his laughter.

"That thing was a *fish?*"

Another zipped by on the other side of the boat, and General Beauregard yelped and ran to the bow.

West grinned. "Cool, huh?"

"Do they bite?" I pictured swarms of flying fish attacking the boat.

"They don't have teeth, if that's what you're asking."

"Why do they fly?"

West tipped his head from one side to the other. "They're generally trying to escape from a predator," he admitted.

I twisted my head in the direction they had come from, but I couldn't see anything. I edged to the rail and looked into the water.

West slid behind me and plastered himself against me, wrapping his dripping arms around my waist. I turned to protest, and he pressed against my front, soaking most of my sundress.

"Hey!"

"Sorry, did I get you wet?" He grinned unrepentantly.

I pushed him away and pulled the bottom of the damp cotton away from my thighs before turning my accusing green gaze on him. "Are you trying to get me to strip down to my bikini?"

"Maybe."

I tugged the dress over my head and laid it over the back of the center console, next to his shirt. "You could have just asked me, you know."

"Would that have worked?" He raised his eyebrows, one corner of his mouth edging into a smile as he took in my bikini—seafoam-green edged with black lingerie-seamed detailing. Yes, I matched my bikini to my nail polish.

"Probably."

"What else will you do if I ask?" He walked toward me slowly.

"What else do you want?"

He kept moving until we were almost touching. He bent his head down, stopping just short of my lips. "Everything," he breathed, closing the last centimeter separating us.

His lips met mine, tasting of salt and sugar. Hands cupped my face and slid into my hair as we devoured each other. I wrapped my arms around him and grabbed his ass, pulling him snug against me until his hardness nestled into my softness. He cursed and ground himself against me, his tongue mimicking what his cock clearly wanted. I lifted one thigh and wrapped it around his waist, needing to get closer, my arms circling his back, and my hands clutching his shoulder blades.

We ate at each other, not bothering to pause for breath, and when his hands cupped my ass, lifting me and urging me to wrap my legs fully around his waist, I groaned with satisfaction, pressing my hips against him, desperate for friction. I nipped his lower lip, pausing to steal a breath, and he rested his forehead against mine, his beautiful eyes closed. Bending my head, I ran my tongue down his neck and trailed kisses along his shoulder as my hands explored his upper back, kneading his hard muscles and feeling them flex in response. Changing directions, I ran my palms up his neck, forcing his head back, and dug my fingers into his scalp until he opened his eyes. He groaned.

"I didn't bring you out here for this."

He rolled his hips, and I couldn't answer, except to squeeze him tighter with my thighs.

I moved my lips to his ear. "Why the fuck not?"

His lip curled, and he tugged on my braid, carving a few inches between us. He took a deep breath, and his chest expanded with the movement, pressing into my breasts.

"I was serious earlier. I really do want to get to know you

better—not just in the carnal sense. But, fuck, if you don't make me forget all my noble intentions."

"I like your intentions. I like your mouth too. Can't we do both?" I was shameless as I squirmed against him.

He swore long and hard as he lowered me to my feet. "I'm a fucking idiot. I don't have a damn condom here, babe."

A rustling noise interrupted my response, and we turned to see General Beauregard nosing the now empty Krispy Kreme box across the deck. West moved around me, hollering a sharp reprimand at the dog, who beat a quick escape to the front of the boat. After tossing the remains of our lunch back in the cooler, West returned to my side, hooking an arm around my waist and pulling me to him, and I rested my arms against his tempting chest.

He lifted a hand and cupped the side of my face. "You—you're so fucking sexy right now with your lips all swollen from my kisses. You make me forget everything else."

I gripped his biceps, one inked and one not, and leaned my cheek into his palm. "What are you forgetting? Do you have to be somewhere?"

"I just have to bartend tonight—fuck! What time is it?"

Leaning over to grab his phone off the console's dash, he powered the screen on, checked the time, and groaned.

"We have to head back if I'm going to make the start of my shift."

I frowned, not ready for our time together to end.

He dipped his head, dropping a kiss on the tip of my nose.

"Come with me tonight. Hang out at the bar."

I sighed. The man did not know how to ask.

But he sure as hell knew how to kiss. Which was more important.

"And watch you flirt with half-dressed girls for tips? That sounds fun."

"So I can flirt with *you*."

I squeezed his tattooed arm. "Need some practice?"

"Not really."

His ego was truly boundless.

"Hmm. I'll think about it." I tapped my chin for effect.

West's smirk was too arrogant for my liking, and I left him in suspense for the time being. Turning around, I plopped back down into a bean bag. He was right. It was the best seat on the boat.

Muttering something I couldn't hear under his breath, West positioned himself behind the console and started up his wannabe yacht, powering us back to reality. I settled farther into the vinyl and closed my eyes against the brutal wind rushing past me, content and happier than I remembered being in a long time.

The next thing I knew, West was shaking my shoulder, waking me up. Disoriented, I sat up and tried to regain my bearings.

We were back at the marina.

Shit, I'd fallen asleep. Again. I swiped at my mouth, checking for drool.

As I got to my feet, the bean bag made an awful peeling sound as it fell away from me. My sweat had glued it to me, and I was pretty sure I left a layer of skin behind on it.

"Sorry 'bout that." I cringed.

"My fault," West offered. "I don't normally bore my dates to sleep."

I ducked my head in embarrassment and made a show of gathering up my bag. As West helped me over the side of the boat and onto the dock, General Beauregard patiently waited, leash pooled at his feet and his tail wagging. We made our way back to the parking lot, and that traitorous dog walked beside West the whole time, never once even tugging against the leash.

"So he behaves for you, and he's a heathen for me?" I nodded at the furry creature responsible for the ache in my shin.

"He recognizes authority and responds to it. He was testing you."

"Well, I don't think I passed," I said.

"That's okay. He's not the one you need to worry about responding to you."

I lifted my eyebrows at him, not following him at all.

West ran his eyes down my bikini-clad figure and laughed. "You want to check out my response?" He dropped the cooler with a loud bang on the aluminum walkway and set the beach bag on top it, before taking mine and putting it with his. He tugged my hips forward until our thighs brushed and dropped his chin. His fingers dug in, until nothing but Lycra and nylon fabric separated us.

Oh yeah, he responded to me.

And if size mattered, then I was impressed.

Cheeks heating, I put my hands on his chest, creating a little space. General Beauregard read my mind and nosed in between us.

"I'm not ready for this date to end," West admitted, one hand coming up to smooth my tangled hair off my face, trying to tuck the wind-snarled strands behind my ear. "Come to the Wreck with me."

West's skin sizzled against mine, and I couldn't help sliding my hands up to his shoulders and behind his neck. My breathing was faster when I raised my eyes to his. "Would that be our second date then?"

He tilted his head, and his eyes followed the path of his fingers down my neck. "Does it matter?"

He said nothing physical on the first date. If we could skip ahead to our second . . .

I licked my lips. "Maybe."

His eyes flickered down to my mouth, and his hand gripped the back of my neck, forcing me to look up at him. He was grinning at me.

"I know what you're thinking. The bar will abso-*fucking*-lutely be our second date."

chapter fifteen

Our second date kind of sucked. Yeah, it was fun to sit on a barstool and stare at West and watch his ass shake when he mixed cocktails and bent over to scoop up grog. It was far less amusing watching all the ladies, and I use that term loosely, offer themselves up to him as not-so-virgin sacrifices. The Wreck clearly did not have self-respect on tap. I sighed as a girl just happened to spill her drink down her shirt. A sheer white tank top. Her big doe eyes widened as she pressed the cocktail napkin to her breast, rubbing at the damp spot until her nipple hardened. Oh, look! West had more napkins to save the day.

How nice.

West sent me a pained look and rolled his eyes. The girl looked barely legal as it was. It was like a guppy taunting a shark.

Stupid girl.

Sharks like to chase their prey.

Needing a break from all the calculated desperation clogging the bar area, I escaped to the bathroom. The stall I picked had a working lock—thank God for small favors—and I forced myself to take a deep cleansing breath as I sat there. Okay, yeah, that was poor planning on my part, since the bathroom reeked of covert cigarettes, drugstore perfume, and stale urine, but it was the thought that counted.

Like the rest of the bar, the bathroom was covered in graffiti. I never understood how people always just seemed to have Sharpies handy when they felt like marking their territory. I looked over the scribbled messages that peppered the wall.

Ohmygod—West lives up to the hype, every inch of it! <3 Jaymie

Wyatt is mine 4ever. The *mine* had been crossed out and *Kim's* was written above it.

Right below that it said, *Kim's a slut-faced hoebag.* Huh, eloquent.

Several seemed to echo the popular sentiment, *West is so hot.*

I spotted a bubble-lettered, *Theo is a sweetheart,* which probably wasn't what he was hoping the girls bathroom said about him, considering the other notes about male anatomy it was tucked between.

But what started to piss me off was the drawing of an erect cock with the words, *West* and *life-sized* scrawled next to it. Other inscriptions saying, *agreed!* and *totally!* and *yum!* had arrows pointing to the image.

The artist was accurate too. Whoever the slut-faced hoebag

was.

I did a quick survey of the other wall of the cramped stall and saw my date for the evening was the star attraction and, boy, did he shine.

Just as I started to flush and rearrange my bikini bottoms under my dress, I heard two sets of footsteps echo off the stained concrete floor.

"Amber, did you see that hopeless blonde that's been hovering at the bar all night? I think West feels bad for her or something, he keeps going to check on her."

"Yeah, but I asked him about it. He said she was his *date!*" Her sarcastic tone conveyed how ridiculous she considered that. They snickered and the sound of running water gurgling in the sink did little to muffle their words.

I stilled, shamelessly eavesdropping.

"She doesn't even look like she's taken a shower today."

"I know! And her skin looks creepy under the lights! Maybe West had too many shots or something tonight. He has better standards than that. It's an insult to all of us who've come before her."

They dissolved into laughter, and the water turned off.

"Let's try offering him a combo. He's gone for it before."

"Mmm, you know I love a good BOGO deal, Tipper. It's worth a try. I think his *date's* disappeared anyway. She must have gotten the hint."

Their laughter faded and a hollow *thunk* of the door closing signaled their exit.

Wow.

Just—wow.

My mind whirled, and I was annoyed I hadn't been able to see them through the crack between the stall door and the wall. How many other girls out there had already screwed my West? I made a face as I flushed the toilet, berating myself for letting things with him go past a quick fuck-and-duck.

I finished adjusting my admittedly wrinkled dress, opened the stall door with more force than necessary, and peered at myself in the crappy mirror. What the hell had that slut said about my skin?

Oh.

Oh!

I looked down at my arm, pressed the fingers of my other hand onto my skin, and let go. Five fingerprints glowed white before returning to an angry, lobster-red hue. The skin around my eyes seemed okay, thanks to the protection my gold-rimmed aviators had provided, but the rest of me looked almost fluorescent, like a raccoon in reverse. My hair was crinkled like old straw, frizzed and barely contained by my sad excuse for a braid.

I *might* have been so caught up in West earlier that I had forgotten sunscreen. And to look in a mirror once we got off the boat.

Maybe. Possibly.

No wonder those girls had been mocking me. I looked like a hot mess. Like, roasted.

Running a cautious fingertip over my shoulder, the tenderness of my skin confirmed the extent of my sunburn. I needed to roll like a pig in a puddle of aloe, stat.

The time had come to call this date a failure and make a quick exit, only I didn't have my Wrangler. We'd dropped off the dog and picnic supplies at West's place and come straight here in his oversized truck.

Twisting to see the back of my head, I finger combed my hair as best I could, letting it fall around my face to try to hide my Ray-Ban tan lines. Then I took the coward's way out and sent West a text that I wasn't feeling well and was taking a cab back home.

Slipping my tote bag over my shoulder, I skirted the perimeter of the bar, escaping out the front doors without looking back. I was standing on the front sidewalk and searching for the number of the cab company on my phone when it was suddenly snatched right out of my hands.

I gasped, taking a step back, and tucked my bag to my side.

"Running away?"

How the fuck had West gotten out of there so fast?

I dropped my gaze and let my hair hide my eyes, trying to disguise the worst of the damage.

"Yeah, I think I got a little too much sun," I mumbled, not wanting to meet his eyes. Even though it was after eight, the sun was just beginning its descent, and there was still plenty of daylight.

He hooked my hip with his hand and tugged me closer. Using his free hand, he tipped my chin up, exposing my face. Eyes widening, he touched my cheek with the tip of his finger, wincing as he removed it. "Shit, Sadie, you've got to be in pain. Hold on, let me tell Wyatt I've got to get you home."

I snorted. "Wouldn't you rather stay here? I'm sure there are other toys you can play with instead."

"What the fuck are you talking about?"

"Amber and Tipper would be more than willing to entertain you tonight. Together."

West glanced toward the bar then back at me, annoyance splashed across his face. He moved closer, invading my personal space, and loomed over me, his eyes flashing gray storm clouds, but I stood my ground, refusing to step back. "I'm two inches from the person I want to be with tonight. Two inches. And I'd be happy to erase those two inches if you're still not clear on that."

I watched as he called his brother. I tried protesting that I was capable of taking care of myself, but he just talked louder and put a finger over my lips until he finished. After pressing the end button, he shoved his phone in his pocket and nudged me farther under the overhanging roofline, into the shadows. "Stay tucked back here out of the sun while I pull the truck around," he instructed, his narrowed eyes daring me to argue.

I sighed and crossed my arms, my chin jutting out, but I nodded once in defeat.

When we got back to the cottage, and I tossed my beach bag on the kitchen table, I found a note stuck on the fridge from Rue, telling me she had gone out but would be back in the morning. I tried to crumple it up, but West had already seen it.

His lazy smirk was out in full force as he plucked the wad of paper from my hand and threw it in the trash. "Good. Because I plan on taking care of you tonight."

"West, really, you can head back to the bar. I'll be fine. I'm just going to take a shower and aloe up."

His eyes darkened, and his lips twitched. "Sounds like a good plan. I'll help."

Muttering to myself about stubborn men, I headed to the bathroom and turned the shower on, adjusting the temperature to lukewarm. I eased my sundress over my head and dropped it in a heap on the floor, ignoring West as he lounged in the doorway, watching me.

Nudging the door with my toe, I tried to edge him out of the small room, but he pushed it back open and planted himself in the opening. With one hand, he pulled his shirt over his head, adding it to the pile I had started on the tile floor. When he started unbuttoning his jeans, I covered his hand with mine, stilling his motion.

"What are you doing?"

"Assisting you. It's my fault you're burned. I had sunscreen on the boat—I should have thought of it. I didn't even think about your skin being unprotected while you napped on that bean bag."

Reaching behind my neck, he tugged on the strings of my bikini until the top loosened and fell, exposing my breasts. He sucked in a sharp breath, and I glanced in the mirror. The sharp delineation between my sunburn and my pale chest looked almost cartoonish.

"Fuck, Sadie." West scooted closer but stopped short of touching me. "That looks worse than I realized. You *need* to let me help you."

After undressing and helping me ease my swimsuit bottoms down my legs, he ushered me into the shower and stepped in behind me, blocking the spray from directly hitting my tender skin. Using his hands and some creamy body wash, he bathed me, his touch light as a feather around my shoulders, which seemed to be the worst.

Working efficiently and wincing in sympathy when I hissed out a breath when his fingers scraped a tender area, he soaped me up, rinsed me off, and wrapped me in a fluffy towel before depositing me on the end of my bed. I dragged a brush through my hair and twisted it into a wet bun atop my head. There was no way I was using a hot hair dryer tonight. While I worked on taming my mane, West rummaged around my medicine cabinet and returned with two ibuprofen and a bottle of water to wash it down. I swallowed the small pills and drank most of the bottle before handing it back.

Flicking off the lights when he returned from putting the medicine up, he spread two large towels on top of my quilt and then moved me to the middle of the bed, my damp towel still draped around me. The muted yellow glow of the streetlight filtering through the curtain left most of his face in shadow, making the angles and planes harsher. Holding the oversized bottle of aloe, West settled next to me on the mattress, sympathy coloring his expression. He squirted a glob of the green gel into his palm and twisted to face me.

"Ready?"

I nodded, bracing myself for how cold it was going to feel.

Starting from the top, he smoothed his fingertips over my forehead, down my nose, and across my cheekbones, tracing the contours of my face. I bit my lip, the coolness of the aloe warring with a small spark of arousal as his fingers set off tingles and goose bumps everywhere he touched. His palm slid down my throat, cupping it, before following the curve of my shoulder. I shivered, my nipples hardening into buds under the towel. He worked his way down one arm and then the other, discovering my inner elbows were ticklish in the process. His lips quirked when I drew back, but neither of us broke the silence.

Taking my right hand in both of his, he turned it upwards and dug his thumbs into the meat of my palm, rubbing from the center out. Then he moved higher, working the tender flesh at the base of my fingers and between the joints before finishing with each individual finger from base to tip, never hurrying but taking the time to go over every area two or three times. You know the way your scalp tingles when someone plays with your hair? I was feeling that times a hundred. By the time he had repeated the process on my left hand, I was boneless.

I'd never in my life had a guy spend so much time on just my hands, never realized how erotic it could be, how many nerve endings could light up as his callused fingers abraded my tender skin. My breathing became slower, heavier, and my eyes closed, all of my focus on where our bodies touched.

I missed when he let go, although the dip and sway of the mattress as he shifted around on the bed told me he hadn't gone far. When he picked up my foot and started a good, old-fashioned rub, I couldn't stifle the quiet moan that escaped my mouth. His touch wasn't sexual, but everything about the moment seemed heightened.

The darkened room. The soft rustle of our cotton towels as he moved. The ball of his hand pressing into the arch of my foot. The heavy thud of my heart. It was overwhelming and not enough at the same time.

He gave my toes the same treatment he had my fingers, focusing on each individual digit as well as the soft skin in between. The back of my heels came next and then he started a path up my legs. He pulled my feet into his lap, and his hardness strained against the towel wrapped around his waist. My lips parted.

His strokes became more gentle as he moved upwards, where the sunburn was worse. Knees, thighs. He moved all the way to my bikini line, and I couldn't help spreading my legs a little. A rough sound left the back of his throat, my motion not going unnoticed.

The towel was suddenly removed, leaving me naked, bare to his eyes. I inhaled sharply. The urge to cover my chest was strong, knowing my stark tan lines looked garish at best, but I forced my hands to stay at my sides.

The chill of the aloe along my collarbones made me gasp in surprise. I'd expected him to still be working from the bottom up. My nipples tightened even further, and I bit my lower lip. He smeared my chest with the aloe, staying clear of my unharmed skin, which meant he touched me everywhere but my aching breasts. His fingers stroked my stomach, tracing the curves of my waist and hips, drifting lower before again stopping where my sunburn ended.

It was such a fucking tease.

I arched my back, reaching for his touch, wanting more. He settled his palm on the rise of my left hip, pushing me back down into the pillowtop mattress. As he stretched out on his side next to me, I reached around him with my right arm and clutched his back, wanting more contact with his warmth. My eyes lowered partway, peering at him hovering over me, his finger drawing a line between my breasts.

He settled a thigh between my spread legs, and I realized his towel was gone. I couldn't stop my hips from circling, seeking friction, warmth pooling in my core.

His thumb tracing my lip distracted me, and I met his gaze, my own eyes begging.

He breathed my name.

"Please," I whispered.

He shook his head, his eyes moving down my body. He shifted closer, his lips almost brushing mine. "You're too burned for fucking, babe. But your best parts—" he skimmed a nipple "—they're okay. So I'm going to take care of you tonight. Like I said I would."

I scraped my nails down his back in protest, wanting his heavy weight pressing me into the bed, but he just kissed the tip of my nose before pulling back. Even my lips were burned.

His right arm reached across me, a single finger moving to circle my left breast. He started wide, moving in ever-tightening rings, but stopped short of the eager peak. He teased the other one, until they both felt swollen and heavy, and I squirmed beside him, trying to get his hand where I wanted it most.

"Patience, Sadie. I promise you'll sleep well tonight by the time I'm through."

I wrinkled my nose and huffed in annoyance and was rebuked with a sharp pinch to my nipple.

I hissed his name in surprise, narrowing my eyes, but ended on a moan when his lips closed over the tight bud. He mouthed me, licking with the flat of his tongue, his actions a delicious torment. I speared my fingers through his hair, the spiky strands too short to grip properly, my nails raking his scalp and urging him closer. His lips smiled against my hot flesh before tightening over me, pulling and sucking the way I needed him to.

My hips bucked, and my eyes closed, heat coursing through me and settling low.

More, more, more.

The thought was the only one in my head, looping.

He switched sides, and his talented hand cupped the other breast, squeezing it and teasing the sensitive tip. I pulled his head tighter, not wanting to be teased any longer, and he nuzzled closer, his day-old scruff a welcome torment as he buried his head against me.

"West." His name was a mere sigh, and he hummed in response, the vibration adding another level of bliss.

He released the breast he had been caressing, his hand lowering to my damp core. His middle finger ran the length of my slit, top to bottom, bottom to top, before easing inside.

He growled and clamped down on my nipple with his lips, while his finger slipped into me and stroked. My hips lifted, more than ready, but he kept the pace slow, removing his hand after only a few thrusts and circling my clit.

I whimpered his name in frustration, and he laughed once against my chest, his warm breath puffing on my overheated skin.

Giving in to my hands pushing against his shoulders, he worked his way down my body, avoiding touching my sensitive stomach. Settling between my legs, he lifted my thighs over his shoulders and made his first slow pass with the flat of his tongue. I about came unglued.

I moaned and dug my heels into his back, trying to force him where I wanted, no, needed him most. He hummed an acknowledgement and separated my folds, delving deeper until his mouth latched onto my swollen clit. His tongue swirled, lapping gently, and my fingers pressed against his head in time with his slow sucks. I'm impatient by nature though, and it wasn't long before I was using my hips and hands to ask for more.

He responded, his lips pulling more firmly against my folds, his tongue flicking, and his roughened cheeks scraping my inner thighs. I was close, so close, and mindless noises spilled from my open mouth.

Two thick fingers pushed into me roughly, and it was enough. My thighs tightened around his head, clamping him to me, and I whispered an endless chain of his name and "Now, now, *now,*" into the dim room.

He stayed with me, his tongue softening as my hips slowed their grinding rolls against him, not releasing me until my hands fell away from his head. Then he pressed soft kisses over my sex, almost reverently, inhaling and licking his lips. The sound of his appreciation mingled with my ragged breathing.

His hands snaked up my body, plumping my heavy breasts and tweaking a nipple to get my attention.

I opened a sleepy eye and peeked down at him, unable to do more.

His husky voice was a mix of threat and promise. "You get three minutes. Then I'm going in for round two."

chapter sixteen

By morning, my discomfort was gone, although I wasn't sure if the credit should go to the aloe and ibuprofen or the flexibility and stamina of West's tongue. I rolled over toward him, wanting to snuggle and ignore the stubborn sunbeams infiltrating my bedroom blinds.

But the bed was empty—the pillow indentation from his head all that remained.

I frowned and propped myself up on my hands to look around. His pants were gone, but his shirt was still balled on the chest at the foot of the bed. Unable to resist, I grabbed it for myself, slipping it over my head and breathing him in, filling my lungs with his salt and citrus scent. Tugging on some hiphugger panties, I headed to the bathroom to brush my teeth and use the bathroom before I went looking for him.

When I emerged five minutes later, happy to find my sunburn only lingering on my shoulders and face, I was awake enough to smell the scent of bacon drifting through the cottage. Helpless to resist the allure of the crispy, greasy goodness, I followed my nose to the kitchen where West was holding a spatula and a cup of coffee while poking at two skillets. One had bacon, and, at the moment, I didn't care about the other one, because he was *shirtless*, cooking breakfast in *my* kitchen, and it was such a sexy moment that I couldn't help but stop, stare, and take it all in.

Until Rue appeared across the living room, halting when she spotted him. She stalked across the room to my side and snatched my elbow to pull me closer to her.

"What is he doing here?" she hissed. "You know the rules."

I opened my mouth. Closed it. Lifted my hand and dropped it again.

"Cooking breakfast?" I offered in a weak voice.

"Morning to you too, Rue!" West called cheerfully, pointing at the counter with his spatula. "Coffee's ready and the pancakes are almost done."

"Mmmm, pancakes," I whispered, more to myself than to her.

Rue elbowed me in the ribs.

I made my eyes big and pleading and then hit her with the full force of my puppy dog expression, sticking my lower lip out for emphasis. "He made coffee and bacon and pancakes. Can't we bend the rules just this once?"

She looked at me flatly, then clomped to the coffee pot, pouring herself a mug and dumping several spoonfuls of sugar in it.

Turning from the stovetop, he squinted in her direction. "Someone," he started, "did not have a good evening. Unlike the rest of us." He tossed a wink at me over his shoulder, and I held the back of the couch to keep from melting into the floor.

"Someone," she mimicked, "didn't think I would mind waiting while he used his vacuum pump to prepare himself last night." She snorted in disgust and shook her head, as if trying to rid herself of that particular memory.

I gasped, my eyes widening, and covered my burgeoning laugh with my hand.

She shot me a dirty look and grunted before taking a big swallow of coffee and mumbling something that I couldn't catch but had West shaking his head.

"It's not fucking funny," she insisted, but a grin had started to work on one corner of her mouth.

I walked to her side and laid my head on her shoulder, curling my arm around her waist for a quick squeeze. "Yeah, it kind of is."

Working the griddle like he'd been doing it for years, my shirtless date drizzled batter onto the hot pan, making some kind of abstract design. I made my way over to the counter for my own cup of coffee, and by the time I'd added an ice cube to cool it down and taken my first few sips, he was sliding the fresh pancake onto a plate and handing it to Rue.

She took the plate, added a few strips of bacon, and sat on a barstool at the island in the middle of the kitchen. Her sudden burst of laughter startled me, the coffee cup almost slipping from my hands, and I set it down to wipe a few stray drops from my fingers with a paper towel.

"What's so funny?"

She tilted her plate in my direction, showing me the penis-shaped pancake sitting on it, complete with a bulbous mushroom head and two oversized balls.

My gaze flew to West, where he stood grinning to himself as he flipped more pancakes.

He shrugged, sensing my scrutiny "Everyone should be able to start the day with a big dick. This is the best I can do to help her out."

I didn't think my eyes could widen any farther as I was caught between horror and mirth, my lips unsure whether they should tip up or down. Without a word, I snagged the bottle of syrup and walked to her plate, adding a sticky stream of maple from the tip, down the exaggerated erection, and oozing over the balls.

She chuckled as she took her fork, viciously cut off the tip, and shoved it in her mouth. "This is so much better than what was offered to me last night," she whined around the food in her mouth. She sent me a look that told me I was forgiven, at least this time, for breaking the rules.

I grinned back at her, helpless to stop myself from imagining more mornings like this, just hanging around the cottage with my bestie and my . . .

Okay, well, I didn't know what to call him yet, because it seemed way too soon for boyfriend, but friend didn't work either. My mind shuffled through some other possible labels until a plate was dropped in front of me.

With my own penis pancake.

Grabbing the syrup, I helped my breakfast find its own happy ending.

Rue perched on her stool, drinking her second up of coffee and scrolling through her phone, while West and I cleaned up the kitchen—which would've gone faster if I could make myself stop staring at his rippled muscles as he towel-dried the pans, but I wasn't complaining.

His hip bumped mine as I scrubbed the skillets in the sink, and suds sloshed over the edge, dripping to the tiled floor. I watched the path the bubbles were making down the cabinet but didn't move to catch it right away, instead giving him a questioning look.

"I have clients booked all week, but are you free next Saturday?"

I shook my head, my wavy strands falling in my face. "I'm shooting a wedding that morning. I won't be done until late afternoon."

West's face fell. "I wanted to try to take you paddleboarding. I think you'd like it. We could go for a short ride before it gets dark if you get done in time."

I took a deep breath. The man did *not* know how to ask.

"I've never done that before," I said.

"You'll love it," he promised. "We'll stick to the creeks where there are no waves. It's a good place to see dolphins too."

"We'll see if I get done in time."

"I'll wait so you can come with me," he countered.

I laughed. "I think you already took care of that last night."

Rue slapped the counter. "I can hear you, you know." She shoved her empty coffee cup next to the sink, pausing next to me. "*This* is why we have rules!" Shooting a final glare at the bare-chested man next to me, she stomped off to her room, shutting the door. Loud music thumped from that side of the cottage a minute later.

I twisted my lips. "I don't think the pancake penis was enough."

He slanted me a wary look. "I ain't offering her any other kind. She looks like she might bite."

"Mmm. I wouldn't mind giving you a little nibble."

Reaching across me, he turned off the faucet and started pulling me back toward my room, the expression on his face saying it all. I barely noticed my soap-covered hands leaving a trail of puddles behind me as he tugged on the hem of the oversized t-shirt—his shirt—that hung around my thighs. I locked the door behind us and turned up my radio too.

Yeah, rules were made to be broken.

APPARENTLY, SO WERE DATES.

I frowned at my phone, looking at the text from West on Friday. *Sorry, babe, something came up. We'll have to reschedule paddleboarding.*

The whole week had been an awkward series of mixed signals.

Monday morning, I'd found a paper airplane tucked under my windshield wiper, along with a Starbucks gift card. Unfolding the notebook paper, I'd read his sweet message: *Wish I was there to make you breakfast this morning again. This is the best I can do.*

I'd texted him a thank you but had gotten no response. All day. I texted him twice the next day. Same thing.

Radio silence.

Annoyed, I'd put him out of my head on Wednesday, squeezing in another boudoir photo shoot after work for the wife of the president of the local hospital. She'd looked fabulous, but I'm guessing that's one of the perks of having friends who were plastic surgeons.

I assumed Aubrey was responsible for that referral, but I couldn't bring myself to ask the precious older lady how she'd gotten my name. Betty had been adorable, though, feisty and irreverent and more than willing to follow my directions. She'd even brought along a naughty nurse's outfit, and her outrageous personality shined through the poses. It was too bad I couldn't use the boudoir images for advertising purposes—some of my best work recently had come from those bookings.

As I'd slipped into bed late that night after editing Betty's session, a familiar rapping on my window had my pulse skyrocketing. West slipped into the room and joined me for a sleepover, looking exhausted. He'd stripped to his boxers and then pulled me close, holding my back to his front. Mumbling an apology about the texts, he explained that he didn't get a signal that far offshore and had just found my messages and come straight over after prepping the boat for tomorrow. He'd barely gotten the words out of his mouth before he'd fallen asleep, his thigh pinning me down and his hand cupping my breast. When I'd woken up a few hours later, he was already gone, another paper airplane left behind on his pillow.

You're fucking gorgeous when you're asleep.

I didn't text him this time, knowing he wouldn't see it. Instead, after work I found his truck at the marina and left a paper airplane of my own for him.

Google it: Marine wi-fi extender.

Friday morning, I unfolded another paper plane, discovering a creased Amazon invoice, his order for the long range device due for delivery next week. I'd smiled all day about that.

Until I saw his text, cancelling our date.

Unsure what that meant, or where to go from there, I kept my distance. I did the wedding shoot on Saturday, which went better than I expected, and had a girl's night in with Rue, drinking her spiked lemonade, watching Ryan Gosling movies, and talking until the wee hours of the morning.

I refused to think about him that night, even as I stayed on the side of the bed that had become mine, leaving half of it empty.

On Sunday, after texting with my parents and brother back in

Tennessee, I logged onto Facebook to check out the video of a new singer they were working with when I noticed a friend request from Aubrey.

Unsure what to think, I stared at it. That little request seemed loaded, and my gut warned me to ignore it, to go back in time and unsee it.

I watched the video, left a comment, scrolled through my feed, and came back to the friend request. I clicked accept, knowing I did owe her for all the photography referrals and couldn't really afford to snub her.

Curiosity drove me to check out her page. Her cover image was a tasteful shot of her and her parents in Italy, the Leaning Tower of Pisa tipping in the background. The most recent post on her feed was from last night, a shot of her posing next to a palm tree, the ocean in the background.

With her arm around West.

I enlarged the image, dissecting the picture, my stomach churning. Was his stance friendly or affectionate? His mouth was turned up on one side, and he was wearing sunglasses, hiding his eyes, his little smirk the only thing I had to go on. She was leaning into him, showing her teeth, her other arm resting possessively on his chest. West stood straight, no lean. Did that mean something? Nothing? Is *this* why he cancelled on me?

Yes.

Clearly, it was. I refused to be stupid about this.

I scrolled farther down. Aubrey was a big fan of the selfie. And the toothy smile. And the tilted head.

There. Two weeks ago. Another shot with West—at a deli along the boardwalk.

I bit the inside of my cheek, feeling hot tears sting my eyes.

It was happening again. West was turning out like Asshole, hiding another life from me.

Except—was he? Two weeks ago, we hadn't even been on a date yet. Maybe I had misread the situation, but I'd felt like things were building up between us.

That picture, though, her putting her hands on him like she had a right to, him letting her . . . it hurt. I closed my laptop, pushed it across my quilt, and curled into a ball. The faint scent of West lingered on the sheets that I hadn't changed since last week when he'd rubbed aloe and his tongue all over me. I held on to that memory, even as I wondered where he had slept last night.

Because it hadn't been here with me.

Four more days passed without a word from West.

I changed my sheets.

Took photos of kids with first birthday cakes smashed on their faces. Shot images of a couple celebrating their fiftieth wedding anniversary, their hands never letting go of each other. Captured stills of two foolish teenagers getting engaged far too young, thinking they had some clue about what love was and how to hold onto it forever.

Idiots.

I had two meetings with Grady about photography opportunities at Water's Edge, and he had my hopes up, alluding to a big project he wanted to assign me to but was just waiting for the final approval from his boss. As I left our meeting that Thursday, I asked Grady if he'd had a falling out with Rue.

His face blanched, and he froze with his hand on the doorknob to see me out. "Why? What did she say?"

Interesting.

"She didn't. But things seemed tense between y'all the other week."

His knuckles turned white, and his lips pressed into a hard line. "I have no problem with Rue. If something seemed off, it must be on her end."

Riiiiight, nothing weird going on there at all.

I smiled at him and slipped out of his office, leaving him to his thoughts, and unable to stop myself from wondering what Rue had found wrong with him. I'd almost asked last weekend, after we finished *Crazy Stupid Love* for the millionth time, but something stopped me every time I went to open my mouth. Meddling never helped, in my experience.

As I left the resort, I ran into Theo in the parking lot as he was headed to his car, which was parked a few spots ahead of mine.

"Hey, Sadie! What are you up to tonight?"

I shrugged. "Maybe a run down on the beach? Nothing much."

"Have you been to the drive-in yet? I feel like getting out of town for the night. Want to see if Rue wants to go, and we can make a night of it? If we leave in the next hour or so, we have time to grab some munchies and get there before the show starts."

My eyes widened. "There's a working drive-in movie theater around here?"

"Yeah, about an hour inland, past the Air Force base. There's a double feature at sundown."

I hesitated and checked my phone. No messages. My fingers tightened around the device, as if it was its fault I hadn't heard from *him*. "You know what, Theo? That sounds perfect."

If he could detect the forced enthusiasm, he didn't show it.

"Great!" He stubbed his rubber flip flop against the asphalt and peeked up at me from under his floppy hair. "Do you mind driving? The Wrangler would work better than my piece of shit here. I'll spring for gas and food."

My eyes softened. "No problem. Want to swing by after you change?"

By the time I got home, took a shower, and threw on some comfy clothes—Nike shorts and a faded Vanderbilt shirt—Rue had packed us a cooler of beer, and Theo had arrived with two Piggly Wiggly bags of junk food.

This was exactly what I needed. A night with friends, way too many calories, and physical distance from everything that reminded me of West.

On the car ride, we cranked up the radio and sang along to Top 40, failing horribly at the hip hop songs but singing louder just the same. Well, Theo and I failed. Rue held her own, the pink tips of her hair whipping around her as we flew down the highway.

Dusk was falling when we pulled into the field, and we divvied up the snacks. Little Debbie cakes, kettle chips, and more candy than we could eat littered the dash and console, and freshly-cracked beers were ready in the cup holders.

"What's playing tonight, anyway?" Rue asked, taking a sip of Bud Light.

Theo shoved half an oatmeal cream pie in his mouth before answering. "Who cares?"

They clinked beer cans, and we settled back against the seats, Theo propping his legs up on the armrest, and Rue and I reclining the seats back.

We chatted while the opening credits rolled and trucks and SUV's parked around us, gorging ourselves on artificial flavors and additives, washing it down with mind-numbing alcohol.

"We need to pace ourselves, guys. I've only got one more thingy of beer left." She held up the empty plastic rings from the first six-pack.

The previews were just starting when two trucks pulled into the row behind us, about half a dozen vehicles down. One was a black extended cab pickup, the other a familiar jacked up dually.

My heart thudded, beating against my ribs and threatening to split my hard won indifference into something wide open and gaping.

The cellophane from my honey bun package crinkled in my clenched fist as I sat upright, squinting through the growing dark at the new arrivals.

Wyatt, Trevor, Aubrey, and two other skinny girls spilled

out of the black truck, laughing and hauling gear with them. The door to the dually remained stubbornly closed for another dozen painful heartbeats.

Finally, it eased open, and there he was, looked deliciously rumpled in a wrinkled tee and cargo shorts.

West.

chapter seventeen

My chest expanded sharply, humid air filling my lungs and forgetting to leave, and my foot reached for the brake pedal as if that would stop this whole scene unfolding before me.

I couldn't look away as they lowered their tailgates and part of the group settled into cheap folding lawn chairs in the back of Wyatt's truck. Aubrey skipped over to the dually and waited until West lifted her up to the high truck bed, his hands spanning her whole waist. She dropped down into one of his orange bean bags, wiggling her barely-covered ass into the vinyl, and stretched her long legs out in front of her, angling them across the space.

West hopped up into the truck bed, plopped on the other poof, and rested his head back against the toolbox, staring up at the sky, his whole body sagging.

A twinge of sympathy swelled—he looked exhausted—but I

smothered it, burying it under a thick layer of I-don't-give-a-shit.

The movie started, and I forced myself to face the oversized screen, although I couldn't help stealing covert peeks. The brightness from the projector did a decent job of lighting the field, and I was a glutton for punishment, intent on watching how my own personal horror show was going to play out.

After my fifth or sixth glance to the side, Rue got annoyed.

"Sadie!" Her loud voice carried over the background music of the opening credits. "What in the hell do you keep looking at?"

She stood up on the seat of the Jeep and turned to her left, her chestnut and pink hair a beacon, causing several heads to turn in our direction.

My face burned hotter than last week's sunburn, and I slunk as low as I could in my seat, wishing I could bury myself under all the wrappers on my floorboard.

From a few spots down the field, I heard Wyatt's voice answer. "Rue? Are y'all here too?"

Rue lifted her hand in greeting, squinting in his direction, and then she turned her big brown eyes to me, silently asking me questions I didn't know the answers to.

I focused on my breathing, squishing my eyes shut in mortification. In, out. Slow and easy. Repeat.

A whoosh of air signaled my door being yanked open, and I grabbed the steering wheel as if I was in danger of falling out.

His presence was palpable as he loomed over me—I could feel his eyes raking down my body, a hot caress that had my traitorous thighs pressing together in response. Only West had ever made me feel that way—a visceral awareness that seeped through me, saturating my limbs with pure, unadulterated desire. I fought it, battling it into submission.

My body was weak. I knew it. *He* knew it.

I needed to let my head handle this conversation, not my worthless fluttering heart.

"Sadie?" His voice sounded low and rough, and I bit my lip, ignoring the curl of desire flaring inside me at just the sound of him.

Oh, now he wants to talk to me?

My inner bitch reminded me of the Italian princess currently warming his truck bed, and the flame fizzled out. My fingers relaxed, uncurled, and dropped back into my lap.

Tilting my head up to him, I responded in a curt voice. "Yes?"

"What are you doing here?" He sounded thrilled, a grin slashing his face, and he ran a warm hand down my cheek, cupping my jaw.

Rue snorted beside me. "I think the better question is—what is *she* doing here?" There was no mistaking the distaste in her tone as she nodded toward West's truck.

He glanced over, running his hand through his hair and gripping the back of his neck. Turning back to me, he shrugged. "Wyatt brought her. I didn't even know she was coming."

I looked him in the eye and kept my question soft, fighting my growing need to yell at him from sheer frustration. "What are you doing here?"

He snagged one of my hands and starting tugging me from

the Jeep. "Now? Watching a movie with my favorite girl."

One foot was on the ground, one still in the Jeep when I pulled free, shaking my head. "Nope. You gotta do better than that." I picked up my beer and took a swallow, needing to break physical contact with him.

The body is weak, the mind is strong.

Propping his arms on the doorframe, he leaned down, catching my gaze. He opened his mouth to speak, but Theo interrupted before any sound escaped.

"Damn, this is better than the movie. Is it going to be R-rated too?" He crunched on a handful of chips and held the bag out toward Rue.

I ignored him.

West moved closer and ran his fingers along my hairline, pushing a chunk behind my ear. "Sadie?"

My chest rose and fell as I gritted my teeth against the instinct to lean into his hand.

The mind is fucking strong.

Crossing my arms over my chest, I pushed my skull farther into the headrest. "It was a good question, West. What is she doing here?"

"Watching a movie, I guess. What are you getting at? I already told you I didn't know she was coming. She rode with Wyatt." His brow furrowed, and he backed up a step.

"And what about on Saturday?"

He regarded me steadily, meeting my gaze head-on. "My grandmother called me on Friday to ask Wyatt and me to please join her for a family dinner on Saturday. I didn't realize she had invited the Perottis over for dessert to discuss the gala."

I forged ahead. "And the picture?"

"What picture?"

"Palm tree, her wrapped around you, ring a bell?"

West clenched his jaw. "Her mom asked to take our picture. I didn't want to cause a scene at my grandparents, so I posed for the damn picture. Hailey and Wyatt were standing right there too. We took a group shot after that. What's going on here, Sadie?"

"Why haven't I heard from you since Friday?"

Just then, Aubrey slipped up behind him, wrapping her arms around his bicep, tugging on him and licking her lips while staring straight at me, her eyes bright with victory.

"West, baby, you're missing the movie. Come back to the truck."

I saw red.

I saw motherfucking matador red.

"Hey, Sadie. I hope you've been getting the referrals I've sent your way."

I attempted a smile of acknowledgement in her direction but ending up baring my teeth at best.

Sneaky bitch.

Aubrey pulled on his arm again.

Theo mumbled something behind me, and Rue shifted, pressing against my side, but whether it was to urge me on or to hold me back, I couldn't tell. Holding my breath, I kept my attention fixed on West.

He inhaled and shot an irritated glance over his shoulder before pulling his arm free. "I'm good here."

The corner of my lip twitched, but he saw it.

And then he swooped.

I was cradled in his arms and most of the way to his truck before I figured out what was happening. My hand pressed against his chest, and I froze, paralyzed between holding on tight and pushing him away. I couldn't see where Aubrey ended up, but really, I didn't give a fuck.

"Don't even think it." The warning fell hot against my temple, and my fingers curled into his shirt, still indecisive, fisting the worn cotton.

His muscles flexed beneath me, and I failed to stop the shudder that ran through me.

The body is weak, so fucking weak.

West set me on the tailgate before vaulting up next to me and pulling me into his lap on one of the beanbags. My ass rubbed against his crotch as he settled deep into the seat with me across him, stretching his legs out wide to cradle me in between them. He buried his face in my hair and took a deep breath, his chest pushing outward, and then he exhaled with a happy sigh.

Like a recurrent nightmare I couldn't shake, Aubrey appeared at the tailgate with her hands on her hips, glaring up at me. Rearranging her sneer into a pout, her voice dripping honey, she appealed to West. "You gonna help me up too?"

I stiffened, my eyes narrowing to slits, but he wrapped his big arm around my middle, forcing me to conform to his relaxed posture.

He yawned before answering. "Nope. Why don't you go sit with Wyatt and them? Do you want the other bean bag? I think me and Sadie can make do with one." He flexed his hips and pressed his growing length against my side.

She couldn't have seen his movement, but she must have noticed the change in my expression because her eyes widened and she stepped back, sucking in a breath and stumbling as she turned toward the other truck. Her words were ripped away by the breeze, and, while I didn't catch the specifics, her angry tone wasn't lost on me. I didn't watch the rest of her retreat.

Instead, I rounded on West and pinned him with a flat look.

He gazed back at me through sleepy eyes, one side of his mouth hitched up. "You didn't want her to stay, did you?"

I huffed out a breath but didn't respond, continuing to watch him.

His brows drew together, and he brushed his thumb over my cheek. "Are you mad at me?"

My tongue traced my upper teeth in sheer frustration, and I pushed his hand off my face.

"I don't get you," I seethed. "You cancelled our date, ignored me all week, met other girls here, and now you're acting like we're together?" I tried to shove off his lap, but the slippery vinyl under me made it difficult.

West sat up straighter, leaning down until our noses were almost touching, his eyes glittering. His voice was dangerously soft. "You sound an awful lot like the whiny girl who just slunk away from here. And that's not you. Now what's going on?"

It wasn't a question, it never was with him, and I swore under my breath.

His curse wasn't as mild or quiet as mine when he yanked me closer, putting his full lips close to my ear. They brushed against me as he spoke in an angry, rapid whisper. "It's been a week from fucking hell, and I'm not sure what's got your panties in a twist, but running into you here has been the best goddamn thing that's happened to me since I crawled out of your bed a few nights ago. I know I haven't texted, but I left you two paper planes explaining—"

"You what?" I interrupted, my body betraying me and turning pliant in his arms.

His arms softened around me, and he tugged on my earlobe with his teeth, his gentle caress at odds with the growl in his voice.

"Didn't you read my notes? I told you it was going to be a crazy week, and then yesterday someone fucked with my boat, sliced my bean bags, and fucked up one of my engines. I've spent two days driving all over three damn states tracking down parts and getting these new seats from the manufacturer. Last night, when I crashed for a couple hours in the back seat at some shitty truck stop along the interstate, all I could think about was your soft bed and your long, sexy legs wrapped around me. I was heading home to you when Wyatt called and told me him and the guys were coming out here to hang tonight. Asshole guilted me into stopping by for awhile."

Long fingers snagged my chin and turned my face so he could

look into my eyes. I lifted my hands up to hold his wrist, my thumb rubbing over my hair tie that was still there.

"I didn't know she was coming, Sadie. I don't give a fuck about her. I was going to drink a beer or two with my brother, catch a nap, and come knock on your window. *You* were my destination."

His last words echoed in my mind, and my eyes raced over his face, taking in the bags under his eyes, the harsh set of his jaw, the fierce slash of his brows as he waited on my reaction.

"I didn't get the planes."

He scowled at me. "What?"

"I haven't heard from you since you cancelled our date."

His face fell, and he leaned his forehead against mine, his arms tightening around me. Then he pulled back, putting space between us so I could see him in the dim light.

"I'm sorry."

His whispered words, sincere and simple, floated between us.

Unexpectedly, my eyes filled with hot tears, and I sucked in a shaky breath, determined not to let them fall. He swore and hauled me against him, nothing between us but two thin layers of cotton, and rubbed his hand over my back and through my wind-tangled hair. "Sadie. You make me crazy. Did you really think I could just forget about you?"

His mouth pressed against my forehead, my eyelids, the tip of my nose, the corner of my mouth.

"What about tonight?"

His brow crinkled in confusion.

"Why didn't you call me?"

His gaze softened, and he traced my bottom lip with the rough pad of a finger. "Babe, Wyatt called me when I was twenty minutes from here. He bitched about not hanging out much recently and made it sound like a guy's night. I was gonna make a quick appearance and bail. I had no idea those chicks were tagging along. Aubrey said she needed to talk about the gala real quick. You fucking saved me from dealing with her shit any longer."

I bit my lip hard, emotions swirling within me, but it all boiled down to him, the way it felt in the places where our skin touched.

His lips brushed mine, dissolving the last of my anger.

Exhaling, I mumbled against him, "Is that why you smell like General Beauregard? 'Cause you slept in your truck last night?"

He stilled against me. Then his chest vibrated with the force of his laughter. Setting me away from him, he leapt over the side of the truck and pulled open one of the doors. When he ripped his shirt over his head, my mouth fell open in appreciation. The reflected lights danced over his torso, highlighting sharp planes and ridges that I wanted to map, to memorize. Pulling a fresh shirt over his head, he rejoined me on the bean bag, settling me in his lap with my back to his chest, his legs framing mine.

"Better."

Since it wasn't a question, I stayed silent, but reached back and ran my hand over the two-day scruff on his cheek. He nuzzled my palm before nudging my hand out of the way to rub against the sensitive skin on my neck. His lips kissed a path along the angle of my jaw before stopping just below my ear.

"What do I have to do to wake up tomorrow smelling like

you, hmmm?"

His teeth nibbled a retreat, a hum of approval buzzing in his throat. Callused fingers crept under the edge of my long tee, tracing the waistband of my shorts and dipping just under the top.

I slammed my hand on top of his, cutting his exploration short. "Easy there, tiger. This is a bit of a public venue."

Leaning forward and forcing me to do the same, he opened the toolbox behind us and withdrew an oversized striped beach towel, throwing it over our lower bodies and draping it across our bent knees.

He moved my hair until it all fell over one shoulder and then placed hot kisses along the nape of my neck, sending a shiver straight down my spine.

"I've been fucking dying to touch you again, to feel you clench around me and smell you on my fingers. Have you thought about that this week, Sadie? When you were washing your hair with that watermelon shampoo, did you think about my hands on your tits? Did you play with those tight little nipples, wishing I was there?"

His hands snaked under my shirt, teasing the soft skin of my stomach and stroking just under my bra. I squirmed against him, his words making my breasts swell and bead against my cotton bra. His thumb slipped just under the elastic band, brushing the bottom swell on my left. I moaned, and he withdrew his hand, lowering it to circle my belly button.

He tsked in my ear and nodded toward Wyatt's truck, where our friends drank beer and laughed, barely paying attention to the movie. "Can you handle this, Sadie? Can you keep quiet while I touch you?"

I looked around us. The truck bed came almost to our shoulders, and his truck was higher than most to begin with, but with the lawn chairs in the back of Wyatt's truck, we weren't totally hidden. Especially if someone was trying to watch us, like the way Aubrey was glaring at me over her shoulder.

Smirking at her, I raised an eyebrow in her direction, catching her attention, and she whipped her head back around, her hair flying around her shoulders.

I licked my lips and nodded.

He groaned behind me and pulled me against him, pushing his cock against my back. "Do you know what you're doing to me? I've been hard for you every night, aching to sink inside you again, feeling your hot pussy squeeze me."

I spread my legs under the blanket and laid my head back against his chest, surrendering to him, to the moment, to the heat building in my core.

"Take your shorts off. But leave those little cotton panties on that I felt earlier. I want to feel how wet I'm making you."

Wiggling under the terry cloth covering us, I slid my nylon shorts down to my knees and slipped one leg out, giving him full access. Rough palms slid down my stomach, over my hips, and across the tops of my thighs, his fingers spread wide.

He moved his hands between my legs, skimming me as he approached my center. Unable to help myself, I lifted my hips, my pulse thrumming an erratic beat in my throat.

"Easy, Sadie. All in good time. I've waited all week for your sweet pussy. You can wait a few more minutes."

Using just his middle fingers, he followed the lacy trim on my panties, teasing the crease where my thighs met my mound, before following the lace lower, his fingers just outside my sensitive folds.

Shifting, I ground against his cock and felt it pulse against me.

"Which do you want more? My fingers, thrusting deep inside you, stretching you, filling you? Or do you want me to play with your greedy little clit? Is it swollen for me? Begging for attention?"

The palm of his hand cupped me fully, and I stilled, my eyes falling shut at the sensation. The heel of his hand ground against my nub, and his fingers stroked me through the wet cotton.

"You're ready for me, aren't you."

Not a question. Because he knew. He could feel it.

His breath rushed past my ear, hot and heavy, and his rough hands gripped my thighs.

Moments later, he shoved a hand under my soaked panties, two fingers pushing deep, and I arched against him, helpless to stop myself. He brought his other arm across my chest, pinning me to him, and I buried my face against his bicep to keep from crying out.

Working my slippery channel, he twisted his fingers, plunging in and out at a pace that had tension building like a tornado inside of me, focusing all of its power on one tiny spot, swirling higher and faster.

A whimper escaped my lips, and I clenched around his fingers, wanting more, wanting less, so it wouldn't ever end, wanting West.

"Fuck, Sadie. Do you know how hot you feel? Can you feel how hard you make me, just touching you with my fucking hand? When we get back to your house tonight, I'm gonna wrap those silky thighs of yours around my waist and bury my aching cock in your wet heat, and I'm not stopping until I've pumped myself fucking dry. It's gonna be hard, fast, slow, rough, and any other way I can think of between now and then. Are you ready for that, Sadie? Do you need that as much as I do?"

His words had me balancing on the edge, ready to fall, and the light scrape of his thumb over my clit was all I needed.

I bucked in his arms as he held me to him, my long, low moan smothered against the hard muscle of his shoulder.

As aftershocks rocked my limp frame, he lifted his hand to his mouth, licking my wetness off his fingers, his eyes bright and his body taut underneath me.

"I hope that sweet body of yours is ready for me, Sadie. Because I haven't even started yet."

chapter eighteen

TAPPING OUT THE final few keystrokes, I finished the setup of my new Facebook page for Paper Plane Photography. A couple of posts with recent images highlighted the scope of services I offered. Cody's cake smash at West's grandmother's house, the headshots from the realty company, a black-and-white photo of the line of a woman's bare back—a cropped view from a boudoir session from one of Aubrey's friends, the engagement session. I left out the wedding I did six weeks ago because as lucrative as wedding photography could be, I didn't want to immerse myself in that genre again. Thinking about it still brought back too many painful memories of my time in Nashville with Asshole.

Switching back over to my personal page, I scrolled through the last month's worth of posts, reliving the events in reverse, starting with a few days prior.

A picture of a frayed hammock under the moss-draped oaks edging the shoreline.

West and I had lounged there for hours the other day, too lazy and too comfortable to get up and go out, positioned head to toe so he could rub my feet. We'd shared silly anecdotes from our childhoods and even discovered that one of my brother's friends was someone he knew from college. I'd moaned my pleasure as he'd dug his thumbs into the arch of my foot and squirmed against him, my calf rubbing against his groin where my leg had rested between his. Teasing him, I'd arched my back and rotated my hips, pressed against his swelling length with my foot.

Holding my ankle, he'd dug a Sharpie out of the pocket of his shorts and drawn on my sole. A sun on my big toe, waves on the ball of my foot, and a heart with an arrow through it on my heel. My breath caught when I saw the heart.

We hadn't said the words, not out loud, not to each other. I didn't know if I was there yet. But I was getting closer the more time I spent with him.

The more I ached when I wasn't with him.

"How am I supposed to get that off?"

He'd pointed at the beach. "We'll take a walk. The wet sand will—what's that word girls use?—exfoliate it or something."

It'd taken two miles to erase the sun and the waves. The heart had lingered, and I'd traced it with my finger that night before I went to bed, smiling like a loon.

Two-and-a-half weeks ago. A picture of him standing beside his old truck, a small Grady White on the trailer behind it.

He'd motored us through the creeks one afternoon, and a pair of dolphins, leaping out of the water and splashing back down, performed a show only we saw. A pop-up summer rainstorm caught us off guard, so we anchored in a sheltered cove and made love behind a veil of raindrops, the rocking of the boat dictating the rhythm, slow and steady and as endless as the tide.

When we'd gotten back to the boat ramp at dusk, West had put me to work. After backing the truck into position, I'd taken over the driver's seat. The window was down, and I'd been waiting for him to tell me when to pull forward. The boat ramp was crazy steep, and I hated knowing the exhaust pipe was almost underwater. Standing next to the boat, knee deep in the water, he'd yelled and waved for me to go ahead, so I'd punched the gas pedal.

And the truck peeled farther *down* the ramp. The ocean lapped the tailgate as I slammed the brakes and then threw the truck into drive and jerked forward again, stopping partway up the incline, my knuckles in a death grip on the steering wheel.

A white-faced West had approached me, set the emergency brake, and pointed wordlessly to the passenger side. Sliding across the bench seat, I'd faced him wide-eyed.

He'd cut off my whispered apology, his words clipped and abrupt.

"You backed over my shoe. You about ran me over. I think I'll take over now."

Later that night, I'd apologized again, my lips wrapped around his cock.

He forgave me. Twice.

Three weeks ago. Feeding doughnuts to the gulls with Rue.

I'd tragically forgotten about half a box of glazed, and we'd walked the block to the beach, tossing stale pastries in the air as the birds flocked around.

Three-and-a-half weeks ago. A panoramic of the Water's Edge entrance.

That was the day Grady delivered the news that officially began Paper Plane Photography. I'd been chosen to shoot the stills for the ad campaign for the newest Water's Edge property opening in Grand Cayman six weeks from then. It was a huge assignment—three weeks on-site, and I had some artistic control. I'd been shocked, stunned, grateful, excited. I may have cried in Grady's office, turning my face away to look out the floor-to-ceiling window at the ocean. He may have pretended not to notice.

Four weeks ago. The sunrise from West's balcony.

A new comment under the picture caught my attention. Aubrey telling the world, "I love that particular view."

I froze and checked the timestamp.

Earlier fucking today.

Unable to help myself, I clicked on her name and navigated to her page, creeping through her endless parade of toothy selfies.

I stopped and scrolled back and forth. There were three of West on there from the last month. All in public, at casual restaurants I recognized. He'd mentioned working on gala stuff more in the last few weeks, but I hadn't realized he'd been meeting with *her*. One was him in profile, leaning back in a chair, one foot resting on the opposite knee. Another was taken at the Wreck, the pile of peanut shells in front of him an indication of how long they must have been together. Most recently, four days ago, was at Starbucks. Two cups of coffee sitting next to each other, their names scrawled on the cardboard, his big hand wrapped around the one labeled his.

I closed the laptop. It didn't mean anything. Well, it did, but not like that. Being the main sponsor of the gala was huge for his growing business, considering it was the biggest social event of the year on Reynold's Island. He had a lot riding on it, and the fact that it was being held on his grandparents' sprawling estate only made him more anxious to have everything go well.

I knew he was nervous about it—about proving himself, especially to his parents, who would be flying down for the big event. He'd tried to brush me off that day in the hammock, telling me he didn't get nervous. But his hand had gripped my foot as he'd said the words, and I heard the hesitation in his voice, his usual cockiness missing.

STILL, IT RANKLED THAT he hadn't mentioned the meetings with Aubrey, even in passing.

"So are you and West official now, or what?" Theo asked around a mouthful of glazed doughnut. We were walking up the driveway to West's house, where the Fourth of July barbecue was already in full swing. I was contributing a couple boxes of Krispy Kreme's to the event, and Theo had insisted on sacrificing one for quality-control purposes.

I slipped my sunglasses on, stalling for time.

Were we? We hadn't had *that* talk yet, but I wasn't seeing anyone else, and most nights found us sharing the same bed. Work had been good for West the last few weeks, and a lot of nights, by the time he knocked on my window, it was too late to do anything but fall asleep wrapped in each other's arms. Usually, he was gone before me in the morning, a paper airplane left behind on his pillow with his daily note to me. If for some reason we slept apart, I found the plane tucked under my windshield wiper.

So, yeah, at this point, I kind of expected us to end the day together.

Maybe we *were* a couple, but I wasn't sure about the official part.

I mumbled something unintelligible and broke off a piece of his doughnut for myself, popping the sticky mess in my mouth and licking my fingers to keep from having to say anything further.

He raised his eyebrows, reading the evasion perfectly. "Don't worry about it, Sadie. He doesn't do girlfriends—don't take it personally."

Ouch.

It stung to be lumped in the same category as all the other women who had passed through his life. Like the chicks in the bar bathroom. Like Aubrey.

I wanted to believe we had something special. That we *were* something special.

Even if we hadn't put a label on it.

A small crowd was already gathered on the patio by the grill, but I needed a drink first to wash away the sudden sour taste in my mouth from Theo's innocent question. Grabbing the boxes from him, I climbed the stairs to the front porch. Ever the gentleman, Theo bounded ahead of me to get the door, holding it open for me to pass.

His question shouldn't have taken me by surprise—the majority of the time West and I had spent hanging out had been just the two of us. Besides a few times at the Wreck and the drive-in a month ago, most people hadn't really seen us together, other than Rue, who still glared daggers at me in the morning when he lingered after she had woken up. Our friends were curious, especially with West's tendency toward flings, not relationships.

Hell, I was curious how he was going to act today. This was his house, his friends, his party.

Was I his girl? Or his dirty, little secret?

When I entered the kitchen, Theo on my heels, people were standing three deep around the counter, tapping the keg and mixing drinks with stronger stuff from glass bottles. I headed for the telltale red cooler, hoping it was full of the Wreck's signature grog.

Jackpot! I filled a red plastic cup, chugged a third of it right there, and topped it back off. Glancing around, I took in all the bodies milling around the small bungalow. I didn't recognize most of them, and it made me uneasy, wondering if that was an indication of how little I knew about West.

Slowing down, I nursed my drink and reminded myself that wasn't true.

I knew West.

I knew the important stuff.

I knew he took his role of big brother seriously, that family, especially his siblings, was his main priority. I knew he had ambition, choosing to carve his own path with his own money instead of following the easy road, but it wasn't driven by greed or vanity. I knew he had a soft side—his airmail messages to me were all the proof I needed. I knew he was stubborn and sexy and smart. I knew that while he was comfortable in a suit with society's upper crust, he was more comfortable in a rundown bar, eating peanuts from a plastic pail. I knew he had the patience of a saint, determined to make me love the ocean with the same passion he did. I knew his heart was his biggest muscle because he put it into everything he did.

I knew the little things too.

I knew he never let his gas tank fall below half-full. I knew he liked plain M&M's, but not the red ones, because he swore they tasted different from the rest. I knew he was ticklish if I ran my fingers over the base of his spine. I knew he couldn't sleep well at night if the ceiling fan wasn't on. I knew he liked my hair down and wild around my face, because he was always tugging my hair tie free if I had it pulled back. I knew how his voice sounded groaning my name into my throat when he found his release between my thighs.

I smiled to myself, taking another fortifying sip. I might not know these people, but I knew West. And I liked all his pieces and parts.

The hair on the back of my neck stood up, my body responding to his presence, and my eyes searched for him. I spotted him coming out of his bedroom, a beanie pulled low over his forehead. His gaze raked me from head to toe, and I held still for his heated inspection. Getting ready for the party earlier, I'd used the standard girl technique where you take way too long to look like you just threw something on at the last minute. My faded tee hung casually over a comfy cotton skirt, a hot-pink tank just peeking out under the shirt's hemline. Trusty rubber flip flops, a purple hair tie around my wrist, and the messy-on-purpose waves I'd managed to coax my hair into completed the look.

He approved, if the way he pushed through the crowd was any indication.

Reaching my side, he curved an arm low around my hip, pulling me against him, before dipping his head to nuzzle below my ear.

"I missed you," he murmured, running his nose along my jaw before dropping a quick kiss on my lips.

I hooked two fingers under the waistband of his board shorts and tugged. "You allergic to shirts again today?"

His bare chest was inches from my face, his skin tanned from his time on the boat. My palm itched to stroke the expanse of muscle, to trace the ridges of his abdomen.

A soft chuckle escaped his lips, pulling my attention higher.

"Maybe I like the way you can't concentrate on anyone but me when I don't wear one."

I made a show of looking around the living area. "There are a lot of good-looking guys here," I mused. "Feeling insecure?"

He smirked. "Should I?"

I wrinkled my nose at him and poked his stomach, making him take a step back, before throwing the question back at him. "Should I?"

"Should you what?"

"Feel insecure?" My voice wobbled just a little, my uncertainty from Theo's remark bleeding through.

The heat in his eyes changed, from a bright flare to a low steady flame, the blue more prevalent than the gray today. He leaned down until our foreheads touched and cupped my cheek with his free hand. "Never."

His thumb stroked my cheekbone, and I closed my eyes, melting against him. Pressing a kiss to the top of my head, he eased back, putting some space in between us. "Come with me. I gotta help Wyatt with the grill or there won't be anything edible to feed all these people."

The next hour was a blur of introductions, burgers, bratwursts, and beer. Josie, who had helped rescue me after my parasailing fiasco, and Kendra, my fellow lifeguard, were both there, and the three of us began setting out the prepped food on a picnic table that had been borrowed from the Wreck, judging by the graffiti that covered it. We filled disposable aluminum trays with buns, toppings, and condiments while we waited for the men to finish grilling the meat. Josie was showing us a new tattoo along her ribs, a Shakespearean quote written in script, when the sound of crunching aluminum caught my attention.

Whipping around, I saw General Beauregard wolfing down huge slobbery mouthfuls of bread. Clapping loudly to startle him, I hollered and shooed him away, tail tucked between his legs, and managed to save the hotdog buns. The hamburger buns, on the other hand, were a total loss.

Walking over to see what all the commotion was about, West stared down at the mess. Scratching his chest, he yelled to his brother, "We got any more upstairs?"

Wyatt shrugged and poked at the grill, raising his beer to his lips.

Rolling my eyes, I headed for the stairs.

"Thanks, babe!" West called out. A small grin curved my lips as I walked away. He hadn't hesitated to call me that in front of his friends. That meant something, right?

Upstairs, the kitchen was mostly deserted, except for a couple making out in the corner. I poked around the cabinets, but I couldn't find any extra bread. Eyeing my doughnuts, I carried them back downstairs.

West chuckled when he saw the green-and-white boxes in my hands. "Skipping straight to dessert?"

Ignoring him, I got a plate and stacked a doughnut, burger, bacon, cheese, and another doughnut. "Buns!" I told him in triumph.

He looked at me dubiously. Narrowing my eyes, I picked up

my sandwich and opened wide, trying to get a full bite of the tall burger. Sugary, greasy perfection filled my mouth, and I moaned, the burger juice dripping down my hand without anything to absorb it. I licked my pinky to get the mess and then took another huge bite.

Leaning over, he took a bite for himself, surprise filtering across his face as he chewed.

"Admit it, it's awesome," I said, gloating.

"It is," he said, stepping closer and lowering his voice. "And I don't know why, but you look fucking hot trying to eat it."

Closing my eyes halfway, I made a show out of taking the next bite, tipping my head back while I chewed, and swiping my tongue down the side of my hand again. He held his beer bottle in front of his crotch, and I wondered if he was trying to hide something.

"Damn, woman. I need to get my girlfriend one of those."

The unfamiliar voice startled me back to the present. Conversation had died down around us, and a handful of guys were looking between my mouth and my half-eaten doughnut burger. My face flamed, and I dropped the burger onto my plate, snatching up a paper towel to wipe my mouth and fingers off.

The same guy, broad-shouldered with the start of a beer belly, kept watching me. "Are you gonna finish eating it? I can wait."

"Maybe later," I mumbled, my hands fluttering, and West stepped to the side, blocking me from the guy's view.

"Food's ready!" he announced, pointing at the picnic table and moving out of the way of the surging crowd. "Doughnut burgers are the specialty of the day."

We moved to the edge of the patio, and he made short work of the rest of my burger. I was too self-conscious to eat another bite in public. "We fucking have to make these again sometime. Privately. Where only I'm around to watch you eat it."

I laughed and nodded my agreement, and a heated look passed between us.

He started to bend closer, and I closed my eyes in anticipation. A loud greeting and the sound of someone slapping West on the back ruined the moment. I sighed, swallowing back my budding arousal. Arguing good-naturedly, a motley handful of his fishing buddies had joined us, wanting to talk shop. He'd introduced us earlier, but I'd forgotten most of their names already. They started talking about the big tournament coming up in Charleston next weekend, and I pretended to listen and understand what they were saying. Mostly, I was happy to just watch West in his element.

He talked with his hands a lot when he joked, and I was distracted watching the muscles in his shoulders bunch and flex, the waves on his tattoo undulating with his movements.

"Is that an elastic hair thing?" The question yanked me back to the present. One of the guys, wearing a Salt Life shirt and a backwards baseball hat, was pointing at West's wrist, at my royal blue hair tie that had been there for weeks now.

West held his arm, twisting his hand back and forth. "This? Yeah, it's Sadie's."

The guy looked at West out of the side of his eye and laughed a little, confusion written on his face, before he took another swallow of beer. "Right . . . so why is it on *you?*"

West furrowed his brow at the guy like he was being dense. "I just told you, because it's Sadie's."

The guy laughed again and changed the subject.

I froze.

My hair tie.

It was his way of claiming me. Publicly.

And he had done it weeks ago.

Lost in thought, I put my hand to my mouth, my mind whirling. Frowning at the motion, he tugged me to his side and leaned down to whisper to me, "You okay?"

"Yeah," I answered, still distracted by his simple statement from a minute ago. It wasn't eloquent as far as declarations went, but it felt real, significant, weighty. "I'm gonna go get a hot dog. I'll be right back."

Swearing, he pulled me back from the group a few steps. "You are fucking crazy if you think I can watch you eat one of those right now."

"No?" Sliding my eyes up to his, I gave a teasing pout.

"No," he said with a growl. "But if you're hungry, I can take care of that problem."

I raised my eyebrows. "I don't think *now* is the right time for that."

His lips spread wide to Cheshire-cat proportions. "Oh, Sadie. I think you just issued me a dare."

Without pausing to say goodbye to his friends, he caught my hand in his bigger one and tugged me through the crowd, threading us through the haphazardly-parked cars and the stilts of the house. Ignoring the stairs leading to the front door, he picked the staircase beneath the house that emptied into the back hallway by the bedrooms instead.

Shutting the door behind us, he turned the lock and pressed me back against the door, lifting me up so my legs wrapped around his waist. His hot lips peppered my neck with kisses, and his hands cupped my breasts over the thin cotton of my shirt.

Laughing, I tried to push him back and put some distance between us.

"Let's go to your room, you crazy horndog!"

"That's too far away. We're doing this right here." His fingers made quick work of the front clasp of my bra, and my freed breasts swelled to fit his hands, begging wantonly for more.

I moaned, unable to resist sagging against the door as he brought my nipples to attention, dipping his head to take one in his mouth.

"People upstairs," I argued, distracted by his tongue for a long moment before I could continue. "Could open that door any minute."

He released my aching bud with a pop and caught my gaze, his eyes burning into mine.

"Then I suggest you stay quiet."

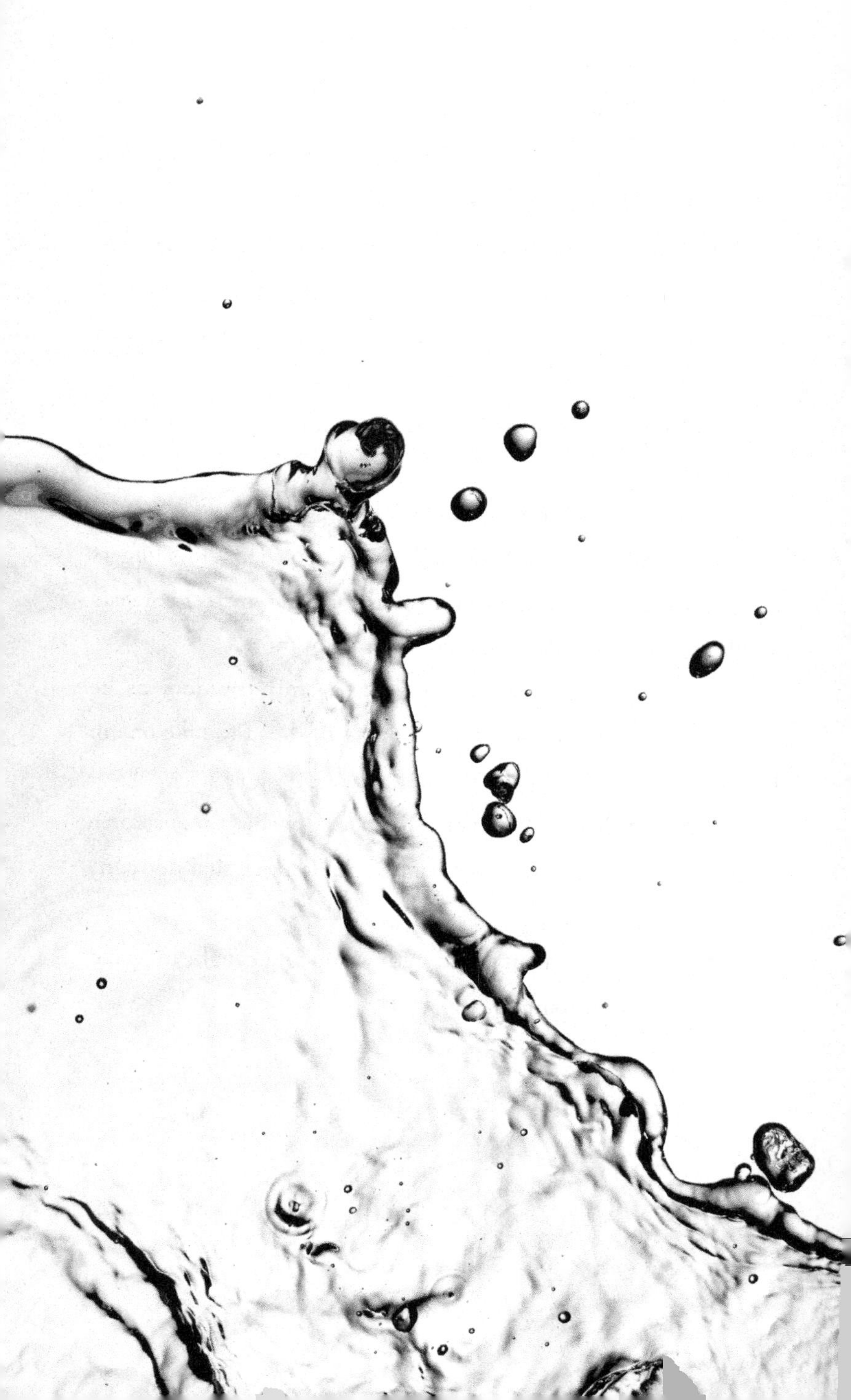

chapter nineteen

"Not. A. Problem," I whispered in his ear, rotating my hips against his groin.

Spinning me around, he placed me on the step above him, making us the same height, and caught my mouth in a searing kiss, his tongue staking claim to mine, his lips wild. I matched him, tilting my head and scraping my nails along his upper back, sucking his tongue into my mouth. Leaning closer, I took everything he had to give.

Breaking away for a breath, he ripped my shirt over my head, letting my unhooked bra fall by our feet. He licked a wet path along my jaw and down my neck, tracing the length of my collarbone. Heat flared hot and fast between us. This was no slow-burning flame.

This was an inferno.

I hooked my leg around his hip, and he pushed between my legs, his hard length evident through his thin boardshorts. Panting with desire, I yanked his face back to mine, nipping his lower lip before he took control again, his lips devouring mine, forcing my head back in submission. He tasted faintly of doughnuts, and I couldn't get enough.

My nails raked his chest, and he fisted a chunk of my hair and tugged. I bucked against him, wanting more. He ran his nose back up to my ear, nuzzling the soft skin.

"Impatient?" He chuckled, his eyes hungry, his hands returning to knead my aching breasts.

"I thought *you* couldn't wait."

Grunting, he closed his teeth over the sensitive slope of my shoulder, nipping me in warning. Running his hand up my smooth thigh and beneath my skirt, he slipped a finger under my panties, finding me already wet for him.

His eyes dilated as he watched another digit disappear inside me, readying me for his invasion. I rocked against him, meeting his rhythm and urging him to go faster. Withdrawing his hand, leaving me throbbing, he gripped my hips, forcing me to turn around on the narrow stair to face away from him. The flat of his hand pushed on my lower back, and I bent over, presenting him with my lace-covered ass.

Wasting no time, he bunched my skirt around my waist, not bothering to remove it, and groaned as he palmed my butt, massaging my cheeks. I rocked back against him, needing him to touch me, take me, fill me. Biting my lip, I remembered his warning to stay silent and fought against the temptation to say his name, wanting to beg.

Frustrated, I glanced over my shoulder. His face was a mask of concentration, focused on his task. One hand ran along my wet slit, the other loosened the drawstring of his shorts.

Freeing himself, he stroked his cock, and raised his eyes to mine.

"Hold on," he rasped, warning me, and squeezed my butt hard before rubbing the sting away.

My fingers curled around the edge of the step under me, and I braced myself for his delicious onslaught. "Waitin' on you," I breathed.

Moving the soaked material covering my sex to the side, he slid deep, seating himself fully inside me, his fingers digging into my sides for traction. My thighs muscles tensed, and I sucked in a breath, going up on my tiptoes to take him and relishing the feel of him pressed close. I sensed his restraint as he waited for me to adjust.

I lowered back down to my heels, accepting the last of his length. Moaning in pleasure, I lifted my head, pushing back, ready for more.

That was the only signal he needed.

Widening his stance, he plunged into me, no waiting, just like he'd promised. With powerful thrusts, he took me roughly. I don't even know if he realized the words that spilled from his lips, praising my body, worshiping me.

I met his tempo, opposites attracting in the most primitive

way. Back and forth, in and out. Male and female.

Reaching back, I cupped his balls, massaging him, and he wrapped my hair around his fist in response, forcing the bend of my back to curve farther. My hand dropped away from him. Above me, he swore under his breath at the change in position.

I gasped as the head of his cock hit the perfect spot inside me, rubbing it with each advance. My panting accelerated, and he picked up his pace another impossible notch, the sound of our skin slapping together echoing through the empty stairwell.

Time stretched endlessly as he worked my willing body. The pressure inside me climbed to an impossible height with him pushing me higher, faster. Releasing my hair, he bent over me, reaching around to pinch my clit between his thumb and his finger, pitching me over the edge. My mouth opened in a wordless scream as I bucked, utterly consumed by the tsunami crashing through me.

West came with a shout he didn't even try to muffle. Tensing behind me, he pulsed into my core, joining me in my release, his embrace the only thing keeping me from collapsing.

Gathering me in his arms, he pulled me onto his lap, sitting sideways across the bottom step with his back against the wall and my skirt bunched between us. Aftershocks rocked my body, and his ragged breaths tickled against my ear. Pushing my tangled hair off my damp neck, he dropped soft kisses along its length, the motion almost reverent.

I sank into him, too spent to do anything but exist. The whole party could conga line past us in that moment, and I still wouldn't budge, satisfaction seeping through every inch of my body.

I ran my hand down his strong thigh, relishing the hard muscle bunching underneath me. His arms looped around my waist, and he hugged me to him, his soft sigh the only sound I needed to hear.

My heart fluttered in my chest. I ran my thumb along the hair tie circling his wrist, hoping it meant what I thought it did, but too scared to ask. Theo's casual comment kept me from diving headfirst into the fantasy of us, together and finding a happily ever after that easily.

But for now, in this dim stairwell, I'd settle for this feeling of completeness. Closing my eyes, I savored the moment. His skin hot against mine, our limbs tangled together, our chests rising and falling in sync. Who needed promises of forever when right now felt so damn good?

THE NEXT MORNING, I was on my first cup of coffee, sitting at the kitchen island in my cottage, when my phone rang. Forcing my eyes to focus, I saw Hailey's name flash across the display.

Sliding my finger across the screen, I hit the speaker button so I wouldn't have to hold the phone. "Mornin'," I managed.

"Hey!" Her bubbly voice filled the kitchen. She was clearly a morning person. Perky freak.

I waited, fortifying myself with another sip of coffee. If

someone called me before ten on my day off, they should keep their expectations low.

"You there?" Her voice was more hesitant this time.

I summoned up some energy. "Yup."

"Cody and I are visiting Uncle West this morning. He's going to teach us how to fly a kite on the beach. If you aren't busy, I was hoping you'd come too." She paused. "And maybe bring your camera?"

I smiled into my mug, the lure of hanging out with all three of them too much to resist. "Sure. Give me a bit to finish my coffee, and I'll head over."

Thirty minutes later, I parked the Jeep next to West's big dually. Checking the time, I saw it was still a few minutes to ten. I mentally congratulated myself for being productive this morning as I gathered my equipment and headed for the beach.

West already had the kite airborne, Cody perched on his shoulders, as they watched it flutter high above them. Something sharp caught in my chest, watching West with him. Hailey stood next to the duo, helping to steady Cody. It took me a moment, but I realized it was some kind of special stunt kite, with two lengths of string running between it and West. By pulling back one arm at a time, he had it dancing in the sky, performing an infinite series of figure eights.

They hadn't noticed me yet, and I stayed back out their sight, putting the camera to my eye and capturing some images without them knowing it. Candids like these always turned out the best and felt the most real. Cody's innocent delight was evident—

listening to him giggle the way only toddlers can. He threw his arm up to the sky and then grasped West's head again when he wiggled off balance. He pointed at the kite and pulled on his uncle's ear, ordering him around. West followed his directions obediently, chuckling along with him.

A sudden gust of wind made the kite shudder and pulled West forward a few steps. Cody teetered and slipped but fell uninjured into Hailey's ready arms. Spinning him around in a few circles, their laughter filled the air. When they stopped, they were facing my direction, and I was caught.

Hailey waved, signaling me to join them. Heading in their direction, I took a minute to enjoy the display of West's bare back, his muscles flexing as he adjusted the kite.

"Where's General Beauregard?" I asked, coming up next to him.

He glanced over, his eyes running a quick path down my body. I blushed, remembering our adventure yesterday.

Afterwards, by the time we'd rejoined the party, Rue had arrived and was talking with Theo. We'd been chatting for ten minutes when Grady walked in with the anime pixie. She didn't say anything outright, but Rue's posture had stiffened, and when a few minutes later she suggested heading to the waterfront in town to watch the fireworks instead, I didn't have the heart to tell her no. Theo had rounded out our threesome, and we'd left, but not before West had given me a lingering kiss goodbye and warned Theo what would happen to him if he didn't watch out for me and Rue.

Theo'd rolled his eyes. "These two? What could possibly happen?"

Nothing but the inevitable. Rue had picked up a scruffy guy who swore he played drums in a band rolling through Charleston, and she'd disappeared, leaving Theo and me drinking cheap beer and watching the sky glitter.

West nodded at his nephew.

"I left him inside with Wyatt. I didn't want him running down Cody."

A quick glance confirmed that the oversized hound was taller than his nephew.

"Good call."

"I'm a good uncle."

I wrapped my arms around him from behind, using the pretense of giving him a hug to run my hands over his taut abdomen.

He made a noise in the back of his throat and shot a glance at me over his shoulder. "Don't think I don't know what you're doing."

"Don't think I don't know you're enjoying it."

His hum of agreement vibrated through me where I pressed against him. Pinching his side, I moved away and picked up the camera again, pointing it at him.

"Gonna pose for me, stud?"

He leaned closer, lowering his voice so only I could hear. "You want some private shots for your collection? That could be arranged. But not with the squirt underfoot. And only if you're in them too."

My breath caught, imagining what we would look like, tangled and thrusting, frozen in black-and-white.

Nudging me with his shoulder, he waited until I met his eyes. "Exactly," he murmured, pressing a kiss to the top of my head.

"What are you going to take pictures of?" Hailey asked as she sidled up next to me.

"You," I answered. "And Cody. And Uncle West. Wanna smile for the camera, little man?"

I snapped photos for the next thirty minutes or so, until Cody's attention waned. I don't know how Hailey found ways to keep him entertained all day.

She and Cody settled down to build a sandcastle, and West switched into teacher mode, instructing me in the finer points of flying a stunt kite. I mastered the figure eight—it was easier than it looked—and was enjoying making it swoop low to the ground, kamikaze-style, before jerking it back up just before it hit the sand.

I tried to get fancy, attempting a barrel roll by stepping over the strings. It didn't work. At all. My foot got tangled in one of the strings, and I lost my balance, tumbling into the sand and dropping the kite strings, although not fast enough to catch myself from landing face first. Pushing to a sitting position, I had just enough time to see the kite nosedive onto the beach, thudding to a stop.

"Crash!" Cody yelled, pointing at his fallen toy, looking thrilled. Jumping to his feet, he ran over to me. "Uh oh. You have a boo-boo." After pausing to press a wet kiss to my nose, he took off down the beach. "Kite fall down. It has a boo-boo too!"

West helped me to me feet and dropped another kiss to my gritty nose. "Better?"

I nodded, brushing sand off my face and clothes. "Sorry for messing up the kite."

"We'll get it flying again," he said with a shrug.

"You think?"

His eyes caught mine. "Oh, ye of little faith."

Ten minutes later, it was airborne again, and he showed off some advanced tricks that sent the kite dipping and twirling through the cloudless sky. Cody gasped every time West yanked on the string, the rainbow kite performing an intricate dance for its captive audience.

He nudged my side with his elbow. "Told you we'd get it in the air again."

"I should have known you'd come to the rescue." I rolled my eyes.

"I'll always rescue you, Sadie. Always." The unexpectedly rough tone to his voice caught me off guard, and when I looked up at him, his eyes were dark and serious.

Swallowing hard, I excused myself to take some more pictures, not wanting to read too much into his comment, his stare.

Cody lit up around his uncle. It pained me that his own dad was missing out on this, sacrificing this time with his child to keep us safe by serving in the military. And West seemed comfortable with Cody, taking the time to play with him in a way I bet most guys wouldn't.

After awhile, Hailey drifted over to me where I was standing about twenty yards down the beach. "Can I see?" She pointed at the camera.

As I showed her some of the better ones from today's session, she smiled big, laughing at some of the goofier moments between her son and brother.

"He's good with kids, isn't he?" She tipped her chin toward West.

"He is," I admitted, knowing he'd be a great father if we had kids one day.

If we have kids one day?

I gasped and put my hand to my chest, rubbing hard at the ache there. Where the fuck had that thought come from? My eyes were drawn to him in that moment, as he tossed Cody in the air like he weighed nothing. The little boy's squeals hit me squarely.

Would our kids have his gorgeous eyes? Would our daughter get his laugh or our son his broad shoulders? Would they share his sense of humor, passed along with his DNA?

I loved him.

It was sudden and undeniable in that moment.

The sun shone brighter, and the sand felt warmer beneath my feet. The camera hung forgotten in my hand. The roar of the ocean swelled, providing the bass line, while the gulls sang soprano, celebrating my revelation. Behind the man—my man—and the boy, the lone cloud in the sky shifted in the breeze, almost resembling a heart if you tipped your head and squinted a little. I froze, unable to take it all in, everything suddenly overwhelming. It was too much, too bright, too big to absorb.

Hailey waved her hands in front of my eyes, looking between me and West, a concerned expression on her face.

"Hey! You okay?"

"Yeah," I replied faintly. "Everything's perfect."

Behind us, a door banged open, shattering the moment.

Hailey and I both swiveled, turning toward the sound.

General Beauregard barreled across the sand, baying as his big body stretched out between strides. Behind us, I heard Cody giggle, his exclamation of "Dog!" making me smile.

Raising my eyes to the beach house door, I faltered.

Aubrey was standing there, hair wild, holding her hand to her eyes to shield the sun and wearing oversized gym shorts and a shirt that I was sure had come from West's drawer. She was on his balcony, leaning against the rail like it was the most natural position in the world.

"Heeeeeeey!" The drawled greeting and finger wave she sent our way were like nails on a chalkboard.

Wide-eyed, I turned to West.

He was moving in her direction, storm clouds brewing in his expression.

I paused and then followed him. Hailey called for me, but I ignored her. My field of vision had narrowed to the man I loved and the woman determined to ruin it all.

He climbed the stairs, growling at her to get inside, with me just steps behind.

Closing the sliding glass door behind us, he glared at her, hands on his hips.

"Why are you wearing my clothes?"

She tittered, her gaze glancing off me.

"What did you want me to come outside wearing?"

He growled. "What happened to *your* clothes?"

"You know what happened," she shrugged with a suggestive smile, running her fingers through hair that clearly hadn't seen a brush today.

My breathing was shallow, but I waited. My dream come true wasn't going to morph into a nightmare before my eyes. That wasn't how it was supposed to work.

Stepping forward, he rose to his full height.

"I know you showed up late to the party, already wasted, and drank even more. And Wyatt offered you the couch, despite my objections. I know you slept there last night—alone, and in your own damn clothes."

She shrank a little under his fierceness.

"I didn't think you'd mind," she said finally, peeking up at him from under her lashes.

"I mind."

She pushed past him toward his bathroom, rubbing her body along his as she passed.

I hissed, narrowing my eyes, and West yanked me to his side, giving me a reassuring squeeze. While she gathered up her clothes from the tiled floor, he leaned down to me. "I promise you, I didn't touch her."

I nodded, but kept a careful watch on her. Underestimating her would be a mistake. So would pushing her too far. We were locked in a fierce game of tug-of-war with West as the prize, but the bitch didn't seem to realize she'd already lost.

Aubrey didn't look at me as she swept from the room, but she paused in the doorway, her eyes sly. "Enjoy him while you have him. It won't last. It never does. And then he'll come back to me, like always."

I started forward, but he stopped me, blocking me to keep me from advancing. Smart man. My hazy plan of bitch-slapping the smile off her face probably wasn't my brightest.

"I'll handle this," he said when he bent down and caught my mutinous gaze.

If looks could kill, I would've already handled it.

Raising his eyebrows, West squeezed my hand. "Give me five minutes."

I huffed in disbelief, tearing my face away, and crossed my arms over my chest.

Sighing, he turned back to where Aubrey was lounging against his doorframe, studying her perfect fucking manicure. Lowering his head, he caught her arm as he strode out the door and down the hall, cursing under his breath. Their footsteps echoed as they moved farther away.

Left behind, alone, I sat on his bed and looked at my hands absently, unsure what to think. Out of the corner of my eye, I noticed his nightstand drawer wasn't shut all the way, and as I went to close it, something familiar caught my attention. Yanking it all the way open, I stared down at a glossy stack of photos.

Aubrey. Her boudoir session.

chapter twenty

West: Where'd you go?

Me: Now you want to know? Three hours later? That must have been some talk you had with Aubrey.

West: I was gone less than ten minutes. I thought you'd gone back outside with Hailey, but you were just gone.

Me: How long did it take you to figure that out?

West: Not long.

Me: So why are you just now texting me?

West: You left. Was I supposed to come find you?

Me: I wanted you to *want* to come find me.

West: I do want to come find you.

Me: No, I wanted you to come find me then, not now.

West: You don't want me to come over now?

Me: No, now I'm pissed.

West: Why?

Me: I don't want to talk now.

West: But I thought you wanted me to come find you.

Me: I did.

West: But not now?

Me. Nope.

West: Ok.

I stared at my phone for another hour. He didn't text again. Didn't reach out the rest of the night. But the next morning, there was a paper airplane and a box with a single glazed doughnut and *I'm sorry* written in chocolate on it waiting on the front porch.

I wanted to talk now.

Well, after I ate the doughnut.

Swallowing my pride and a cup of coffee, I headed over to his house. He was waiting for me on the hammock, reading a tattered book with a fish on the cover. I paused, taking a moment to just look at him. Was there anything hotter than a guy reading—shirtless?

No. No, there wasn't.

Walking closer, I nudged his feet where they were crossed at the ankles. "Hey."

He lowered the book, watching me with wary eyes. "Have you had coffee yet?"

I grinned. I loved that he knew it wasn't smart to approach me before I'd had caffeine. I held up one finger.

"Just one? You're lucky I'm prepared." Reaching down beside him, he retrieved a thermos I hadn't noticed on the ground and handed it to me.

I started to lift it to my lips and then hesitated. He drank his black.

"It's the way you like it."

Unexpected tears pricked my eyes. Sometimes, it was the little things that mattered most.

"Don't just stand there. Drink it. For my safety, if nothing else."

I mock glared at him, but followed orders, the laughter chasing away the sappiness. The coffee was perfect, strong and sweet.

Shoving his legs to the side so I could climb on next to him, I kicked off my flip flops and settled my feet across his chest, wiggling my toes to get his attention.

He peered at me over the top of the book, raising his eyebrows.

"I'm sorry about last night. The texts. I just got scared you weren't telling me the truth."

"Have I ever lied to you?"

Raising the thermos to my mouth, I took a long, slow swallow, thinking about his words. Technically, I didn't think he had. But omitting things? The walls of the bathroom at the Wreck came to mind. The meetings with Aubrey about the gala. And the pictures in his nightstand. I don't know that he'd ever lied, but he wasn't as honest as he could be either.

I shook my head, wondering what else I might not know.

"What's that face for?"

Choosing my words carefully, I focused on my hands when I answered. "I'm not sure not lying and being truthful are the same things."

He marked his place in the book with a postcard and dropped it to the ground. Scooping one of my feet into his strong hands, he dug his thumbs into the arch, making it hard to concentrate on the conversation.

"What are you talking about?" He met my eyes, confusion written across his features. He didn't look like a man trying to hide a secret.

I didn't want to admit I'd snooped in his drawers. Or creeped on Aubrey's Facebook wall. Stalker, much?

"She just caught me by surprise yesterday is all." I forced myself to keep the accusation out of my voice.

"Yeah, sorry 'bout that. I thought she would've left by then."

So you weren't planning on telling me, I mused, irritated. I didn't want to sound like a clingy girlfriend. Even though he'd kind of claimed me at the barbecue, we'd still never officially had a talk. Had never discussed being exclusive.

I wanted to ask, get it all out in the open, but, at the same time, I was scared of his answer. I didn't want to hear him say he was just looking for a good time and that it was nothing serious to him when it was becoming everything to me.

Gritting my teeth, I tried to withdraw my foot, but he wouldn't let me, holding on tighter and massaging the tendon on the back of my heel. Damn him, his fingers felt good too. Lying there, sipping coffee, having him pressed against me while he rubbed my feet. It was hard to stay upset when I wasn't even sure we were a couple, if he had even done anything wrong. Yeah, I had fallen in love with him, but that was *my* problem, not his.

The moment stretched. He was relaxed beside me, his body harboring no tension to make me think he was lying. I started to feel foolish for my paranoia. His hands switched to my other foot, giving it the same thorough treatment as the first one.

"What are your plans this week?"

I wrinkled my nose. "Lifeguarding until Thursday and a photo shoot on Friday. I'll probably spend most of Saturday packing before the flight Sunday."

The hands around my feet squeezed. "Your trip to Grand Cayman is next weekend? I thought it was two weeks away. *Fuck.*"

"Problem?"

"Yeah, I just booked a big tournament out of Charleston for Thursday through Saturday. I wouldn't have done it if I realized you were about to leave for three weeks."

I made a face. "Can you get out of it?"

"Not easily. It's a new client for me, one who does a lot of business around here in the summer, and he could turn into a great repeat customer if the weekend goes well. I could see if one of the other companies can do it instead, I guess—"

"No, don't do that," I interrupted, hating to see his business suffer. We both needed every booking we could get. I nibbled my lower lip. "Do you want to go out Wednesday night, before you leave? What time are you done Saturday? Will you be back in the evening?"

He resumed working on my foot, giving each toe individual attention. "Wednesday night, I'm all yours. And I can just leave the boat at the marina on Saturday night. I'll go up on Sunday to get it out of the water and bring it back to Reynolds."

"That'd be nice."

"If *nice* is the word you're using to describe it, I'm not doing something right," he teased, leaning down to suck my toe into his mouth.

Surprised, I pulled back, my leg jerking down the length of

his body and over his hard—*oh!* I stared at his erection tenting his shorts.

"Hey, Sadie?"

"Yeah?" I asked, my attention still focused on his lap.

"You got any plans this morning?"

I peered at him from under my lashes. "You have something in mind?"

"Yeah. A little water desensitization exercise I think we should try. It involves the outdoor shower."

"If you think it'll help . . ." I ran the sole of my foot over his hard length.

"We can keep practicing until you feel comfortable with it. No matter how long it takes."

It took the rest of the morning.

Getting clean had never been so dirty.

The first part of the week dragged, the only highlight being when West slipped into bed with me late on Tuesday night for a sleepover. By Wednesday afternoon, I was counting down the hours until our date. I hoped he planned on taking me someplace other than the Wreck, but honestly, I was happy just to spend some time with him.

Kendra grew annoyed with me checking my watch every few minutes and, at four o'clock, told me she'd finish solo and to get the hell out of there because I was making her crazy. Wrapping her in a quick hug, I grabbed my gear and scooted back home to get ready.

Even though we were going to see each other Saturday night too, I knew that'd probably be a group event, and I used the extra time I had to prep to go all out. Conditioning treatment for my hair, straightening iron, shaving all the necessary places, more makeup than normal. I slipped on a dress and shoes that weren't flip flops for a change, knowing he'd like me no matter what I wore, but wanting tonight to be special.

Settling onto the porch with my laptop to browse Pinterest while I waited for West to text that he was ready, I lost track of time as I scrolled through hotel pictures for inspiration for my big trip. The new board I started pinning to had over sixty images on it before I checked the time again.

Six-fifty.

What the hell?

Pulling out my phone, I checked for missed calls or texts.

Nothing.

Irritated, I called his number, waiting as it rang and rang. I didn't leave a voicemail. After shooting off a quick text, I checked his Facebook page—and Aubrey's. No recent posts from either of them.

Clenching my jaw in irritation, I tried to resume my research on Pinterest, but I couldn't get back into it. Fifteen minutes later, I went inside to make myself a drink—Rue's signature basil hard lemonade. I was on my second glass when seven-thirty rolled around.

At eight, I got tired of waiting and drove to the Wreck, wondering if maybe I was supposed to meet him there. No sign of him, and Wyatt confirmed he wasn't scheduled to bartend that night.

At eight-thirty, he finally texted back.

West: Sorry, lost track of time. I'm not going to be able to make it tonight, babe. Can I get a raincheck?

Seething, I ordered my second cup of grog and chugged it like a man, using the back of my hand to wipe off the dribble of punch dripping down the corner of my mouth. Wyatt stopped in front of me, concern evident in his eyes, and asked if I needed anything.

Nope, just fucking peachy, thanks.

I shook my head and held up my empty cup for a refill. He got me another drink, but his expression was reluctant. Tough shit. I was a grown-ass woman, and if I wanted to drink alone at the bar, I damn well could.

I glared at my phone, as if it was to blame for the turn my evening had taken.

No, I didn't want a damn raincheck. I wanted a date with the guy I couldn't get off my mind.

Me: Where are you? What happened?

I hated myself as soon as I hit send on that message, sensing the neediness those five words revealed. Two more drinks sank in my belly before I got tired of waiting for a reply.

Fuck him.

Pushing to my feet, I headed for the door, my path not as straight as I had intended it to be. I was drunk. And past caring. And even though I knew I shouldn't be behind the wheel at all, I drove by his house, noticing his car was missing.

Unable to help myself, I took the long way home, the really long way, the one that detoured all the way past Aubrey's fairytale mansion. Her luxury compact was MIA too.

Well, wasn't that just fucking convenient.

It wasn't proof of anything. Not really. I repeated that to myself, trying to believe it.

Not wanting to see anything else, I went straight home, dropping into bed without taking off my makeup. My mind swirled with denials as I drifted off to a restless sleep.

A KNOCK ON MY window woke me up before the sun was even peeking over the horizon. Grumbling, I stumbled to the blinds, squinting out into the gray sky.

West.

I hesitated, my sluggish brain trying to process his appearance. Finally, I sighed and pointed toward the door. Walking through the cottage to meet him, I shoved a hand through the snarls of my hair, knowing I looked like a hot mess and not giving a shit.

I didn't let him in. Instead, I slipped out the door to join him on the porch. Even pre-dawn, the air was already warm and humid. My thin tank and cotton shorts weren't much protection from his hot gaze raking over me. I crossed my arms over my chest, trying to hide the reaction my nipples were having to the sight of his scruffy face and his blatant perusal.

Pulling his arm out from behind his back, he handed me a small bouquet of white and blue flowers. My eyes widened in surprise. He'd never brought me flowers before. I raised them to my nose, sniffing in appreciation. His other hand presented me with three paper airplanes, each folded differently.

I cocked my head in question. We hadn't spoken a word yet, and the silence seemed ominous, even though he came bearing gifts.

Leaning close, he tucked an unruly strand of hair behind my ear. "One for each day I'll be gone."

After a long moment, I accepted them, tucking them under my arm for later. The flowers were nice, but they weren't what I needed right now. I just wanted to know what happened last night.

I waited, leaning against the doorjamb, letting my eyes do all the talking I needed.

"Sadie, I'm sorry about last night." His hands came up to cup my shoulders, but my expression remained unchanged. "I was having trouble with an engine, and I was using my phone to stream YouTube videos on how to fix it, as ridiculous as that sounds. It killed my battery. I didn't find your text until a few hours ago. I haven't even been to bed. I've been working on it all night—look."

He held up his hand near my face, the porch light illuminating a myriad of small cuts around his knuckles and grease under the nails.

"I hate that I missed one of our last nights together for a while. I saw Wyatt when I went by the house to grab some gear. He said you stopped by the Wreck? And you had dressed up?"

I nodded once.

"Did you take a picture?" he asked hopefully, tipping my chin up so he could see me better.

"Nope."

He deflated, and a twinge of conscience hit me.

Studying him closer, I saw the bags under his eyes. And he smelled like motor oil. He didn't look like a guy who'd been out partying and having a good time without me last night.

"Right." He nodded. "I deserve that. I just wanted to apologize in person before I left. I'll miss you. I'll try to do a better job texting while I'm gone, okay?"

I licked my lips, hating that I cared so much, hating the power he had over my mood.

Taking the flowers from me and setting them down on the doormat, he wrapped his big arms around me, tugging me into his embrace. I stood stiffly at first, but my body responded to his heat, melting into it, softening. When he nudged my face up for a kiss, I didn't resist.

His lips were soft, gentle. The kiss was undemanding and slow, a promise of what was to come. I slid my arms around his back and grabbed fistfuls of his shirt, pulling him closer. My lips opened and his tongue swept inside, tangling with mine, but not trying to dominate.

He tasted like coffee. As our lips slanted together, he cupped my face, and I lifted up on my tiptoes to keep the connection. Finally breaking apart, he rained kisses over my nose, cheeks, and forehead.

"I gotta go. I won't make it to Charleston in time if I don't leave now."

The words clawed at the back of my throat. I wanted to tell him how I felt but not like this. Swallowing them back, I bit my lip hard. I couldn't say them. Not until I knew he felt it too.

"Good luck." My voice was rough.

"See you Saturday night. I promise. No excuses."

Brushing one last kiss over my forehead, he turned toward the road. I hadn't even noticed the big dually sitting there, his huge boat hooked behind it.

The first rays of dawn cracked the morning sky as he drove away. I couldn't explain it, but I wanted to cry as he disappeared.

He kept his word. Texts and pictures pinged my phone at regular intervals on Thursday and Friday, helping the time pass faster. We flirted, we teased, we mocked each other. We swapped goofy selfies. On Saturday, I couldn't wait any longer to see him. I hatched a scheme to meet him at the marina when he docked, planning on surprising him.

The only problem was, I wasn't exactly sure when he was going to be back. I knew the tournament ended at one, but the marina he had a slip at was a little farther away, and I didn't know how long it would take in between. I'd tried texting a few times, but he'd been pretty quiet today. He had sent me a "Good morning" text hours before my alarm went off. As I munched on cereal, I received a message saying he wouldn't be around much and that he was going to be pretty busy.

I'd sent a few more and hadn't heard back. But that was okay. At least he was doing a better job communicating.

Feet propped on the chair across from me, I was sitting at the marina café on the edge of the shore, the rows of docks spread out before me. I knew what his boat looked like, so I scanned the water every couple minutes while I played around on my phone. My last text to West had finally gotten a reply four minutes ago.

West: Almost done. Got a few more things to finish doing, and then I'm headed your way.

I sent back a smiley face and ordered a bottle of water from the waiter. I got tired of Pinterest after a while and switched over to Facebook. Rue had some new shots up from her trip to St. Augustine. Hailey and Cody were making fish lips in a selfie. My brother was giving a side hug to a redhead I didn't recognize. Pausing on that picture, I sent him a private message, asking who the girl was. Aubrey had commented on a photo Wyatt had posted of General Beauregard, and I couldn't help but click on her name.

I snorted at the photos she had posted just from today. A view over the water. A selfie of her wearing a plunging bikini top. Her patriotic pedicure. Did she think anyone cared what her toes looked like?

Opening the picture up, I saw it had thirty-two likes and eight comments. Okay, maybe people did care what her toes looked like.

Glancing up again, I saw West's boat pulling in at one of the far slips. He threw a line to an employee and cut the engines as the boat drew up snug to the dock.

A huge smile spread across my face. His expression was hidden under the brim of the baseball hat he had pulled low on his forehead, but just seeing his muscles rippling in the sun was enough to have me rubbing my thighs together in anticipation. I couldn't wait for him to realize I was here waiting for him.

As I packed away my phone and my bottle of water into my bag, a familiar voice drifted across the salt air.

I froze.

No.

It couldn't be.

My eyes had to be playing tricks on me. I lowered my sunglasses to be sure.

West was walking down the dock, carrying a laughing, bikini-clad Aubrey in his arms like a baby, her arms thrown around his bare shoulders. I recognized that bikini. It was the same one from the picture. She reached up and snagged the hat off his head, settling it onto her own. They walked right by me, neither one of them glancing over.

His definition of a *few things to finish doing* apparently wasn't the same as mine at all.

I flashed back to Nashville. To Asshole.

Déjà vu washed over me.

Not again.

Want to know what happens next?

Look for Soaked, the next book in the Water's Edge Series.

SOAKED

Having hope was her weakness.

If Sadie Mullins hadn't started to believe in love again, hadn't let herself fall for him, she wouldn't be feeling this way.

Wouldn't have her heart breaking.

Wouldn't regret meeting West Montgomery

The cocky bastard should have left her alone,

let her forget about him.

Let her move on with her life.

Of course, he didn't.

That could have been the end of it.

Of course, it wasn't.

Damn hope.

Acknowledgements

First of all, if you made it this far, I want to thank you, the reader, for taking a chance on a new author. I went into this whole writing-a-book adventure not knowing if we'd ever find each other. Not knowing if anyone would ever see these words. The gift of your time spent with my characters means the world to me.

Julia, you poor girl. You've heard more about West and Sadie than anybody, and you never doubted for a minute that I could write their story—hell, that I could write a story at all. Thank you for being so unbelievably patient as I navigated this crazy path to publishing. This one's for you.

Emily Snow, thank you for answering an email from a nutty fan. And for working together and asking to see my words and for then believing in those words. And then helping me figure out how to go from having a written story to a published book. You advice has been invaluable.

Erin Noelle—some things were just meant to be. Like us finding each other and just clicking the way we do. Except when it comes to matters of skipping. Then we'll just have to agree to disagree. We're proof that when opposites attract, great things can happen. Let's keep making great things. I love you!

Thank you to my former coworkers who helped along the way—especially you, Hollie.

Mariah Rice, thank you for reading the rough version and being so excited about when the next chapter was coming. Don't worry, I'll be sending you more soon.

Thank you to the authors who I've met along the way, who took the time the answer my endless, endless questions. Brooke Blaine, Aly Martinez, CM Foss, Liz Reinhardt, Rachel van Dyken, my Indie group girls (I would never *skip* y'all).

Thank you, Hang Le, for the beautiful cover and graphics! I love them so hard!

And thank you to Kay Springsteen, for not just editing, but teaching me how to strengthen my writing (and also telling me the different between blonde and blond—who knew?).

Jill Sava and Love Affair With Fiction, thank you for helping me spread my story. And for not making fun of my newbie questions. And handling all the stuff I still don't understand.

Candace Wood, thank you for the tough love. You know I like it rough and you always deliver.

Ella Frank, you saved my butt at the very end. I'm so grateful.

Michelle Ehrlich, my biggest fan, I hope you loved it.

A huge shout out to all the blogs who shared anything at all having to do with my book! Your contribution is priceless.

About Stacy Kestwick

I'm a Southern girl who firmly believes mornings should be outlawed. My perfect day would include lounging on a hammock with a good book, carbohydrates, and the people around me randomly breaking into choreographed song-and-dance routines. It would not include bacon, cleaning, or anything requiring patience.

Come visit me! We can hang out and talk about cupcakes and books, not necessarily in that order.

Need more? I have a secret readers group called The Wreck full of sneak peeks, exclusive giveaways, and all-around awesomeness. Send me a Facebook message to join!

www.facebook.com/StacyKestwickAuthor
www.stacykestwick.com
https://twitter.com/StacyKestwick
https://instagram.com/stacykestwick/
https://www.goodreads.com/stacykestwick
https://www.bookbub.com/authors/stacy-kestwick

Want to get the inside scoop on all things Stacy Kestwick? Sign up for my newsletter to stay in touch!

http://bit.ly/1Zjbn3F

Made in the USA
Las Vegas, NV
20 August 2021